Editorial Reviews For

THE ANDROBIOTICA ADVENTURES

"*David Gittlin's* AndroBiotica 2: Journey in Time *offers an intriguing and timely tale of artificial intelligence and corporate intrigue. Overall, the novella is a fun read with an interesting take on the mechanics of time travel—something very difficult to accomplish these days.*"
Kara Dennison—IndieReader

"*David Gittlin takes sci-fi to a new level! With fantastic tech advancements, right down to color-changing walls and artificial intelligence that is human in almost every way, Gittlin enthralls his readers with attention to detail. It's almost impossible to fully convey the extent of advancements in a novella, but the author focuses on two important aspects of science and delivers an enhanced vision to his readers.*"
Courtnee Turner Hoyle—Readers' Favorite

"*As questions of what constitutes humanity play out against the backdrop of a dangerous mandate and mission to retrieve the Androbiotica File, readers receive a vivid plot that moves from detective work to efforts to reshape the world.*

The AndroBiotica File: Nearly Human is replete with engrossing subjects and considerations that make it highly recommended not only for sci-fi readers looking for original writing but also book clubs that would discuss the moral and ethical boundaries of what makes us all human . . . or not."
Diane Donovan—Midwest Book Review

"*Moving into a space where AI and robotics converge, Gittlin's deft storytelling seamlessly blends complex technical concepts with engaging plots. This book quickly draws the reader into a world both familiar and highly advanced, painting a vivid picture without overwhelming the reader with excessive jargon.*"
Michael Beas—The Book Review Magazine

THE ANDROBIOTICA ADVENTURES

DAVID GITTLIN

Entelligent Entertainment, LLC

Published in the United States by
Entelligent Entertainment, LLC

Cover and Interior Design by
David Moratto www.davidmoratto.com

ISBN: 979-8-9858605-8-0

In loving memory of my mother,
Bernice S. Gittlin

Author's Notes

Dear Reader,

I'm aware that most authors prefer to write fiction in the past tense. For some reason, the voice of this novella came out in the present tense. I stayed with it because it felt alive. I hope it works for you.

I'm also aware that much of the science in this science-fiction tale is pure bonkers. Please indulge me. It's all in the service of your enjoyment. And finally, certain words in this book are intentionally misspelled. You will understand the reason for this once you get past the first few chapters. I have italicized these words to avoid confusion and persecution due to poor spelling.

Oh, and one more thing. I've intentionally left some redundant character and scene descriptions in the second half of the narrative. (Remember, we're combining the first two novellas into one novel here.) I thought the repetition might be helpful as a refresher. If it bothers you, just move on.

Truly yours,

David Gittlin

CHAPTER 1

"What have you got for me, Faulk?"

Observing my supervisor, Clive Borinsky, I wonder, for the four-hundredth time, why he only calls me by my last name. Despite the holes in my science training, I am Deputy First-Class Investigator Derrick Faulk. I hold the highest investigator rank in the *National Science Service*, a division of the National Security Authority. Our organization's primary mission is to ensure that the rapid pace of scientific and technological advancement does not run amok and consequently destroy the world.

Somewhere around four hundred instances of disrespect have finally worn me down.

"Would it trouble you to call me Agent Faulk?"

Sitting next to me, my associate, Aurora Zolotov, turns her head to the wall, which is painted a dismal shade of green. The subtle shake of her body tells me she is trying to stifle a laugh. Aurora is as colorful, beautiful, and phenomenal as her namesake, the Northern Lights.

After working with Aurora for nearly six months, I find it difficult to resist her radiant beauty and personality. The most maddening aspect of the situation is that Aurora makes no effort to affect me the way she does.

Borinsky glares at me. He finally decides to ignore my remark. "It's been twenty-four hours since the unauthorized file copy has been missing. You and your partners better have some good news for me."

"Our forensic IT team has thoroughly examined AndroBiotica's IT systems," I answer. "They have determined that no exterior cyber breach occurred. We've questioned each IT employee extensively. The forensics team scanned their computers. We found no examples of wrongdoing by any employee."

Borinsky places his elbows on the desktop of his workstation, hunches his shoulders, and leans toward us.

"Are you saying the file disappeared into thin air?"

"We are saying it is reasonably certain that the IT Department is not responsible for the theft," Brendt Williams offers.

I cringe inwardly. At this moment, I want to strangle Brendt. He is the remaining member of our team. A handsome, trim, affable man in his mid-thirties with a full head of blond and prematurely graying hair, Aurora and I find Brendt marginally useful, thanks mainly to his overly logical mind. This theory may sound counterintuitive at first, but personal experience has proven it to be true.

Shining through Brendt's resume of qualifications is a conspicuous lack of intuition. Only the top two percent of our profession possess this essential trait sufficiently to handle a crisis of this magnitude. Sadly, Brendt's other capabilities have propelled him to the sixty-seventh floor to complement our team. And so, we are stuck with him. At least he means well.

"Reasonably certain is not good enough," Borinsky explodes. "I want you to be dead sure!"

"We are more than reasonably certain," I quickly interject. "Agent Williams' choice of words is unfortunate. He intended to say we have high confidence in our findings thus far."

Borinsky is a man in his late forties who smokes three packs of *sagarillos* a day and appears to be somewhere in his late sixties. His eyes look like the double-door entrance to a bomb shelter after a cold fusion holocaust. I'd feel sorry for the man if I didn't loathe him intensely.

"Do you have anything to add, Agent Zolotov?"

"I believe Agent Faulk has given you an accurate update on our progress."

"Are you telling me that ninety-five percent of AndroBiotica's employees remain under suspicion?"

"That's one way to put it, Director. I am confident we will find *za* culprit or culprits quickly by *za* aplication of superior deductive techniques and intuition."

I've observed that Aurora tends to revert to her native accent when under pressure.

"Our next target is the Science Department," I add to inform Borinsky and deflect his attention.

Borinsky glances at the gilt-edged computer interface on his super-efficient workstation. Despite his exalted position and expensive equipment, the man has failed to make his office feel like anything but a prison cell.

"Get on with it, then. I have work to do. I'd say you have another forty-eight hours at the outside to get the file back before all hell breaks loose."

We scurry out of Borinsky's office like squirrels evading a predator. Waiting for the bullet elevator, I tell Agent Williams to re-interview the IT employees. I observe him wilt visibly.

"Do you think that's a good use of our time? There are only three of us on the case."

Two and a half, I think to myself.

"Because you opened your big mouth in Borinsky's office, it is now necessary to waste our time. Borinsky will surely ask us if we did the re-interviews."

The elevator arrives. We descend twenty-three floors in a matter of seconds. The elevator's intelligent gimbals make it feel like we are standing still.

As the doors open on sixty-seven, I turn to Aurora. "You'll handle backgrounding the scientists."

She winks at me. "Of course."

Not for the first time, I wish she wouldn't wink at me that way.

We go our separate ways. I head down the long corridor to my corner office.

CHAPTER 2

Unlocking the door to my spacious work abode, I remember the not-so-long-ago days when the acronym AI stood for Artificial Intelligence. AI will soon have a new meaning, namely, Alive Intelligence. The "old" designation for Artificial Intelligence will now be relegated to the acronym MI, signifying Machine Intelligence.

Everyone associated with AI expects these new classifications will take some time to settle into the sinews of society. Conceivably, there will be protests and possibly riots. What else is new besides Alive Intelligence and the latest flavor of Greek yogurt?

Like anyone with half a brain, I knew it was only a matter of time until science came within a hair's breadth of duplicating Human consciousness. Fortunately, I have more than half a brain. I have at least a brain and a half, but I keep this to myself.

I drop into the custom-fitted chair behind my workstation. I had to special order it due to my rangy six-foot-four-inch stature. Lower backs are vulnerable at such altitudes. Before diving into work, my intuition tells me some introspection is in order. I have learned to trust my intuition implicitly.

I recall why my former supervisor recommended that I transfer from the *NSA* to the *NSS*. The latter needed a few investigators capable of resolving cases quickly. I am known for solving crimes efficiently. That's why I'm here. That's why I'm facing the most crucial matter of my career. Despite the size of the suspect population, I see no reason why Aurora and I can't solve this case expediently and quietly. Regardless of my meager science background, solving cases is the bottom line. I've solved a lot of them. I will solve this one. No matter what it takes.

The problem we face is both complex and straightforward: One copy of the file is somewhere in unauthorized hands. And because the information in the file is impossibly sensitive, the President of the Federated Corporations of the United States has allowed only me and two other associates to head the investigation.

I tend to keep my thoughts and emotions to myself. That's another reason I'm in this position. The descriptor "taciturn" may have negative connotations in our society, but it is a virtue in this context. My feelings for Aurora are yet another example of the secrets that I doggedly hide, even though I have long ago tired of keeping secrets. *Such is one of the costs of being in the secrets business,* I remind myself repeatedly. And allowing emotions to cloud professional relationships is strictly frowned upon by the National Science Authority. It can lead to lapses in judgment in high-risk situations. The regular application of emotional discipline helps to keep things in perspective.

Metaphorically, and taken with a grain of salt, I have risen in the ranks with the launch speed of the new Thor Starship, much to the chagrin and jealousy of the many others I have left in my wake. I try hard to be humble and self-effacing with my peers, but they still resent me. *I can only do my job to the best of my ability and let the results speak for themselves,* which is another mantra I repeat to myself. The universe tends to favor those with this attitude, but not always. Trust in my business is a rare commodity, even when it comes to trusting in the sacred principles we assume govern our everyday lives.

Nevertheless, I don't lose sight of the fact that I've come a long way up, and with one wrong turn, I can plummet at the speed of the bullet elevators ferrying thousands of people throughout this tall tower.

I am also keenly aware that the world population continues to balloon despite dire warnings from governments around the globe. Good jobs like mine are as rare as the highest-quality diamonds. And the pressure attendant to this job is almost as severe as the pressure required to form diamonds. However, I endure the pressure because I enjoy my work, and therefore, my deep gratitude is in order.

I swivel in my ergonomic chair to look outside. Observing the imaginatively designed and varied city skyscrapers built upon the bombed-out, resurfaced rubble of old *Manterrattan* helps me to think productively. Although it's a gray and rainy day, I have a clear view, thanks to the monolithic suction towers. Since their installation throughout the city, the ever-present smog has dissipated to negligible levels, like a lethal infection decimated after the introduction of a new wonder drug.

It strikes me that the meeting with Borinsky was the source of my need for revitalizing and reassuring self-talk. I am now ready to go to work.

My attention returns to a file encompassing the events leading up to the crime. I lose track of time. Strands of unrelated thoughts crisscross and form relationships. I glance at my reasonably priced gold *Blenova* watch. The afternoon is waning. Another workday has almost expired. With every passing moment, the situation becomes more critical. We cannot allow the blueprints for an Android that mimics a Human Being in practically every detail to fall into the hands of anyone or anything besides those entities mandated by the *Federated Government*.

I continue to examine the facts from every angle: Up, down, backward, forward, and all points in between. Thirty seconds later, Aurora bursts into the room unannounced. I cannot help but take in the sight of her.

Aurora stands six feet tall in her plain black sneakers. The *NSA* and *NSS* require all agents to wear mousy-looking sneakers or flats to avoid any hint of sexuality. In Aurora's case, the Service has a big problem. No matter what attire she wears, Aurora finds it impossible to dim her sexuality. She dyes her blond hair brown, and still, the sheen and bounce of her curls radiate through. She once cut her hair boyishly short in a vain attempt to blend in.

The starched folds of her standard navy blue business suit and white shirt cannot conceal the luscious curves of her slender frame and ample bosom. With her almond-shaped ice-blue eyes, high cheekbones, aristocratic nose, and creamy complexion, Aurora can't stop employees' heads from turning. Most women would welcome this problem. Not Aurora.

Approaching my clean and compact workstation, Aurora finds enough space to plant her lovely hands painted in pale blue nail polish. I installed the workstation only last week. I'm still learning how to use it. With their all-in-one desktops, the workstations are expensive, but in the long run, they pay for themselves through increased productivity and savings on office supplies. Due to their expense, the Service only allows grade-one investigators and above to have one. I hope Aurora doesn't begrudge my upgraded desktop.

She leans over and engages my eyes directly. I find it hard to breathe for a fleeting moment.

"I've made a break in the case," she announces.

While paying prudent attention to diversity, the Service generally prefers good-looking men and women of high intelligence, accompanied by a long list of other prerequisites. If you have these traits and skills combined with wholesome habits on and off the job, your future is secure within the *NSS*. Of course, maintaining rare profiles such as these is easier said than done. Due to the pressure inherent in their jobs, a shocking number of agents have fallen from grace by pursuing pastimes such as hyperactive sexual activity and the quiet development of addictions to controlled substances. So far, Aurora and I have strenuously avoided stumbling into crevices such as these.

In all honesty, I don't mind in the least bit sharing the burden of the Alive Intelligence matter with Aurora and no one else. It's a satisfying intimacy without the pitfalls.

I meet Aurora's wide-eyed stare. I admire her curiosity and enthusiasm. I've never told her so, naturally.

"*Dites moi*," I reply with an equal measure of enthusiasm. I am teaching Aurora French as a fourth language to help her lose the remnants of her *Roussian* accent. The method works, even though there is no reasonable explanation for it.

Aurora emigrated from the *Souviet* Republic to *Angland,* where she won a scholarship to the prestigious *Carlton University*. This turn of events spawned her *Rousian/Anglish* accent. Sometimes, it can be unclear, so she's working on her diction.

"Za, oh damn, I mean, *the* assistant to the Science Department head is a woman named Louisa Esperanza. She has been calling a phone number in Bolivia that I've traced to a violent Bolivian Cartel known as *Los Monarcas,* or in English, 'The Monarchs.' We must question her immediately."

"Agreed."

I rise from my desk while casting an eye on the two adjacent walls containing rows of criminology texts I rarely consult. Experience has taught me that intuition and deductive reasoning work far better than arid textbooks. I maneuver around my compact desk and smile. "Give me a chance to wash up. I'll be right with you."

Aurora crosses her arms and nods. "*Vitch* car?"

I hear Aurora mutter something that sounds like a *Rousian* curse word. "I mean, who's driving?"

I glance out of the reinforced plexiglass windows behind my workstation. "I think we'll take the Jet-copter. The traffic looks bad."

The corners of Aurora's mouth turn down slightly.

I've trained myself to notice little details like this. "Is everything okay? You look a bit dejected."

"I'm fine," she replies. "The weather is affecting my mood."

My intuition tells me otherwise, but it's not worth pursuing. It's most likely a trivial matter, and we have urgent work ahead.

CHAPTER 3

We Jet-copter across town at a slow but steady speed. The journey to AndroBiotica is too short to retract the blades and use the jets. On longer trips, the Jet-copter can convert to a small aircraft on the rooftop launch pad as quickly as a convertible car can lower its top. Then it's straight up on dual-thrust engines and off into the wild blue yonder. However, in this case, the yonder is becoming charcoal gray, with the rains growing heavier as we slice through them at an angle.

I turn to Aurora on the seat next to me and catch her staring out into the gloom through her porthole window. I sense sadness cloaking her.

"It's a good thing we decided to fly. The heavy rain chokes traffic like concrete flowing from a cement mixer."

Aurora turns to me. "Are you trying to impress me with awful poetic phrases?"

"I'm trying to amuse you. Depression doesn't suit you, and it's counter-productive."

"It's called deep analysis, Derrick. You should try it sometime."

"That's a cruel and uncharacteristic remark. Something is bothering you. What is it?"

She turns back to her porthole window. "Nothing."

"In answer to your innuendo, I've already done my analysis. Allow me to restate the salient facts."

Turning from the window, Aurora raises an eyebrow. "Haven't we done that enough?"

"It's never enough until answers begin to reveal themselves. Besides, the summary will keep us sharp for our upcoming meeting with a genius inventor."

I begin speaking against the noise of the *whomping* rotor blades.

"The *National Security Authority* commissioned AndroBiotica to create and manufacture Androids that can pass as Humans to infiltrate terrorist cells, illicit drug organizations, extremist political groups, money laundering operations, and other large-scale criminal entities. I assume the synthetic Humans will prove helpful in espionage cases, but the *NSA* is mum on the subject.

"After serious consideration, the *NSA* ordered ten test subjects. They then deployed the Androids on secret missions known only to them."

I check to make sure I have Aurora's attention. By all outward signs, she is listening raptly.

"With the testing underway and the initial results promising, an unauthorized file copy containing patented schematics and manufacturing instructions to create AndroBiotica's Androids has disappeared. The first question is *Cui Bono*—who benefits?"

"We've started with the easiest to trace and most logical perpetrator or perpetrators, Aurora answers. "The first place to look is in the company's backyard."

"Right. We're running the financials for all active and deactivated AndroBiotica employees for the past year. In addition to Louisa Esperanza, we will interview employees in vulnerable financial positions, especially those receiving unusual cash payments."

"To be thorough, we must also check if any *NSA* employee had access to the file."

"Good point, Aurora. We didn't think of that before. It proves the value of this exercise."

Aurora delivers a forced smile.

"This backgrounding will take precious time, but I think we have a window of opportunity to recover the file because there will be a learning curve associated with manufacturing the Androids. The length of time will vary depending on where the plans end up."

Placing her hand on her forehead, Aurora looks down.

"What is it?"

"Something just occurred to me. Whoever has the file will probably copy and sell it to finance the manufacture of the Androids. It means that several different criminal organizations may eventually acquire the plans."

"Which would be disastrous. I suppose there's hope if *Los Monarcas* obtained the file. They have enough money to underwrite the manufacturing on their own."

Aurora stares at me. "Are you serious?"

"Half-serious."

Shaking her head, Aurora regards me with a dubious expression.

I regard her evenly. "It's possible, and maybe even likely, that *Los Monarchas* or another group may attempt to kidnap an AndroBiotica scientist to help them manufacture the Androids. We'll have to put the entire science team under twenty-four-hour surveillance."

As an afterthought, I add, "It probably makes sense to keep an eye on the art team too."

Aurora nods in agreement.

I reach inside my coat for the phone. "We'll implement the security surveillance immediately. We have to stop this threat before it gets underway. After Brendt completes the re-interviews, I'll assign him to the surveillance team. That will keep him out of our hair for a while."

The Jet-copter breaks through the rain clouds and begins its descent.

"Did you find anything else suspicious in the science logs?"

"Nothing besides Louisa's phone calls jumped out at me," Aurora answers.

"We'll do a quick scan of the roles of each employee and the inner workings of AndroBiotica's business. It won't be thorough, but it will have to do. I expect the warrants will be ready within a day."

I sit back in my luxurious seat. "If the Louisa Esperanza lead doesn't pan out, there won't be time to follow many more."

Aurora nods. "I know. It's a good thing we're working on this together."

I turn to her, but she is looking straight ahead. Our seatbelts automatically engage.

"Prepare for landing," the captain says.

CHAPTER 4

We sit in the office of Adrien Mattias, President of the AndroBiotica Corporation. Mattias summoned Aurora and me here before he permitted any questioning of AndroBiotica employees. This ban makes perfect sense. If I were in Mattias' shoes, I'd want to speak to me before I accused any of my employees of espionage and a slew of other dreadful offenses.

Mattias is a trim five-foot-ten-inch *Fraunchman* who looks a bit anemic. His pale appearance is unsurprising since men like Mattias are not in the habit of working on their tans. He wears his black hair in a *Rouman* emperor's cut accented by angular features, a firm jaw, full lips, and sleek glasses. For all I know, Mattias could be an Android designed with the characteristics of a famous *Fraunch* actor.

According to our confidential records, Mattias is forty-two years old, married, and has an eight-year-old daughter. This information is not public knowledge. Mattias scrupulously guards his private life and personal information. He does not make public appearances, nor does he grant interviews. His tightly guarded public persona is over-the-top, but at the same time, it makes perfect sense. Aurora and I are privy to Mattias' private life only because we are with the *NSS*.

The office is impressive. It reflects the ever-changing world of high technology. I notice the desktop of Mattias' enhanced workstation contains four computer interfaces. The interface closest to me displays the *Federated, EuroUnion,* and *Neddeki* stock markets. I can read the current AndroBiotica stock price highlighted on the Federated Techno Board.

I marvel at the rows of Android sculptures on each side of the room, which function as load-bearing walls and radiate an energizing light. Mattias tells us the furniture changes shapes and configurations on voice command to accommodate the nature and number of employees in the various types of meetings he hosts. He proudly explains that the color scheme on the walls can change according to his moods. In short, everything in his expansive corner office operates with artificial intelligence except, hopefully, Adrien Mattias himself.

After we introduce ourselves and present our credentials, Mattias gets down to business.

"Do you have a suspect?"

"We do," I answer. "Her name is Louisa Esperanza."

Mattias slumps back into his black leather executive chair trimmed with an elaborate border of scrolled stitching. The threading appears to be real gold.

"You can't be serious. Louisa is one of my most productive and trusted scientists. She's brilliant. I've never received a complaint about her."

Aurora hands Mattias a blue manila file labeled "Classified" in bold orange letters.

"These are copies of her recent phone log," Aurora explains. "You can see from the log that Louisa has been calling a number we traced to a known Bolivian cartel member called *El Hacedorde Justicia*. Roughly translated, it means *The Justice Maker*. He is a twenty-one-year-old enforcer and a first cousin of Sebastian Marquez, the leader of *Los Monarchas*, a violent drug cartel and a major exporter of heroin and cocaine."

While Mattias examines the file, the lifelike plants and flowers arranged on pedestals throughout the office capture my attention. The artificial flowers open and close in a riot of pastel and elementary colors. The green plants sway as if a subtle breeze moves their fronds. Who wouldn't want these colorful plants and flowers that require no maintenance and live indefinitely?

AndroBiotica holds exclusive patents on the designs and manufacturing process of these products. The NSA chose AndroBiotica for the Alive Intelligence project based on the ingenuity demonstrated by their unparalleled artificial plants for commercial and residential decoration.

A year after the government awarded the $200 billion contract, AndroBiotica presented an "almost Human" Android prototype that surpassed everyone's expectations.

Mattias throws the file on his polished redwood desk.

"Is this all the evidence you have?"

"It's enough," I say.

Mattias removes his glasses to clean them with a tissue. Then, he presses his eyes with his thumb and forefinger. AndroBiotica's President must be registering the same pressure as I am, times ten. He reaches into the top drawer of his desk to retrieve two white capsules and quickly downs them with a glass of water.

In the course of my work, I quickly learned that a bit of understanding goes a long way.

"I understand this is an unusually stressful time, but there are questions I must ask you."

"Ask away. You people are my only hope since the *NSA* forbade me from taking matters into my own hands."

"Only because a matter like this requires a specific kind of training."

Mattias leans forward. "It's not necessary to butter me up, Agent Faulk. Ask your questions and get on with your work, and let me get on with mine."

"Very well, sir. Do you know if anyone at the *NSA* had access to the file?"

Mattias looks at me as if he were talking to an eight-year-old. "Do you think I would be stupid enough to allow that? We write reports to the NSA in general, non-scientific terms. I review each one of them to be sure no proprietary information escapes these walls."

Aurora and I exchange a glance. *Scratch one more possibility off the list.* We ask more questions that do little to help us. By this time, Mattias is frustrated and tired of answering questions. I am about to end the meeting when Mattias surprises us.

"I have *NDA* forms for both of you to sign. After they are properly executed and witnessed, I'll take you downstairs to the central lab. You will get a first-hand look at our Android technology. I hope it will give you a greater sense of urgency to find the missing file. Then, I'll call Louisa to the lab. She won't expect to be interrogated until you begin questioning her. I'd also like to keep the meeting just between us."

"The *NSS* hasn't cleared us to see the Androids in person," Aurora states for the record.

"I'm allowing you to see them," Mattias says. "That's all the clearance you need."

After we get the NDAs out of the way, Mattias leads us to an elevator in the vestibule of his office. He seems preoccupied but not troubled. The man exudes a quiet confidence. I've always wondered how titans of industry like Adrien Mattias can function with a junk pile of problems incessantly weighing on their minds. I'd never trade places with any of them. I notice his expensive *Zandac* suit is rumpled, as if he's worn it while sleeping in a king-sized bed hidden in the floor or ceiling of his office. It's the only evidence I can see of the crisis at hand. I imagine Mattias regularly sleeps in his office after working late into the night. Say a voice command, and presto, your ultra-modern bedroom appears with the quilt folded back and chocolates on the pillow.

I catch my thoughts from carrying me away amidst the monastic silence of our descent into the bowels of the AndroBiotica building.

The elevator doors swish open into what is known as a "clean room." I've been in many of these antiseptic rooms during my investigations. Microscopic robots keep the air and the room's surfaces germ-free. In the antechamber to the lab, we unstrap and store our weapons. AndroBiotica prohibits the use of firearms in all scientific areas and meetings where five or more employees are present.

We strip down to our underwear. It requires a concerted effort to look away from Aurora's semi-nude body. Next, we move to telephone booth-sized UV disinfecting pods. After about a minute, the pods open to a short corridor, where a disembodied voice instructs us to put on the provided lab coats and special slippers. Before leaving the passage, we extract a visitor security badge from a small bin.

Mattias follows us through the safety doors and into the lab. It is primarily white, like an arctic mountain top. I notice plastic-wrapped bodies stacked on shelves on the wall to our right. The place looks more like a morgue than a lab. Workstations equipped with electron microscopes, computers with virtual screens, and honeycombed machinery stand against the other two walls. The body of a male Android lies naked on a gurney in the center of the room. There are no other Humans here except the three of us.

CHAPTER 5

Standing in front of the gurney, Aurora and I surround Mattias. He catches me staring at the Android's fire-engine-red hair.

"We've colored its hair bright red to mark it as non-Human. We apply Android exterior features in layers. During this process, there have been instances where an Android was mistaken for a Human. The bright red color serves as a security measure, distinct from the orange tones of natural red hair.

"When we release the finished product into the field, our teams have updated all of the Android's physical and psychological features according to its intended function. For the time being, this one responds only to voice commands. Soon, it will be programmed to act autonomously within its designated context. Its temporary name is Georges. In *Frauch,* the 'G' is pronounced like 'J'.

"Activate, Georges."

Mattias follows this command with a sequence of numbers and letters. Turning to us, he says, "We embed each unit with a unique name and password. The passwords are restricted exclusively to the science team. We are considering granting password access to Human field agents working with Android partners, assuming the government rolls out the test program."

In response to Mattias' command, the Android rises and moves adroitly out of the gurney. I watch its muscles flex and unflex in a perfectly natural way. I'm no expert on anatomy, but I'd never guess the creature in front of me is anything but Human, except for the flagrant red hair.

"Dress," Mattias tells it.

Aurora turns to me. By her expression, I can see that she is impressed by the demonstration.

There is a set of clothing on a shelf underneath the gurney. Georges bends down to retrieve one piece of clothing at a time. Its body is well-proportioned with clearly defined musculature. It looks fit but not overly developed. Its facial features aren't ugly or handsome. It's the sort of face that would go unnoticed in a crowd. An artist will later add defining features, such as character lines, skin defects, tattoos, and variations in body hair intensity. The finishing touches include skin tone, eye color, and hair dye.

Georges is finishing dressing himself in a black business suit and a light blue shirt. He is tying a Windsor knot in a red and gray striped tie using a cosmetic mirror extending from a pole on the gurney. He has yet to put on socks and shoes.

"Introduce yourself, Georges."

The Android turns to us. His tie is half-made. He glances down at his bare feet before introducing himself. With a non-threatening move, he gracefully shakes my hand and then Aurora's. His hand feels warm, and his flesh feels slightly moist. In a polite and sincere tone, Georges apologizes for being partially dressed. Then he turns back to finish tying his tie. After satisfying himself with how it looks, Georges picks up his shoes and socks. He examines them and then turns to Mattias with a puzzled expression.

"Go to the chair at the first workstation and put them on," Mattias says.

Georges smiles, bows slightly to Aurora and me, and moves off to finish dressing.

"Their hair and nails grow like ours do. As I've indicated, Georges needs some important external finishing touches. You may have noticed that Georges is adapting to his basic programming. When he shows us that he is ready to learn more, we will imbue him with a personality. Then, we'll decide if he needs to know that he is an Android. Some of our creations know their origins, and others do not, depending on their missions."

"If you don't mind me asking, how is it possible to make them so Human?" Aurora asks.

"The breakthrough came when we successfully mirrored a series of Human DNA strands. Then came the bigger challenge of finding a suitable substrate and transferring the recreated DNA strands onto a substrate. The next milestone came after we assembled an embryo of sorts. I use the term loosely. The 'initial building block' is a more accurate description. We chose to call it an 'embryo' for expediency. Having created the embryo, we had to find a way to accelerate its growth into adulthood. After another year of experiments, we struck upon a chemical agent to do the job. We lightheartedly call the ingredient 'baking soda.'

"The rapid growth cycle is a patented process that I can't divulge, even to a government agency. In general terms, it involves energy waves and a chemical solution. As you can imagine, we initially experienced colossal failures, followed by years of lesser failures. This became the norm until two years ago when we made the DNA breakthrough."

"I admire your persistence," I say to flatter Mattias' evidently big ego. I've dealt with high-powered people like Mattias before. Subtle ego flattery is one way to earn their cooperation.

"Your story is fascinating and inspiring," Aurora adds to double-team our genius gatekeeper.

"I've been dreaming of creating Georges since I was a boy of thirteen. I'm proud of our achievements. There were many milestones to reach. At times, the difficulties tempted me to give up, but we eventually found solutions one by one. I couldn't have done it without our science team. Fortunately, the right people showed up at the right time."

"I'd like to know what their insides look like if you don't mind me asking?"

We've pushed Mattias into an effusive mood. He answers Aurora's question willingly.

"We created our Androids to resemble Humans in every way. Their organs, nervous system, muscles, and skeletal structure closely match Human anatomy. Their hearts pump with a miniaturized pacemaker powered by a non-radioactive, proprietary energy source. The power source is a unique concept. It is one of several reasons the competition is far behind our technology. The power pack can last up to fifteen years. We expect to lengthen its life soon."

Mattias is on a roll. He is literally beaming. We encourage him to continue pouring out information. A tiny droplet could break open the case.

"Before an Android is activated, we inject it with blood and initiate the heartbeat. Software programming comes next. We do it in phases to avoid what we call 'traumatic awakening shock.' It took us a while to figure out how to activate our Androids without damaging them.

"The one obstacle we haven't yet overcome is skin. The skin tissue we use degrades rapidly after one year, and we must recall a unit to allow our technicians to replace it in the lab. We've tried extending the skin's life with special oils, but so far, nothing has worked. Currently, the skin issue renders the cost per unit too high for both commercial and private use. Only the government can afford our Androids for organized crime intervention and terrorist group infiltration. A few billionaires may want them as toys, but we aren't going there yet."

A moment of silence passes between the three of us. "I'm sorry if I rambled on," Mattias adds.

"On the contrary," I say. "I appreciate the information, and I'm sure my colleague does too."

Aurora nods. "Surely, you must have given a great deal of thought to the impact your Androids will have on society."

"I've examined the question extensively, Agent Zolotov. I've drafted a document covering the proper uses of Androids, including a set of laws I will propose when the time comes to introduce them into society. It's a work in progress. I'm doing my best to get ahead of the curve and the red tape."

I'm about to ask when we can expect Louisa Esperanza to arrive for questioning when Georges stands after putting on his shoes. He looks to Mattias for further instructions.

"Come with me," Mattias tells him. Then he turns to Aurora and me. "Give me a minute to check on something. I'll be right back."

Mattias walks to a doorway in the far wall with Georges in tow. On an oval panel to the side, he keys in a combination. The door slides open. Mattias ushers Georges in first. I catch a glimpse of a machine inside the room. Constructed of intertwined, curved silver rods, it gleams in the recessed lighting fixtures above. Before the door closes, I can see that the back of the machine is higher than the front, and there is something like a saddle in the middle of it. I get the impression of a giant, streamlined motorcycle. I glance at Aurora. She appears to be as curious about whatever is beyond the door as I am.

We are careful not to speak in Mattias' absence. It's the result of instinct and training. There is a good chance that hidden recorders will pick up anything we say in private. With Aurora at my side, I use the time to take a closer look at the bodies on the shelves. There are male and female specimens. They all have perfect physiques and red hair. I imagine an AndroBiotica team will modify them to fit whatever function they will eventually serve. We know that the science team is field-testing ten Androids. We don't know what the Androids look like or what their assignments entail. As is always the case, the background information the government feeds us for our investigations is on a need-to-know basis.

Mattias emerges from the doorway of what I think of as his secret laboratory. Georges has remained in the other room. I try to look blankly at Mattias to disguise my curiosity and indicate that I respect his privacy.

"I'm working on a pet project in the other room," he says dismissively, indicating the closed doorway behind him. "I enjoy tinkering with my ideas. Some of them turn into projects. Some of them are dead ends. It's a hobby. Helps to relieve the pressure. Once in a blue moon, a project will become a product offering."

Mattias approaches us with his hands clasped in a hand-washing gesture. Then, he touches his right ear. I notice for the first time that our host has an almost imperceptible device implanted in his ear.

"A staff member has alerted me that Louisa Esperanza will be arriving any moment."

CHAPTER 6

The meeting takes place in a makeshift configuration of workstations. Georges has assembled four of them in a square. With Aurora on my left side, I sit opposite Louisa Esperanza. Mattias sits across from Aurora. Esperanza wears a white lab coat. Her long, black hair is piled in a bun on her head, covered with a net. She wears a blue and gold security badge on her left breast. Her dark-skinned features are regular and attractive, but pockmarks from adolescent acne mar her cheeks. The smile on her full lips is warm, and her eyes shine with a curious expression. The hands clasped firmly in her lap tell a different story. She is understandably nervous. Our presence in this meeting is highly irregular for her.

Louisa Esperanza does not strike me as a criminal. Nonetheless, appearances can be deceptive. Aurora reaches across to hand Louisa a file—the same one she showed to Mattias. Louisa takes a moment to scan it. She looks up at me and then across to Aurora.

"Now I know why I am here."

"Good," I say. "My name is Derrick Faulk. My partner's name is Aurora Zolotov. We are here to ask you some questions."

We show Esperanza our credentials. "We are investigators from the *National Science Service.*"

Esperanza settles into her chair. She looks squarely at me and then at Aurora. Her facial expression communicates an unspoken question: *How dare you come here to ask me about this?*

I refrain from glancing sideways at Aurora. I'm sure she is as surprised as I am at Esperanza's reaction. If she is bluffing, she's good at it.

"It has come to our attention that you have been making calls to a member of a dangerous Bolivian cartel known as *Los Monarchas.*"

Esperanza breathes a heavy sigh. "I have been making calls to my cousin, Ramon Duarte. He is not an evil man. He is trying to atone for his sins. He wants to leave his life of crime behind. To that end, he is an informant for the *Federated Marshals Authority.* Why is your agency unaware of Ramon's status?"

Noting the absence of an accent, I can read Esperanza instantly. She is an educated, articulate, and highly intelligent woman. And, she does not appreciate, for one second, our suspicion of her as a wrong-doer. If Esperanza is telling the truth, then it's our turn to explain. Aurora does the honors.

"Sometimes agencies don't share information. I'm sure we can verify your statement quickly and clear up any misunderstandings."

Actually, I tell myself, it's common practice for agencies not to share information, but we leave this dirty little secret unsaid. It is now my turn to deliver some bad news. We have done this dance before.

"In the meantime, it will be best for you to come with us. It's a routine procedure for your security and ours."

"I will not permit Louisa to leave the building, Agent Faulk. I have a business to run, and subjecting this valuable employee to your questions is the result of an interagency screw-up. My company will not be held responsible for it."

"She will come with us, or we will arrest you for obstruction of justice," Aurora says in a neutral tone.

"You wouldn't dare."

"Watch us," she follows with less neutrality.

Louisa speaks up in an agitated tone. "I'm a single mother, and I'm cooperating with the *FMA* to keep Ramon calm and on track. The *FMA* has promised Ramon will be extracted soon and awarded full citizenship in exchange for his undercover work."

"I'm sorry for insisting, but…"

I feel Aurora's hand on my arm. Turning, I see her ice-blue eyes filled with the kind of compassion only one woman can have for another. She turns to Louisa. "I think it will be okay if you stay here until we can sort this out. Just be sure not to vary your routine."

She turns back to me. After some thought, I nod my okay. I can live with Aurora's compromise. My instincts tell me Louisa is telling the truth. We'll have a long conversation with the *FMA*. Maybe Ramon has some information about the missing file. That would be a fortunate coincidence, but probably too much to hope for.

As I prepare to leave, a tall, thin man wearing a lab coat and slippers enters the room. From his straight black hair, matching black glasses, and Asian features, I typecast him as a Japanese scientist.

"This had better be important, Hideki," Mattias calls across the room.

"I believe you will find it most important," the scientist replies.

■ ■ ■

Two hours later, I am sitting across from Aurora in her office. It is half the size of mine. Aurora is a grade two investigator. Technically, I'm her superior. My position relative to Aurora's makes my secret feelings for her even more impossible. If the situation were to become more uncomfortable, I'd consider quitting the *NSS*. It may come to that. I can afford to wait until another desirable job comes along. I don't work for the money. I work for the work.

Before he died miserably of cancer, my father left me with enough money to circumvent the cruelties of economic necessity. His name was Bernard. My father and his brother, Henry, became wealthy from their success as entrepreneurs, although my father never seemed happy about it. Bernard was a company builder, and Henry made wise investments. Together, they made money like a thousand-*Dara* note printing press. Being a Gemini, my father had two sides. He was kind and generous on one side and mean on the other. He cut me with his constant criticism, but I survived to fight another day. Nowadays, I like to think I'm fighting for something worthwhile.

Growing up with money generally leads to feelings of entitlement and a lack of ambition. I fell into this trap for a while. As an adolescent and teenager, I led a charmed life. I didn't have to work for anything except my grades in school. Everything else came to me as naturally as the seasons. I spent my summers playing golf and reading mystery and adventure novels. I read every book published by the authors I liked. I wasn't the least bit lazy when pursuing my hobbies. I attacked them wholeheartedly and energetically. I had, however, a distinct aversion to real work. I imagined I'd become a novelist or a pro golfer when the gravy train ended. No nine-to-five grind for me. Then, in my senior year in high school, a small voice spoke to me. It said: "Criminal Justice." It may have come from my summer reading. Who knows? In college, my interest deepened with every CJ course I enrolled in. Eventually, I majored in Criminal Justice with a minor in Public Administration. The idea of becoming a lawyer tempted me, but only momentarily. I naturally gravitated to law enforcement. I love the art and science of investigation. It's not a job. It's almost as much fun as my adolescent hobbies.

So, here I am, listening to Aurora videoconferencing with a *Federated Marshal* and deciding to buy a few AndroBiotica plants and flowers for our offices. I'll come in early to arrange the plants in Aurora's office. She'll want to rearrange them, but at least the gifts will be there to surprise her. And she'll probably chastise me for buying them, and I'll hope she secretly likes the gesture.

Aurora ends her call. I've overheard every word. The Marshal confirms Louisa Esperanza's story. He has no leads to offer. Why am I not surprised?

An instant later, Aurora's videocom on her computer chimes. She looks up at me, and since I'm on the other side of her screen, mouths the words: *Adrien Mattias.*

Answering the three-dimensional call, I hear Aurora say, "Hello, Mr. Mattias. I'm surprised to hear from you again so soon."

"We can drop the formality. Call me Adrien. It looks like we're going to be working closely on this problem. Where's your partner?"

"He's right here with me."

Aurora gestures to me to join her. As a grade two investigator, Aurora uses an outdated workstation with an upright display and a physical keyboard. If we resolve this case in a timely manner, I will promote Aurora and order her a new workstation. If we fail, Aurora's career will stall, and there is a good chance Borinsky will demote me. And surely, in the scheme of things, our struggles will pale in comparison to the prospect of criminals using AndroBiotica's Android technology for evil purposes.

I cross over to sit beside Aurora. Mattias makes no effort to acknowledge my existence.

"I'm almost positive I know where the missing file went. Hideki Maroukama, one of my top scientists, found a cleverly disguised login to our system. The case now has the earmarking of an unusual inside job. I'll need you two back here right away."

And with that, Aurora's screen fades to black.

CHAPTER 7

Adrien Mattias meets us in his office. Unlike our first encounter, we don't linger there. Mattias instructs his AI assistant, whom he has named *Kopernikus,* to hold all calls while he's away from his desk. Then, we follow him back down to the central laboratory. After the long elevator ride and the decontamination pods, Mattias strides purposefully into the gleaming white room a few steps ahead of Aurora and me.

Georges lies spread-eagled on an operating table in the center of the room. An artist is at work with a tray of brushes and pencil lasers by his side.

As I draw closer, I see that Georges's appearance has changed dramatically. His wavy hair is brown, and so are his eyes. He has aged about twenty years since our last visit. I can make out a slight paunch in his stomach. The other features that strike me are his bulbous nose and handlebar mustache. His skin is pale, almost chalky. His thin lips are liver-colored. Georges looks to be a serious drinker. The artist has inked a faded tattoo on his right arm. To me, Georges appears to be someone who has fallen through the safety net of a good job and into a dissolute lifestyle. I feel sorry for him.

As we pass the gurney, Mattias remarks, "Georges is the last of the test subjects. We've changed his name, of course."

"He's not an under-the-radar type of guy," I remark.

"We typically keep our subjects plain-looking to help them blend in," Mattias explains. "Georges is an exception. He's an example of the differentiation we can achieve with our Androids. We can make them any race we want them to be. Their facial features, physiques, body markings, age, and accents can vary over a broad spectrum of Human variables. The possibilities are endless when you add a customized set of personality traits. No two of our subjects are alike.

"George's primary mission will be eavesdropping. He will frequent a bar known to attract criminal elements of all stripes. We've equipped Georges with special ears that he can use to select, amplify, and record conversations of interest. All the while, he will appear content to drink himself into a stupor."

"That's impressive," Aurora says sincerely.

"I'm trying to impress both of you. I'm not supposed to reveal any details of the test subjects' missions, but I read you in on this one to underline the importance and time-sensitive nature of your mission."

"Seeing first-hand what these machines are capable of definitely emphasizes your point."

"Aurora nods in agreement, then adds, "But no pressure, right?"

Mattias laughs, and I join him.

"Follow me into my private lab. I believe you've already had a glimpse of it."

Aurora and I exchange a look. "There must be hidden security cameras everywhere," I whisper to her.

Standing before the keypad, Mattias opens the door to his private office. Three machines occupy most of the area. They look like the one I glimpsed earlier this morning—an oversized, streamlined motorcycle with the rear end protruding from a tall, vertical panel. The machines remind me of exquisite metallic sculptures.

We are in a clean room identical to the central lab, except the ceilings are higher. I estimate fifteen feet. Recessed lighting shines down from above. In the confines of the room, the machines look enormous. The back panels are about ten feet high. They consist of curved silver rods, electronic devices, and thick, multi-colored wires secured by transparent tubes to the back panel. What I figure is a control panel with a built-in monitor sits atop a solid, shiny metallic front wheel. Positioned in the middle of the machine, I see a gleaming silver saddle with terraced footrests at the base, presumably for varied leg lengths.

Observing us examine the machines, Mattias says, "I haven't had time to cover them with fancy skins."

After we recover from the unanticipated sight of the machines, Aurora asks, "What do they do?"

"They are transporters to a parallel dimension," Mattias answers as if parallel dimensions are as commonplace as butterscotch pudding. "I built them one at a time, improving each successive model. I sent the fourth machine into the parallel dimension."

If anyone besides Adrien Mattias made these statements, I'd think they were delusional. I glance at Aurora. She is taking all of this in more calmly than I am.

"Is there somewhere we can sit down to discuss this?" I propose.

"I have an office behind this lab."

Mattias leads us to a sealed doorway. He opens it by keying in another combination. We are entering a second private room, both behind the central lab. The room sequence is becoming a labyrinth.

The office is small but functional. The ceiling is lower, and the lighting is softer than in the two labs outside. A bookcase of first-edition antique texts lines the wall to my right. I notice a row of oil painting prints by past masters on the wall to my left. Mattias is a man with a deep appreciation for the past and a clear vision for the future. Blueprints cover a smaller version of Mattias' cubed desk in the upstairs office. Strips of gold inlays accent the lustrous redwood. Inset into the surface is a computerized design interface. Like everything I've seen belonging to this man, it's pricey. Four black leather chairs surround a cocktail table in one corner.

"One and two in front of my desk," Mattias says. I'm not sure if he is talking to us or the chairs.

When two of the chairs roll themselves up to his desk, I have my answer.

Mattias gestures to the chairs. We sit in them. They immediately adjust to the contours of our bodies. I can't remember feeling this comfortable in a chair of any kind.

"Give me a moment to take care of something," Mattias says politely. He transfers blueprints into a cabinet of architectural drawers beside his desk. With his desk clear, Mattias types something into his computer interface. When the task is complete, he sits back in his regal executive chair and stares at us.

"Do you mind if I record this?" I ask.

"Might as well. I have a lot to say."

I place a half-*Dara*-sized recorder on the desk. After an uncomfortable silence, I begin the discussion.

"You mentioned a lead you have for us." Mattias laughs.

Maybe the man *is* delusional. "Did I say something funny?"

"No, Agent Faulk. I admire the way you are adjusting to the situation."

"A bit like your chairs."

He laughs again. "I like people with a sense of humor."

Mattias rubs his chin. "Let's see. Where do I begin?" He takes a moment to compose his thoughts. "We'll start with the math. Are you two good mathematicians?"

"I'm okay, but not too far past *Caculars Ona*," Aurora answers.

"Passable," I reply, avoiding my distaste for Math.

"Alright. I'll try to keep it relatively simple. Here we go. I became interested in string theories and parallel dimensions. A thesis by one quantum physicist in particular caught my attention. His name is Anton Bukofsky. I flew to Moscow to meet him. A fascinating man. Brilliant. He proved to me that parallel dimensions exist, at least mathematically. After more research, I began to think in terms of frequencies. I found the writings of both scientists and spiritualists to be congruent and intuitively relevant. To save time, I will condense the ideas into a few sentences.

"Everything in the universe exists on a vibrational level. If I want something honestly and sincerely, and if I am willing to put forth the effort, all I have to do is tune in to the vibration. If I am persistent, I will have what I want. It will come into my life. It may not come in the form I envisioned, but the essence of my desire will appear.

"I wanted to find other dimensions. I built a machine to accomplish this. My research revealed that if parallel dimensions exist, they will vibrate at different frequencies than the one we are in. My machine detected one dimension vibrating at a lower frequency than ours."

"Only one?" Aurora asks.

"It's fortunate that we found only one, as you shall see. I believe there are an infinite number of dimensions out there, but their vibrations are too subtle to detect with the latest model I'm using."

"Can you tell us about the other dimension you found?" I ask.

"I wanted to save that for later, but I suppose we can get into it now."

I sit back in my chair. Evidently, Mattias has decided to give us a full briefing. I'm glad he's allowing us to record it.

"I've named the other dimension Tier Two. The name will have to do until I think of something better. As I said, Tier Two operates at a lower frequency than ours. Essentially, we exist on a higher plane. We are more technologically advanced than they are. There are similarities and differences between our two worlds. For instance, I've been using an Android to study a company in Tier Two called Aerodyne Dynamics. The company is developing AI for the aerospace industry. They are also developing Humanoid robots. Their Humanoids are crude compared to our nearly Human Androids. You might say Aerodyne is in the Dark Ages of AI. The company is owned and operated by a Frenchman. Not a *Fraunchman*. A Frenchman. He hails from the city of Lyon, France. I come from *Liron, Fraunch*. Do you see the similarity? His name is Valerian Simons. He changed his last name from Simonovitch. Valerian is a *Jorish* immigrant from *Roussia*. His background is entirely different from mine. Do you see my point? The variations of names and places between the two worlds vary randomly. I can find no pattern to them."

We acknowledge our understanding of the point.

"Okay, now let's look at some macro examples. There is a country in Tier Two called the United States of America. The high-level agencies there are similar to those in our country. They are called, for example, 'The Federal Bureau of Investigation,' 'The Central Intelligence Agency,' The National Science Foundation, Homeland Security, and The National Security Agency. The currency of the United States is the Dollar. Ours is the *Dara*. And so on. Getting used to the different names is relatively easy.

We nod our agreement. Mattias' eyes brighten with the next topic of discussion.

"I designed a new Android model to explore Tier Two. I chose not to share the details with the science team because I took some liberties with the project that I would not allow them to take. I've been experimenting along the lines of intelligence and free will. The question is: How much intelligence and autonomy can we afford to give an Android before losing control of it? I programmed this advanced model with a comprehensive set of moral and ethical rules to address the issue. I named my new model Romulus. I thought a higher-functioning unit would be useful in certain instances. I must also admit it wouldn't hurt our sales.

"Romulus has traveled to the other dimension eight times to capture strategic photographs and compile notes. I've been debating whether or not it is wise to share the information I'm privy to with anyone. I'm not sure our world is ready for it. However, with what has happened, I'm forced to share the information with you."

After sitting upright during his entire presentation, Mattias slumps backward in his chair.

"I finally stepped over the line with Romulus. I lost control of him. I established twelve-hour check-in times with him. He missed his scheduled check-in time yesterday. I haven't been able to reach him since. I believe he is too intelligent now for his own good. I designed Romulus to evolve, but his mental capabilities are expanding faster than I expected. I suspect he is overwriting his programming in unpredictable ways."

"Is it possible he's missing due to a system failure?" Aurora asks.

"I doubt it. Romulus has backups for all of his critical systems."

Mattias stares whimsically at his bookcase. "I should have seen this coming, but I was so pleased with Romulus' progress. You get attached to them. Can you understand that?"

I nod.

"Of course," Aurora says.

"I want to create more enhanced models like Romulus, but I've learned my lesson. If I play with fire again, it will be with strict control protocols."

Mattias sits forward again. "Here is my primary concern. The IT team discovered an unauthorized duplicate file that had been missing for ninety minutes after Romulus departed on his last mission. My scientist found a suspicious login. I have reason to believe Romulus made the suspicious login. He disguised it well enough to give him time to escape into Tier Two. I'm almost certain Romulus has the file. I'd guess his motive for desertion is freedom. He probably took the file to sell it or to make himself useful to a robotics company in order to land a job. But his motives are irrelevant. The goal is to find Romulus and recover the file. Quickly."

Mattias takes a long look at us. "Your job is to find Romulus and recover the file. Whatever it takes. When you recover the file, I want you to destroy Romulus for the safety of everyone in both dimensions."

A fundamental question occurs to me. "Why would Romulus go to Aerodyne Dynamics if it's the first place we would look for him?"

"As I said, Romulus is evolving. He is learning something new every moment. I can't predict what he's thinking or what he will do next. I can only be sure of one thing: He has a plan that he believes will enable him to survive and thrive. The most logical place to start looking for him is a place he is familiar with: Aerodyne Dynamics."

I'm getting a better picture of what we're up against. "Can you give us a minute?"

"Of course. I'll meet you in the other room."

We wait for Mattias to exit the room.

"You don't have to do this," I tell Aurora.

"Does that mean you want to go alone?"

"Yes?"

"Why?"

"This is a dangerous assignment. As the senior member of the team, your safety is my responsibility."

"What?"

"And someone has to explain my absence to the Director. He won't let me go if I tell him I'm heading off into another dimension to follow a lead."

"I have to tell him?"

"Yes. Once I'm gone, it will be a *fait accompli*."

"It makes no sense for you to go alone. You admit the mission is risky. You need a capable field agent by your side."

I ignore her comment.

"Derrick, you can report me for disobeying a superior. I don't care. I refuse to be left behind to explain what you've done. Borinsky will think I've lost my mind if I tell him you've gone to a parallel dimension. And he will castigate me for allowing you to do it alone. I'm going with you. End of discussion."

CHAPTER 8

After leaving Mattias' subterranean hideaway, we are with him again in his resplendent upstairs office.

"That was a chilly ride up," he says to us once we've taken our seats on a curvilinear pit sofa in an area below Mattias' big desk. From this new seating arrangement, Adrien Mattias appears less like an Emperor and more like an equal.

Aurora and I haven't spoken a word to each other since rejoining our host in the central lab.

"Let's have it. What's going on between the two of you?"

"We had a disagreement. We've resolved it," I answer.

I notice Aurora assumes a more relaxed posture. My statement confirms her forceful request for inclusion on a mission from which we may never return.

Mattias turns his attention to Aurora. "Is that true?"

"Yes, Adrien," she answers, deliberately using his first name as he allowed on the video conference in her office.

"May I call you Adrien as well?"

"As long as I can call you Derrick," Mattias deadpans.

"Of course."

"Good. We're all on a first-name basis. Who knows, we might even become friends?"

Aurora glances at me and then back at Mattias. "Anything is possible," she says with a winsome smile.

Adrien is showing us another side of himself. The reason is apparent. We have to get along and feel comfortable with one another to succeed. Removing barriers leads to a more productive relationship. By "letting his hair down" with us, Adrien is demonstrating a strong leadership skill.

A calm female voice enters the room from a hidden speaker, making it sound as if it is coming from all around the office. To me, the quality of the effect is superior to that of surround sound.

"Excuse me, Adrien. A gentleman by the name of Carlton Whitewater is on the line. He says it is urgent."

Adrien sighs deeply. "It's the Managing Director of the *Euro Police Force,*" he tells us. "They think everything is urgent. I wish I had never included them in the field test. I have to take the call. Excuse me."

Adrien goes to his desk. I think Adrien had intended to fill us in on our mission in the comfort of his main office. He might have to do it downstairs, where a team of Androids is making preparations for our journey to Tier Two.

"Do you mind if I attend to a few things while we await whatever comes next?" I ask Aurora.

She gives me a mischievous look. "Be my guest. I'll call Borinsky and make up a story to cover our asses."

"I'm sorry to lay it off on you."

"Don't be silly. I'm probably a better liar than you." Her expression becomes deeply concentrated. "Come to think of it, I don't think I've ever caught you in a lie."

"That illusion will quickly fade the more we work together."

Moving down the sofa for more privacy, I call my estate attorney. I am establishing bulletproof Trusts for my younger brother and sister in the event of my early demise. It is a task I've been putting off mainly because I haven't, in the past, stared death in the face as squarely as I am now. When I finish the call, I see that Adrien is still preoccupied with his. I decide to use the break to add notes to the two cases I've been working on before this one came along. If I disappear without a trace, my successor will have a better idea of where to pick up the slack. While I'm covering my bases, I can't help overhearing Aurora reciting a fake cover story to our supervisor. In as few details as possible, Aurora is telling Borinsky that we are on the trail of a brighter-than-average male Android whom we believe has the AndroBiotica file. Since the suspect is unusually smart, his whereabouts are unpredictable. Our pursuit requires last-minute decision-making, which can result in irregular or no reporting.

Borinsky has never been a happy man. Aurora's update does nothing to relieve his misery, but from what I gather, he is willing to give us a little more rope to hang ourselves with. That little bit of rope is all we'll need to reach Tier Two. After about forty-eight hours of radio silence, Borinsky will think the earth has swallowed us whole or we've gone rogue. He will no doubt send agents after us, but by the time he unleashes his agents, we will be long gone.

When I finish dictating my case notes, my thoughts turn to something else. The issue has been standing in the background since our first meeting. I turn in time to see Mattias finish his call. He massages his eyes and face to relieve the stress of the call. This is probably the wrong time to address the issue, but I decide to broach the subject because our time together is waning.

"Excuse me, Adrien, but I must discuss a matter that's been on my mind."

Mattias looks up from his desk. It takes him a few seconds to refocus. "What?"

"I've been thinking about the effects your Androids will have if you release them into mainstream society. One issue bothers me in particular. We've already seen technology steal jobs from hard-working people. The use of Androids in business will deprive people of even more jobs. I'm talking about bartenders, waiters, maids, and administrative assistants, to mention a few. This trend has already gone too far. How can we be helping people if we take away their means to earn a living?"

From the corner of my eye, I see Aurora listening coolly.

Mattias takes a deep breath. I get the impression that he's had this discussion many times before.

"I'll be succinct. Unfortunately, what you describe is a byproduct of advancing technology. However, I feel it is a part of the natural order of things. The people you mentioned will have to adapt and survive. The market will push them to upgrade their skills for better-paying and more interesting jobs. I look forward to discussing topics like these with you and your partner once we have resolved this crisis. I'll take you both to my favorite restaurant to celebrate. Then, we can debate these issues until dawn. I sincerely hope that time arrives soon."

Mattias' answer is over-simplified, but I let it slide. He makes a salient point: This is not the time for long-winded debates.

The videocom chimes. The caller identifies herself as the Android team leader. I hear her advise Mattias that the preparations for our mission are complete.

The elevator takes us down to the central lab. Mattias is lost in thought. Perhaps he does his best thinking in elevators. I'm in the moment, feeling the magnitude of the reality we are facing. It is a journey into the unknown with no guardrails or guarantees.

Aurora whispers in my ear. "Are you frightened?"

"Anyone with a scrap of intelligence would be."

She whispers again. "I can hold your hand if it will help."

"How about I take you to dinner if we reach the other side?"

Aurora laughs. "Sounds good, but I doubt we'll have the time for it."

"I wasn't being serious."

Maybe she's playing with me to calm herself down. Or, perhaps she's flirting with me because no one will ever know what happens between us in another dimension. I tell myself to stop thinking about this sort of interplay. The mission ahead of us is difficult enough. Distracting thoughts only add to the difficulty.

After disinfecting, we pass through the central lab into Mattias' private lab. Awaiting us are three machines that look like modern sculptures of giant racing motorcycles. In addition, I notice two hiking outfits, complete with caps and boots, and an Android who identifies herself as Laura, the team leader. She may have a name and perhaps a personality, but she has no outer finishings. Laura is a white figure in a white technician's uniform.

While we strip down to change clothes, Mattias imparts mission directives and final instructions.

"Report to me every six hours with these comms. Mattias pulls two small objects from his pocket. I'll have one of these with me at all times. Laura has programmed your machines with Romulus' last known coordinates. The machines will carry you to your starting point in Tier Two. We call the machines Trans-Dimensional Transporters, or TDTs. I've programmed them to return here upon completion of your mission. You don't, and shouldn't, try to operate them. The

Trans-Dimensional Transporters will do all of the work for you. Just sit still and enjoy the ride."

While dressing, I'm listening intently. It all sounds reasonable if I ignore the fact that we will be traveling inter-dimensionally on monster motorcycles.

"You will land near an abandoned warehouse in a rural area outside of a city called Alexandria, Virginia. The population there is low-density. You can operate in relative secrecy. Hide the machines in the warehouse by removing the weight of the cargo Laura and her team have packed for you in the landing pontoons."

Mattias points to a cabinet in the corner. "We have mobile sanitizers in there to clean you up when you come home."

I like the sound of "when" instead of "if."

"You will find fifty thousand dollars in US Mint platinum bullion coins in the pontoons. Romulus exchanged one-gram gold bars for them on his first trip. The coins are lighter, and they hold their value. You will exchange them for dollars as needed. In addition, you will find fake identification wallets, including passports, driver's licenses, and FBI credentials.

"Along with a gold badge, the FBI leather wallet contains two slots for your photos and an FBI medallion. While in Tier Two, Romulus photographed the essential identifiers needed by the average citizen. I asked him to research and photograph law enforcement credentials in case the requirement arose. The FBI credentials I've given you will pass as authentic. Romulus' work with identification credentials led to him having authentic-looking identifiers, including a driver's license, pass-port, insurance, and business cards. These were necessary items for obvious reasons. We gave Romulus the name Bruce Sanford Dillon for his credentials. Naturally, we gave him no weapons or agency identification. Bear in mind, however, that your adversary is resourceful. He will likely acquire another identity or possibly several identities. He may buy unregistered weapons on the street.

"If Romulus uses a disguise to change his appearance, it will not be radical. He can't go to a plastic surgeon for obvious reasons. I've given you a set of eight-by-ten photos to help identify him on sight.

"I've also packed extra clothing for different occasions. I've included your service weapons for emergencies, plus rations in case you need them. After unpacking the cargo, I imagine your first order of business will be to find suitable transportation. Don't forget to buy suitcases."

The man has a sense of humor when the mood strikes him.

"I've given you a good start. The rest is up to you."

Mattias hands us our comms. They look like Silver *Daras*, only thicker.

"And one more thing."

Mattias hands us each a streamlined silver pen. He points to mine.

"That's an energy weapon disguised as a pen. Point and click it to shut down Romulus' systems permanently. There is enough energy for one shot in each of the weapons. You will not be able to recharge them in Tier Two. Make your shots count. Do not, under any circumstances, use your service weapons against Romulus. The odds are that the impact will trigger his power pack to explode with enough force to bring down a building this size. Am I clear?"

We both acknowledge the danger.

"Any questions?"

I try to think of a question. Nothing comes to mind. I'm sure I will have plenty after we land.

"Have you packed instructions with any of the items we might not be familiar with?" Aurora asks.

"Yes, dear."

Now he's acting fatherly. There are many sides to Adrien Mattias, many of which I'm sure we haven't seen.

"Any last words?"

We smile mirthlessly.

"Bad joke. Let me give you one final piece of information. Romulus knows he is artificial."

"Why is that important?" Aurora asks.

"You will find an enhanced, self-aware Android a more formidable opponent than any Human you will ever encounter."

CHAPTER 9

In the private lab, we take seats on two of the three Trans-Dimensional Transporters. I offer the more advanced model to Aurora. She accepts it after a mild argument about who should have the better machine. Mattias communicates with us from the central lab through speakers. He assures us that the difference between the two Transporters is nominal. I will arrive in Tier Two about thirty seconds after Aurora, assuming all goes as planned.

The dashboard in front of me is simple. It comprises a numbered combination panel on the left, a small red rectangle in the middle, and a translucent computer interface on the right. Mattias instructs us to enter a passcode into the oval combination panel. The passcode releases a red ignition guard in the center. The ignition guard opens, revealing an orange ignition button underneath. After entering another number combination, there is a slight delay before the ignition button glows green.

"Have your ignition buttons turned green?"

We answer in the affirmative.

"Good. When the ignition guard is enabled, the machines perform an automatic final systems check. The green means you are good to go. I bid you a safe trip, safe trip, and good hunting."

After thanking Mattias for his warm wishes, we push our ignition buttons.

From underneath the pontoons, I watch a sheet of molten material issue upward on both sides of my Transporter. It meets to form an enclosure above my head.

A loud *whooshing* sound indicates to me that blowers are cooling the molten material. It slowly resolves into a transparent, oval-shaped bubble surrounding our machines.

"We replace the safety shield after each excursion because it degrades," Mattias explains informatively. "Standby for phase two."

The computer interface on my dashboard comes to life. Through my red-tinted goggles, I see a readout of my vital signs: Heartbeat, blood oxygen level, pulse, temperature, and breathing rate. The body of my Transporter rotates to a forty-five-degree angle. My feet rest on metallic stirrups. Synthetic straps slither into place around my torso. Instantly, the Transporter blasts me into total darkness.

Has the machine malfunctioned?

I wait in a black void for about thirty seconds. If Mattias didn't tell me about this, something has gone wrong. I can only hope he forgot amidst the last-minute instructions.

A tiny light appears in the distance. Suddenly, it expands into a bright portal with diaphanous edges. The Trans-Dimensional Transporter catapults me toward the light. It becomes so bright that I have to close my eyes, even with my light and radiation-canceling goggles affixed.

My seat rotates to a horizontal position. I open my eyes. Gratefully, I realize I've made it through the void. A landscape of rolling hills under a bright and clear sky surrounds me. I turn around to see a hole in the fabric of time and space fade and disappear behind me. *I'm not in Heaven, thank God.*

The TDT thrusts me over the hills toward a farm and open fields stretching to the horizon. The fields rush toward me at breakneck speed. I close my eyes again and affirm to myself that the Transporter knows what it is doing.

The subtle vibration of my saddle ceases. As far as I can tell, I'm still in one piece. Tentatively, I open my eyes. My straps release and disappear into the sides of the saddle. To my left, an exit door in the oval safety shield swings open. I glance at the dashboard. The computer interface reads Cullen, Virginia. A map displays the city of Alexandria marked with a star to the south and a highway leading to it. Hoisting myself up and through the exit, I step to the ground one foot at a time. Turning to my right, I see Aurora standing beside her TDT. Beyond her lies a warehouse with rusted corrugated walls and a slanted roof. A ground fog surrounds it. The temperature is chilly.

Aurora approaches me with a smile. It was worth the trip to see that smile. She slaps me on the arm. "*Ve* made it."

We are both too relieved to worry about her pronunciation.

Unexpectedly, Aurora hugs me. I return the gesture gingerly. We disengage awkwardly.

"Sorry," she says. "That was unprofessional. If Mattias were here, I'd be hugging him for getting us this far."

Pointing over my shoulder at the warehouse, Aurora says, "Check out the lock on the double doors."

I turn around to face the warehouse. The padlock is large enough to be seen clearly from thirty yards away.

We walk together toward the doors. From a few feet away, the padlock looks brand new against the rusted door handles.

"Are you thinking what I'm thinking?" Aurora says.

"An agent never goes anywhere without a set of lock picks. And the padlock probably belongs to Romulus."

Aurora nods. "Quick. Open it."

After probing the lock for five minutes, I conclude the tumblers are too thick to be breached by lockpicks.

"There might be an opening in the roof for dropping heavy crates or bales of hay through by crane," I tell Aurora. "I can boost you up there to take a look."

She nods again.

I give Aurora a leg up. She is heavy but agile from hand-to-hand combat training. Her height is another advantage. I've seen her train. She is a powerful fighter. With the traction of her hiking boots combined with her flexibility and strength, she boosts herself over the ledge easily. I hear her scrabble up the incline.

"You were right," She calls to me. "There's an opening up here."

"Wait a minute," I call back to her.

Walking around to the far side of the warehouse, I see a pile of discarded wooden boxes. I assemble a few of them to make an improvised staircase. Cautiously, I ascend the makeshift stairs. I see across the slanted roof. Aurora crawls to me on her hands and knees. Reaching down, she helps me up with one arm. I am surprised by her strength. I may be slim, but I'm not a lightweight.

I take a minute to adjust to the incline of the roof. From here, I can see the farmhouse in more detail. Weeds and untended grass have overrun the yard and driveway. Vines cling to the white siding. Acres of fallow fields extend beyond the run-down dwelling. A red-lettered sign in the yard reads: "Bank Foreclosure." A phone number and a realty company logo appear underneath. No one is in a hurry to buy a small farm without government subsidies. With the town of Cullen's low-density population, developers are not snapping up the land for commercial projects.

I look at Aurora. She looks back at me. "We're on a rusted roof in another dimension," I say straight-faced.

"Who *vould* believe it?"

Together, we converge on the door on the roof. There is no lock on the outside. The handle is closest to me. Taking in a deep breath, I pull it. The door screeches open a few inches. I yank on it harder. It opens halfway. Rain must have rusted the frame. With a final heave, I open the door.

Small pieces of debris fall into the semi-darkness below. Sunlight shining into the space reveals the outlines of a Trans-Dimensional Transporter.

My phone is equipped with a powerful flashlight. Aurora edges closer to me. Her phone flashlight peers into the darkness with mine. I notice the Transporter pontoons are open and empty. Our suspicions are confirmed. Romulus landed here. We're on the right track. I point to the empty pontoons.

"I don't think Romulus has any plans to return here."

"He must be staying in town," Aurora says. She looks at me. "This is almost too easy."

"I'm sure it will get harder, but at least we've narrowed the search grid. Let's go into town, rent a car, and buy some suitcases, padlocks, and a boltcutter. We'll have to risk leaving our machines exposed until we return. Then, we'll unpack our cargo, stow the machines, and secure this place. After we've settled all that, it's back into town to find Romulus."

"Sounds great, except my watch says it's a twenty-mile walk to Alexandria."

"We'll use our credentials to stop a car and declare an FBI emergency."

"*Zhat* will create waves of gossip in this small town. Word of our presence could reach Romulus."

"Would you rather walk?"

After a beat, Aurora shakes her head. "You're right." She turns in a circle with her arms outstretched like a ballerina. "But we can take a little walk. It's a nice day for it. We might as well enjoy ourselves while we can."

CHAPTER 10

Romulus surveys himself in the full-length mirror in room 232 of the Indigo Hotel in Old Town Alexandria. He likes what he sees. A six-foot, athletically built man in his mid-twenties stares back at him. The man's features are unremarkable but not unappealing. He wears a gray, striped suit that he has just bought and pressed. His navy blue tie matches nicely with his pale blue shirt. He has cut his wavy black hair shorter for a more conservative look. His black loafers shine. Oakley designer glasses with prescriptionless lenses complete the ensemble. The LensCrafters salesgirl thought him odd for buying non-prescription lenses until he told her he was an actor auditioning for a role in a movie. She asked for his autograph. Laughing to himself, he signed his name as Adrien Mattias in a bold, artistic script.

Pulling the cuff-linked sleeves out of his black suede jacket, he notices the messiness of the room behind him. He hasn't found time to straighten it up. Romulus knows himself as an orderly Android. The clothing and towels strewn about the room are out of character. But the excitement of the project has absorbed his attention entirely. The life he has planned so carefully is about to begin. Unlocking and opening the door, he steps into the hallway on his way to the parking lot.

The drive to Aerodyne Dynamics takes only fifteen minutes across the quaint city of Alexandria. He knows the route by heart. He has practiced it repeatedly on his excursions in Tier Two. Reviewing the past twenty-four hours in his mind, Romulus is surprised at how easily he passes as a Human Being. He moves about largely unnoticed, except for the amorous stares of a few lonely women. Everything is going according to plan.

On his previous trip, Romulus cased the lobby of Aerodyne Dynamics, memorizing every detail and paying particular attention to the chart of departments on each floor. When he noticed a security guard watching him, Romulus pulled a notepad and pen from inside his jacket and pretended to jot down a few notes. Then, he walked confidently out of the lobby and back to his car.

His exit is coming up. Smoothly, he guides the rented Chevrolet Impala down the ramp. Passing by middle-income colonial homes, Romulus arrives at a modern industrial campus. The Aerodyne Building is located here amidst a few other prestigious company headquarters. The Aerodyne building is impressive. The fiber cement exterior is painted in a natural earth tone and accented with tinted windows. A magnificent early morning sun frames the edifice. Romulus finds the chill in the air refreshing. He does not need an overcoat.

Grabbing his sleek leather briefcase, Romulus locks the car. From the parking lot, he can see Aerodyne's arched front entrance. The company logo is elegant. The graphic suggests a source of free-flowing ideas.

Entering the lobby, Romulus advances to the circular security desk. It is the first time he has done so.

A male guard in a gray uniform stands in the middle of the circular counter. He is dark-skinned with tightly curled black hair. The man is middle-aged but in excellent shape. As he approaches, Romulus notices a gun holstered on the guard's hip.

Romulus steps confidently up to the desk. Above the logo emblazoned on the guard's left shirt pocket, a nametag reads Jamal Hendricks. The words *How May I Help You* are stitched in white thread underneath Hendricks' name. A gold security shield rests on Jamal's right breast pocket. From the bulk of his shirt, Romulus can see that Jamal is wearing a protective vest. He calculates Jamal's height at six feet one-and-a-half inches. The security guard regards Romulus with a polite but no-nonsense look. His first words are, naturally, "How may I help you?"

"I'm here to interview for a position," Romulus says politely.

"And you are?"

"Bruce Sanford Dillon."

Hendricks asks for identification. Romulus produces his driver's license. After examining it, Hendricks squints at him. "Have I seen you before?"

"I have an ordinary face. You must be confusing me with someone else. It happens every so often."

"Who are you seeing?"

Romulus has memorized every employee on the lobby chart. "Jonathan Winslow in HR."

Jamal looks down at the monitors below his counter. After a moment, he says, "Mr. Winslow isn't here today. Are you sure about the date?"

Romulus remains poised. "Then I'll see Judith Baumgarten."

"But your appointment is with Mr. Winslow?"

This is unexpected. With some effort, Romulus remains calm.

"What's the difference?"

"The HR people are very busy. Everyone is busy here. People apply for jobs from all over the world. If your qualifications suit our requirements, it typically takes six weeks to see someone after we notify you of our interest. If I were you, I'd check your interview date and hope you've made a mistake."

Hendricks hands the driver's license back to Romulus. "I can't permit you to remain in the building. Please leave immediately. Have a nice day."

Despondent, Romulus leaves the building thinking, *This is unplanned. I have never looked for a job before. I did not anticipate that an appointment was required to interview for a position. I am unfamiliar with corporate customs. Perhaps I've made a mistake by leaving Androbiotica?*

Romulus pauses for a split second to analyze his actions. He quickly arrives at a conclusion.

What is done is done. I cannot go back to my old life. I will have to devise an alternate approach to securing an interview.

With the issue resolved, Romulus strides purposefully toward the arched main entrance.

CHAPTER 11

Since we are risking our lives on this mission, Aurora and I reward ourselves by staying at the stately Morrison House Hotel in Old Town. On the lobby wall, we find the story of the hotel's origin. An enterprising hotelier established the Morrison over two centuries ago. Management, overseen by the city council, restored the property to combine the best of the old world with the new. We like the accommodations. If only we had the time to avail ourselves fully of the amenities.

While unpacking a few articles of clothing in my bedroom, I notice the date and year on the clock radio: September 19, 2006. Aurora and I have not asked anyone about the date to avoid arousing suspicion. However, the date and everything we've observed up to this point are clues. Romulus traveled to a window in the past related to the timeline in Tier One. I'd estimate the technology here is at least forty years behind ours. These facts confirm our suspicions. Romulus came here with the AndroBiotica file to use as a bargaining chip.

We've discovered another curious fact. The people we've encountered speak with a distinct accent. They call it a Southern accent or a Southern drawl. We don't have anything similar in Tier One. It's an example of a random difference between the two dimensions. Our lack of an accent marks us as suspicious foreigners—another reason to be on our guard.

Now that we've settled in, there is time to catch up with ourselves. We sit opposite one another in leather lounge chairs in the spacious living room of a two-bedroom suite. It has been a long and fruitful day.

We are both drained from our activities. On the way into town, a kindly stranger asked us if we needed a ride. We accepted and offered the Good Samaritan a plausible cover story, not far from the truth. We said it was a fine day to walk, but we had miscalculated the time and fallen behind schedule. When asked why we were in town, we said we were high school science teachers here for a Robotics conference. The Good Samaritan was unfamiliar with the robotics industry. Still, he told us that the people in the area held the Aerodyne Dynamics Corporation in high regard, thanks to the jobs and training programs they offered during difficult economic times. Many of the locals took advantage of the training programs to upgrade their skills.

After the Good Samaritan dropped us off, I remarked to Aurora that Adrien's theory about individuals out of work due to advancements in Technology proved true, at least in this area.

Once in town, we exchanged platinum coins for dollars at a Citizens National Bank branch. After renting a slate-gray Jeep Grand Cherokee, we purchased every item on our list, including a boltcutter, heavy-duty locks, and, of course, suitcases.

Returning to the warehouse in Cullen, I used the bolt-cutter to break the padlock and open the double doors. Then, we transferred the cargo from the pontoons into the four suitcases we bought. Finally, we dragged the empty TDTs into the run-down warehouse. After sealing the roof and entry doors with new locks, we loaded the Jeep and returned to the city.

Shortly after renting the hotel suite, I called Mattias on my special comm and gave him an update on our progress. He approved but reminded me that "time is of the essence." He likes that phrase. I told him we accomplished everything we could fit into our first day in Tier Two.

During the day's activities, I couldn't help but notice that something was weighing on Aurora. I didn't want to interrupt our errands by getting into it with her. Now that we're alone with our chores completed, I decide that this is the right time to explore the matter.

"You aren't yourself. Tell me what's bothering you."

What's the plan for tomorrow?" she asks to deflect the question.

"We go to Aerodyne Dynamics bright and early. Romulus is somewhere in this city. I can feel it. Aerodyne is the most logical place to begin our pursuit."

Aurora nods, but I can tell her mind is elsewhere.

"Let's talk about what's on your mind. Something is distracting you. We have to resolve it. I need your total concentration on the mission."

Aurora looks out of the living room window. I follow her gaze. Rows of blazing streetlights and loblolly pine trees line the cobblestone street several floors below. She turns to me.

"I think I'm artificial."

This utterance comes as a complete shock. I stare at Aurora in disbelief.

"I keep having the same dream. I'm in a room. I think it's a hospital room, but I'm not sure because my vision is blurry. Tubes with multi-colored liquids in them run from my arms and nose. A pump works silently by my bedside, forcing liquids into me. I want to talk, but I can't speak. I want to sit up, but I'm unable to move. I have no sensation in my body. A sheet and blanket cover me from the waist down. I want to leave the room, but I'm powerless to do so. A woman in a white lab coat enters the room, but I can't make out her features. Then, I lose consciousness. The same dream repeats itself sporadically. Each time I wake up from it, I feel intense fear, and then relief when I realize it was only a dream."

"The source of your dreams must be job-related. We are under constant pressure to perform at a high level. Borinsky and his superiors closely monitor us. No wonder your mind created the metaphor of a hospital where you can't move and where an attending nurse observes you. We are literally under a microscope. The intense scrutiny can be paralyzing at times."

"The dreams are so real, Derrick. I sometimes think they aren't dreams but buried memories coming to the surface that a tech failed to erase."

"Don't take this the wrong way, but why would AndroBiotica create an Android with your face and body? You attract too much attention."

"Maybe I'm on a mission to test you? Maybe the *NSS* wants to know if you can resist temptation."

"I'm not that important. The *NSS* wouldn't waste time, energy, and money just to find out if I'm a good boy. Why do you assume I find you irresistible?"

"Because you are a man who doesn't strike me as a Gay man."

"Maybe you give yourself too much credit?"

"It's not worth arguing about."

"We've never talked about our formative years. Do you mind discussing it?"

Aurora eyes me with a plaintive expression. I sense that she doesn't want to talk about her past, but she goes ahead anyway.

"I grew up in a port town on the North *Roussian* coast. My father was a kind and gentle man, a professor of linguistics. He died of radiation poisoning when I was twelve. I was an only child. It took me years to recover from his unexpected death. As a child, my mother explained my father's death in non-political terms. When I started my advanced education, my mother told me the truth. She said the government assassinated my father for speaking out against the regime of an inhuman dictator."

I make the connection between the fate of Aurora's father and her motivation to go into law enforcement. She is subconsciously seeking justice for the cruel and unjust death her father suffered.

"I still talk to my mother once a week," Aurora continues. "She has always been warm and encouraging to me. She lives in *Angland* now. She never remarried."

Aurora pauses before finishing her thoughts. "I am unaware of any lingering childhood trauma besides the tragic loss of my father."

I give Aurora's last statement room to breathe before asking my next question.

"What were your parents' names?"

"Vadim and Irina."

Aurora starts to cry. I take her hand in mine. It is a reflex. "If you talk to your mother, how can you be an Android?"

Aurora sniffles. "I don't know. Maybe the woman I talk to is an actor."

"That's preposterous. How can you be anything but a Human Being? These dreams are a form of mild psychosis. It's something you will have to deal with after the mission. I'm sorry that I brought this up now. You have to stay strong."

I want to hold her in my arms to comfort her, but I know I can't.

She bends over and holds her face in her hands. She looks up at me. "I'm afraid."

I've never seen this side of Aurora. I suddenly realize the unusual pressure of the mission has brought us closer, but probably not in a good way. I am at a loss for words until I remember a vital part of my life.

"It would help if you had a healthy outlet to calm you down. Have you ever tried meditation?"

She looks at me with a puzzled expression. "No."

"Regular meditation can help to alleviate deep-seated feelings of grief and anxiety. It promotes inner peace. I find time to meditate daily, no matter what's happening in my life. I recommend that you try it."

Aurora picks her head up. She gives me one of her typical intense stares, but this one is laced with desperation.

"I've never considered taking up meditation. Tell me about it."

"The subject of consciousness is as vast as consciousness itself. I'll give you an abridged answer that may be helpful. What I say might conflict with your beliefs. I can only tell you what I believe based on my reading and experience."

After a thoughtful pause, Aurora says, "Go on."

"It is my experience that we are much more than a physical body. There are dimensions of consciousness, just as we now know there are multi-dimensional worlds. In higher states of consciousness, we can access levels of peace, joy, love, and knowledge that are not present in our normal waking state. The more we access higher consciousness through meditation, the more peace, happiness, and compassion become part of our daily lives.

"Essentially, our consciousness is as limitless as our universe. We have the potential to be superconscious and individually conscious simultaneously. Admittedly, only a small number of dedicated seekers have attained infinite states of consciousness. It is rare, but it is possible. And that, dear partner, is the *Five-Dara* tour of consciousness."

"It sounds wonderful," Aurora says. "I'll try it."

"Please do. With practice, meditation will convince you of your Humanity. Something glorious, profound, wondrous, and powerful resides in every cell of a Human Being. Who or what put it there is an open question. One thing is for sure: Matthias will never be able to duplicate it, no matter how hard he tries."

"If I'm an Android, then I won't be able to attain these elevated planes of consciousness."

"Aurora, you haven't given me the slightest indication to make me think you might be an Android."

"We've only been working together for six months. You don't know me that well."

My patience is waning. It's my turn to level a penetrating stare. "Stop thinking about this until we return to Tier One. Stay focused on the mission. Okay?"

Aurora looks away. My last remark stung her, but it had to be said.

She turns back to me. "Will you kiss me?"

I'm taken aback by the request, but I go with it.

"As a test of your Humanity?"

"Yes."

"Haven't you been kissed by a man before?"

"Of course. I'm not a prude. But those kisses and what follows them could be implanted memories."

My resolve finally crumbles. "I can't say this is a difficult test." Gingerly, I bend to kiss her. I let the kiss linger before I pull away.

"Take me to bed," she says with another intense look in her eyes.

Her request comes as a complete shock. Sensing my reluctance, Aurora says, "We may never have this chance again."

Is it possible that Borinsky is testing me, as Aurora speculated?

I eliminate the thought. We are away from everything and everyone in Tier One. No one will know what goes on here except Aurora and me, and I am sure that she is a Human Being. Despite rigorous mind control, I've fantasized about a moment like this. I find Aurora's invitation irresistible. Taking her by the hand, we head toward my bedroom.

CHAPTER 12

Nightfall. A pale half-moon overlooks the Aerodyne Dynamics parking lot. Romulus sits in the front seat of his Chevy Impala, reviewing his strategy for the last time. *The risk is worth the reward,* he encourages himself.

Exiting the car, Romulus resolutely walks to the impressively arched front entrance. He finds the sight of a white Rolls-Royce Phantom parked under a canopy near the entrance reassuring. On his previous expeditions, Romulus has confirmed that the man he really wants to meet works late almost every night.

At eight in the evening, the front doors remain unlocked to permit late-working employees to exit the building. Passing through the lobby is another matter. Romulus expects the same security roadblock he experienced earlier.

He has chosen his clothing with an abundance of forethought. Romulus wears a blue silk suit with matching loafers. A pink tie and breast pocket handkerchief accent the outfit, complemented by a gold tie pin and cufflinks. With the right face, Romulus believes he could pass for the wealthy CEO of the company. His fashion statement is deliberate. A well-dressed man triggers no alarms upon entering the lobby. His late arrival is easily explainable as an opening to engage the guard. Thieves and terrorists wear camouflage, not expensive, impeccably coordinated outfits.

As he nears the security station, Romulus realizes he has lost the element of surprise. The security guard recognizes him. The difficulty of the job ahead has suddenly doubled.

"You again," Jamal Hendricks says. "What're you doing here?"

"I have an appointment to see Valerian Simons, the president of your company."

Romulus says this with an air of superiority to get under Hendricks' skin.

"What are *you* doing here?" he adds. "It looks like they work you long hours."

"I'm working a double shift, and it's none of your damn business. What was your name again?"

Romulus picks up the innuendo. *Tell me your name again, Mister Nobody.* "Bruce Sanford Dillon."

As he speaks his fake name, Romulus scans the lobby with an imperceptible move of his head. He is alone with Hendricks.

"You were in here earlier trying to apply for a job. Do you expect me to believe you have an appointment with Doctor Simons?"

"Call his office. He's expecting me."

Before Hendricks can retrieve his phone, Romulus shoots an arm across the counter. The action is so quick that it is barely noticeable. He grabs Hendricks by the throat and squeezes, crushing his larynx in one smooth motion. Romulus holds Hendricks off the ground for fifteen seconds. Hendricks chokes and spews saliva. With a deft twist, Romulus breaks the muscular guard's neck.

Releasing his grip, the Android lets Hendricks collapse to the floor. Placing his left hand on the counter, Romulus glides over it with the ease of an Olympic hurdler. Without the sound of voices or employees scuttling about, the lobby is as quiet as a crypt. Romulus looks up. Security cameras spaced at intervals look down in patterned clusters from the ceiling. Bending down, Romulus turns to a locked cabinet under the circular counter. A set of keys hangs from Hendrick's belt. Snapping the keys off the belt, he finds the key to the cabinet. Opening the cabinet doors, Romulus finds what he's looking for: Six compact disks recording the input from the security cameras in the ceiling and most likely other parts of the building. Romulus removes the disks from their cradles and places them in the inside pocket of his suit jacket. Then, he unclips Hendrick's security pass.

From a crouching position, the invader looks over the top of the circular desk in every direction. The lobby is empty. Someone may be monitoring the cameras from a remote room, but there will be no recorded evidence of Romulus' presence. He expects to be at his destination before anyone can stop him.

Pushing the rear gate of the desk open, the nattily dressed Android, who easily passes for a human, hurries to a bank of elevators across the lobby to his right. Rushing to them, he presses the button on the nearest elevator. It opens immediately. The building comprises twenty-five floors plus a lower lobby and a basement. At the top of the column of floor numbers, Romulus sees the letter T. He figures the letter stands for Tower, where he will find the executive offices. Romulus places Hendrick's security card against a round metal security plate. It blinks green. He presses the Tower button, and the doors close. Pleasant symphonic music accompanies Romulus on his way to meet the president.

Everything up to this point is going according to plan, but Romulus knows the next stage will be the hardest. The phrase his creator overuses pops into his head: "Time is of the essence." He must get in to see the president before the building is locked down.

There are five offices on the floor. All of them look deserted. Finding Simons' office poses no problem. His name and title are engraved in silver lettering on the doorway of the glass wall surrounding his office. It is the largest one on the floor. The outer office clearly belongs to his administrative assistant. From the dim lighting, Romulus can tell the assistant is gone for the evening. Burnished wood double doors stand behind the assistant's long desk. An old-fashioned computer sits atop it. The desk is otherwise clear. The assistant has locked away all confidential paperwork.

Romulus opens the outer glass door. Passing through it, he hears an electronic chime. From speakers somewhere in the room, a baritone voice demands: "Who's out there?"

Rather than answer, Romulus takes three long strides to the double doors. Grabbing the silver handle, he opens the door on his right. The locking mechanism springs, but Romulus has already opened it. Another second, and the doors would have locked him out. Romulus steps into a spacious office with no windows. All of the lighting comes from white tiles on the ceiling. Valerian Simons sits behind a sleek black desk scattered with documents and no less than three laptop computers. The computers appear to be custom-made, although

Romulus can't be sure. He is not familiar with the antecedents of the computers in Tier One.

Simons is a big-boned man. From his anatomy studies, Romulus has learned that big-boned bodies tend to be overweight. A home gym in the corner to the left of Romulus evidences Simons' attempt to stay in shape. The windowless office, coupled with an abundance of security measures, suggests a degree of paranoia in the man looking up at him. He wears a gray sweatshirt emblazoned with the Aerodyne logo and a tagline underneath: "The Future is Now."

"I'm sorry to intrude like this," Romulus says tentatively. "It is the only way I could get to see you."

Simons reaches for the phone near him.

"Please don't call security. What I have to say will be of great interest to you."

Simons pauses. Romulus believes deeply in his words. They have resonated with the man behind the desk who, unknowingly, holds Romulus' future in his hands.

"With the knowledge I have to offer, your company can be the unquestioned leader in robotics globally."

Romulus observes Simons in detail. He is a man somewhere in his fifties. He dyes his hair and eyebrows jet black, making him look like an unfinished Android. Romulus estimates his height at five feet ten inches. His muscular shoulders and arms speak of regular weight training. Simons is, literally, no slouch. He sits upright in his chair with a hawk-like stare. As Romulus anticipated, the next few moments will be critical.

"Young man," Simons says derisively. "You're wastin' my time. You've broken into my office with no preliminary paperwork to justify your presence, only to make a wild and unsubstantiated claim. Give me one good reason why I shouldn't have you arrested?"

"Robotics has advanced exponentially in the timeline I've come from."

"Now you tell me you're from the future?"

"In one sense, I'm from the future, but not exactly. I will tell you about my world in time. All I ask from you now is a little patience."

"Are you some kinda' alien?"

"No, sir, I—

"Tell me who you are and why you are here, and make it quick."

"My name is Bruce Sanford Dillon. I am an Android. The proof of my claim is standing right before you."

Simons reaches for his phone again.

"Wait." Romulus reaches down to the desk. He picks up a statuette of a man thinking, rendered in meticulous detail. Before Simons can object, Romulus grinds the piece into dust.

Valerian Simons eyes him warily. "How dare you? That was an expensive sculpture."

"I can tell you are a man who is not convinced easily. I had to do something dramatic."

Simons glowers at him. Romulus points at a legal document on the desk. "May I?"

"You certainly may not."

Disregarding Simons' reply, Romulus snatches the document. It is in his hands before Simons can say another word. After speed-reading the first three paragraphs, Romulus drops the document back on Simons' desk. He then proceeds to recite the first three paragraphs verbatim.

Leaning to his left and supporting his chin with his left hand, Simons says, "If you are an Android, you don't follow orders very well."

"With respect, Doctor, I am not a typical specimen. My creator has given me the unique ability to think for myself within a broader context of restraints."

"Who is your creator?"

"Adrien Matthias."

"I've *nevah* heard of him, and I know everybody who is anybody in this business."

"You don't know him because he lives in another dimension."

"Oh, come on." Simons makes another move for his phone. Romulus darts his hand to Simons' wrist. Simons looks at the hand on his wrist, then up to Romulus. "Take your hand off me."

Romulus complies. "I'm here to help you. Don't throw this opportunity away."

"Who are you? Really?"

"My real name is Romulus."

"They have long-dead Roman generals in your dimension?"

"There are similarities and differences between our two worlds."

There is a knock at the door.

"Where is my assistant when I need him?" Simons mutters. Then louder, "Who is it?"

"Security."

"Come in."

Two security guards enter the inner sanctum. "Is everything all right, sir?"

Simons hesitates, then, "Why wouldn't it be?"

"The lobby security guard was murdered ten minutes ago."

Simons' hand covers his mouth."Oh, my," he utters. He remains in that position until turning to Romulus with a look of suspicion.

Romulus looks down at the handcrafted beige carpet. When he looks up again, Simons is staring at him intently. It seems to Romulus that the president is replaying their conversation in his head.

After a long moment, Simons looks past him and says to the guards, "I'll be downstairs as soon as I finish my meeting with this young man. If the authorities arrive before me, tell Chief Fitzroy to keep his mouth shut until I get there."

CHAPTER 13

"Have a seat," Valerian Simons commands from behind his curved black desk.

Finding a sleek black leather and silver-framed chair in a grouping behind him, Romulus drags it opposite Simons.

"Feel free to call me Romulus, sir."

"I'll call you whatever I damn well please. I'm the founder and sole owner of this company."

Making no reply, Romulus looks into the hazel eyes staring back at him. If he could read minds, Romulus is sure that Simons is cataloging every move he makes and every word he says.

"Let's assume everything you've said is true. Tell me, then, how you came here from another dimension."

Romulus sighs. He planned to ease into this discussion, but Simons has made it clear that he controls the order of business. Removing three photos from his jacket pocket, he lays them on the desk. Simons picks one up and studies it.

"What am I looking at?"

"It's called a Trans-Dimensional Transporter."

Simons squints at him.

"I come from a parallel dimension. In that dimension, Science and Technology have advanced far beyond this one."

Before Romulus can continue, Simons cuts him off. "And you've come here, out of the goodness of your Android heart, to help my company and advance your career and financial status. Am I correct?"

"I'm here, first and foremost, to find refuge. Agents from my dimension will be here soon, looking for me. Secondly, I'm here to be a free entity with the opportunity to determine my future. Thirdly, I want to find a place in this world. I'd like to find it at Aerodyne Dynamics."

Romulus reaches into his hip pocket. He holds up a flash drive. "This file contains the schematics and documentation to create Beings like me. You won't be able to do it without me as your consultant."

Simons leans back in his executive chair. Dropping the photo back on his desk, he points to the three images depicting the Trans-Dimensional Transporter taken from different angles.

"Where is this machine?"

"In a small town not far from here. I can take you to it."

Simons' following statement is not a question. "You killed the security guard."

Romulus uses his hands to make a pleading gesture. "I had no other option. A man in his position has no latitude or authority to make the decision I needed him to make. Initially, I tried to earn the right to see you by applying for a position here. I quickly learned that that pathway was not a viable one."

Simons leans forward in his chair. Romulus can only anticipate that his straightforward explanation will have the desired effect.

"Your logic is flawed, Romulus. You killed a Human Being without the slightest bit of remorse. That makes you a dangerous entity."

"I know that killing Jamal Hendricks was wrong. Please understand that my actions were born out of sheer desperation, as I've explained."

"You are dangerous, Romulus, but you are also valuable. I'm *gonna* keep a close watch on you. Your proposal intrigues me. If what you say checks out, we can find a way forward. The first step will be to cover up this murder. I'll have to remove the lobby tapes before the police get to them."

Romulus is quickly learning how to deal with this Human. "I already have the recordings in my possession."

"I'm impressed."

"How do you suggest we proceed, sir?"

"We have a suite of rooms on the floor below this one that we use for various occasions. Come with me. I will personally show you to your new accommodations."

CHAPTER 14

Early morning. The crisp, clean air rushes through the Jeep's window. The autumn weather is sunny, clear, and brisk, with temperatures in the low fifties. My open window may be a subconscious attempt to clear the air between Aurora and me. Last night, our lovemaking was passionate and too brief. Aurora left my bedroom immediately afterward. We have not spoken a word about it since. Consequently, there is an underlying tension between us.

Turning into the Aerodyne Dynamics parking lot, the scene confronting us puts my relationship concerns in the background. Police cruisers with flashing lights ring the front entrance of the building. A yellow crime scene tape stretches across the front doors. A crime scene investigation van is parked nearby. I share a concerned look with my partner.

Wordlessly, we exit our Jeep. Besides the police vehicles, I see only three other cars in the lot. One of them is a white Rolls-Royce parked near the entrance.

We approach an officer standing near the arched entryway holding a clipboard. She sees us coming and motions for us to stop. We don't obey. The officer puts a hand over her holster. Pulling my credentials, I hold them over my head. The officer relaxes. We advance toward the gatekeeper confidently yet cautiously. I hand her my identification. She registers surprise.

Looking at me, she says, "What's the FBI doing here?"

"I'm afraid the answer is confidential."

Aurora hands over her credentials. After checking our ID wallets, the officer hands them back to us. She is a small woman, slightly more than five feet tall. Her features and complexion suggest that she is of Latin descent. Her nameplate confirms it: Antonia Fernandez.

"I applied to the Academy," she says. "They rejected me because I wasn't tall enough."

I give her my best sympathetic look. "I'm sorry to hear that. The FBI's loss is Alexandria's gain."

She hands me the clipboard. I sign the attendance log and hand it over to Aurora. She signs it and hands it back to the officer.

Lifting the yellow tape, Officer Fernandez says, "Don't mess up my crime scene."

When we duck under the tape, the lobby doors open automatically.

The lobby is as impressive as the building's exterior. The flooring consists of large, gray tiles. Panels of faux black granite line the walls. Behind the security kiosk, I see a long, multi-station reception desk. I imagine Aerodyne Dynamics receives a lot of visitors.

Three men stand around the circular security kiosk. The shortest one is dressed casually, unlike the other two men, who are uniformed. The shorter one is arguing with a tall officer, who wears a police uniform featuring a silver bar on his collar and five hash marks on his sleeve. The man beside him wears a gray uniform with a gold star on his breast pocket. The three men look up at us in varying degrees of surprise.

Upon reaching the security post, we identify ourselves. From the nameplate, I can tell that the gray uniform belongs to the head of security. He is a few inches shorter than I and stout. Unlike the other two men, he has allowed himself to go to pot. His curly red hair is an obvious dye job. It matches the color of his handlebar mustache and manicured goatee. I get the vibe he is impressed with himself. His nameplate reveals his name: Charles Fitzroy.

The blue uniform is a police lieutenant. He relaxes noticeably when I tell him that the FBI has no intention of taking over the investigation. The man wearing a gray sweatshirt with an Aerodyne Dynamics logo and tagline below it acts like he is in charge.

I peek over the security countertop. Fingerprint powder, cotton swabs with blood on them, and vials of crime-detection chemicals litter the floor. A crime scene tech looks up at me from the middle of the mess. He wears protective clothing from his boots to the top of his head. I smile back at him.

I speak to the Security Chief first. "Can you bring us up to speed on what happened here?"

"You don't know?"

"I wouldn't be asking the question if I knew the answer."

I've already succeeded in arousing Charles Fitzroy's suspicion.

The gray sweatshirt answers for the Security Chief. "A highly valued security staff member was murdered here last night."

"I see. And you are?"

"The president and sole owner of Aerodyne Dynamics. My name is Doctor Valerian Simons."

It figures that the guy in charge is the least likely one to be, judging by his size and casual attire. He looks more like a janitor than the head of the company.

"Thank you, Doctor Simons. Is there somewhere private where we can continue this discussion?"

Simons looks at Charles, who shrugs. Turning to the police lieutenant, he says, "Please complete your forensics investigation by noon today at the latest. I have a business to run."

"We'll finish when we finish," the lieutenant answers calmly.

"Then don't waste time doing it."

Turning to us, Doctor Simons says, "Come with me."

We follow Simons and Charles Fitzroy into an elevator. Minutes later, we are sitting in the president's office. I find the place depressing without windows to let the glorious day outside in.

I begin by asking Simons about the curious lack of windows. "Are you afraid someone will steal your ideas if you allow windows in your office?"

"Exactly. I am also concerned that my competitors will try to assassinate me. Bullet-proof windows are not foolproof, and besides, *they'uh* expensive. As the *sayin'* goes, 'When there's a will, there's a way.' It applies to doing something good *or* bad. I am a walkin' example of applyin' my will to do something good."

From his file, I know that Doctor Simons is a *Dannishe* immigrant with a Southern accent. That's quite a combination. It means Simons has been in the South long enough to absorb the accent. I have a feeling

Simons intentionally uses the lazy undertone of the accent to invite his adversaries to underestimate him. I glance at Aurora with a faint smile. Considering the overall picture, Valerian Simons is a prime example of the eccentricity that accompanies genius.

Aurora speaks up. These are the first words she has uttered since last night. "Help me to understand something, Doctor. Last night, someone entered the building and murdered an armed guard. I assume your security guards undergo training to deal with violent behavior?"

"They are *thouraly* trained."

"Yet someone entered the lobby and murdered a highly trained guard without stealing anything?"

"It would seem so."

"Then it stands to reason that the guard knew his murderer."

"I think that's a fair conclusion."

"Do the police have the security recordings?" I ask.

"The security discs were removed, presumably by the *perpatrator*." Aurora and I exchange a long look.

"If nothing is missing, what do you think the murderer wanted?" I ask.

"It would seem only to murder the guard," Simons replies. "The killer either had a strong motive to kill him or maybe an argument escalated outta' control."

Simons' last statement registers a direct hit on my inner manure meter. The man is lying. Shamelessly. It's time to ask the primary question we came here to ask.

"Do you know someone by the name of Bruce Sanford Dillon?"

Before Simons can answer, his assistant enters the room. He whispers something to Charles Fitzroy. He, in turn, nods to Simons. Apparently, Simons is the only Aerodyne representative allowed to speak in this meeting.

"Let's drop this little charade, shall we? I had my assistant check you out. Due to the nature of our work, we have a direct line to the FBI. Hidden cameras in my office captured your images, and we have the names you gave us. The FBI has no record of you in their database. I'm sure representin' yourselves as *Gov'ment* Agents carries a long prison sentence."

Simons turns to his Security Chief. "Charles, detain these people until I can get a police escort up here."

CHAPTER 15

Unclipping the handcuffs from his belt, Fitzroy reaches out to Derrick. He holds the open handcuffs, ready to clasp them around Derrick's wrists resting on the arms of his chair.

Aurora hears the words "Activate, Aurora," followed by a sequence of numbers and letters. The command comes from somewhere inside her mind.

Automatically, Aurora rises from her chair. As Fitzroy turns his head toward her, she swipes the handcuffs out of his chubby hands.

"What do you think you're doing?" Simons demands.

In response, Aurora shoves the chair over with Charles Fitzroy in it. She catches Derrick's surprised expression while turning to Simons.

In a voice she has never heard before, Aurora says, "Where is Bruce Sandford Dillon?"

Simons reaches for his phone. "I don't know what you're talking about."

Aurora twists the phone out of his hand before he can raise it to his ear. Simons pulls his hand back, massaging his wrist.

"Don't make me ask you again."

Simons can only stare back at her.

Grabbing one of his laptop computers, Aurora heaves it against the wall.

The screen of the laptop breaks away from the keyboard before crashing into the carpeting.

"Aurora?"

She ignores Derrick.

Rubbing the back of his head, Fitzroy struggles to his feet.

"Don't move," Aurora says authoritatively. Fitzroy freezes.

Aurora turns back to Simons. She has become someone else. She can only be a spectator to her actions.

"You have thirty seconds to answer before I break your left arm."

"Okay. Relax. I'll take you to Dillon. Wherever the hell you Androids come from, it must be a very violent place."

Aurora's thoughts and emotions are swirling. She turns to Derrick. By his expression, he must be sensing her confusion. He also looks confused by her actions. Then, Aurora realizes that only a part of her is confused.

The other part knows what to do.

"Lead the way," Aurora says to Simons. She looks over to his Chief of Security, who now looks decidedly insecure. "You will come with us and behave."

Simons turns nervously to Fitzroy. "Do what she says."

Aurora turns her attention to me. Her eyes are vacant. I feel an urge to reintroduce myself.

"I'm your partner. We are here on a mission."

Aurora tilts her head. "I know this. Follow me to Romulus."

CHAPTER 16

I go with the flow, no matter how surreal it is. It's heartbreaking for me to learn that Aurora is an Android who previously thought of herself as a Human. It will be much worse for Aurora once the shock wears off and she has a chance to reflect on her situation. Still, the cruel reality is that the mission goal is more important than either of us.

I walk down the hallway behind Aurora, who holds Valerian Simons by his arm. I walk next to Charles Fitzroy, keeping a keen eye on him. He studies the carpet. I believe Aurora has dispelled any doubt about who is in charge.

The twenty-fifth floor of the Aerodyne Dynamics building looks more like a five-star hotel than an office building. We pass one lacquered white oak door after another, each with a bronze suite number. I noticed Simons used a gold-coded security card to access the floor. It differs from Charles' purple-coded card and our red-coded visitor cards. The gold-coded security card must be for the highest security areas. Simons may be the only person who has one. He points to the door three suites away. "He's in there."

"Do you have the master security card to gain entrance?"

Simons fishes in his pants pocket and holds up the gold-coded card.

"You will enter the room first," Aurora tells Simons. "Stay close to the front door so we can hear you. Talk to Romulus casually. Give us an idea of where he is in the room. If you try to warn him of our presence, I will detect it, and I'll break more than your arm."

Aurora may be bluffing, but if I were Simons, I wouldn't want to test her. He is clearly unused to this type of treatment. I observe Simons struggling to maintain his composure. I gather he is smart enough to know that his only choice, for the moment, is to follow Aurora's instructions.

We gather in front of suite twenty-two. I reach into my hip pocket to wrap my fingers loosely around the silver pen Mattias gave me before we left on the mission. I watch Aurora make the same move. Turning to Simons, Aurora mouths the words, *"Open it."*

Using his card, Simons opens the door halfway.

"It's me, Romulus. Doctor Simons. I'm alone."

Simons enters the room. Aurora holds the door slightly open with her foot. I hang back and signal Fitzroy to stay put. We want the target to feel comfortable before we surprise him.

"Ah, there you are. Nice and comfy, flipping TV channels like a real man."

Simons' voice comes from the other side of the door. He is astute for a civilian with no situational training. He's giving us a picture of what to expect. I nod to Aurora. She pushes the door open. We rush into the room, taking positions on either side of the front door.

The living room is empty. I see one streamlined sofa and two leather lounge chairs circling an entertainment center. A fully stocked mini-bar occupies the far corner. I notice the door is open to a room that must be a bedroom. I close the suite door quietly, with only the sound of the lock engaging.

I motion to Aurora, pointing two fingers at my eyes and then to the bedroom doorway. Staying out of Romulus' view, we creep toward the door.

"It looks like you want to spend some time relaxing. I'll come back in a while," Simons says.

I hear Romulus say, "If you have something important to say, we can talk now."

"I mainly wanted to check on you to make sure you're comfortable. We'll talk later. I'm sure you can use some quiet time. It's been a taxing night and day."

Taxing, my ass. Romulus killed a man in cold blood, I tell myself.

"I'm actually starting to get bored, Doctor Simons. I'd like you to stay and talk."

"I have a pressing meeting upstairs, Romulus. I'll be down as soon as I can."

We wait for Simons to exit the room. As soon as he does, I lead the charge into the bedroom. Romulus faces me, leaning against pillows and the headboard. Reacting immediately, he shoots to a sitting position and heaves the remote control at my head. The distraction gives him enough time to fall off the far side of the elevated mattress. From there, we hear him scramble on all fours into the bathroom. I hear the *click* of the bathroom lock. Rushing to the bathroom door, Aurora kicks the center of it with the sole of her boot. The door doesn't budge. It's another hardwood door. Simons spares no expense for his VIP guests. With two more ferocious blows, the door frame shatters.

Romulus bullies his way back into the bedroom by launching himself at Aurora. His momentum knocks her over. The velocity of the impact dislodges the silver pen from her hand. I watch it tumble a few feet away from her on the Berber carpet.

Romulus straddles Aurora. He raises his right arm and fist to strike her. I have a shot, and then I don't. Arching her hips up from the floor, Aurora pushes Romulus off of her. While hand-fighting with her adversary, she kicks one leg out from under him. Quickly, Aurora straddles Romulus before he has a chance to react. Wasting no time, she raises her fist and smashes him in the face. I move to pick up the silver pen on the carpet. Aurora's head swivels.

"Stay away," she says flatly, making me feel like a helpless, total stranger. Then, I realize she is protecting my vulnerable Human body from lethal body blows.

Romulus pummels Aurora's midsection. The punches come in double-time like a film with the frame rate sped up.

Aurora stands suddenly. Looking at me, she moves deftly out of my line of sight. She's setting me up for the kill shot. In less than a second, Romulus jerks to a sitting position. As I squeeze the trigger, Romulus twists his torso to rise quickly from the floor. It's a lucky move. My shot hits Romulus square in the shoulder instead of his chest, but it rips his arm off from the shoulder.

Romulus hesitates for a moment to examine his missing arm with an expression of detached disbelief.

That's it. I've used my only shot. Romulus turns to me. Blood spurts from an artery where his shoulder should be. Standing now, he takes a step toward me. Then, he looks down at the silver pen on the floor. By now, Romulus knows it is a deadly weapon. He bends to pick it up. I step toward the bedroom door, but I'm kidding myself. If he doesn't bleed out first, I'll never make it out of the room. The rogue Android is too quick.

A second later, Aurora slams into Romulus with the force and momentum of a pickup truck.

I dive to the floor to secure Aurora's pen. I retrieve it.

One shot left. Make it count.

Rolling to my opposite side, I see Aurora and Romulus exchanging vicious punches in front of the closet. The full-length mirror shatters. Aurora has her back to me. I have no shot. I hear her grunt as she absorbs the blows.

"Get down," I yell at her.

Instead, she wheels away from Romulus. As he turns, I see the expression on his bloodied face is one of molten fury. He sees me aiming the silver pen at him. He leaps toward me, covering half the distance between us in an instant. I barely have time to squeeze the trigger.

Romulus' chest explodes. Blood, bones, and organs splatter against the closet doors and the adjacent walls. The Android's legs crumble underneath him. He crashes backward to the floor. His chest is a bloody, empty shell. It is a ghastly sight. I've never killed anyone before. I suppose killing an Android is as close as it gets. I step away to avoid the pooling blood. As I'm looking down, I see splotches of blood on my shirt and pants. I can't leave the building covered in blood. I'll have to deal with it later.

Aurora has slumped to the floor on all fours, panting like a spent lioness. Going to her, I help her stand. Her battle with Romulus has left her face badly bruised, but there is recognition in her eyes.

She looks down at the remains of Romulus and then back at me.

"What happened, Derrick?"

"You don't remember?"

She shakes her head 'no.'

I hold her battered head in my hands. "We'll talk about it later. We have a mission to complete."

Aurora places her right hand on her left side. She winces in pain. "I think I have a few cracked ribs."

I can see in her eyes and movements that Aurora's sense of identity as a Human Being is returning. I didn't expect it, but then, I've only met Adrien a short while ago. Who knows the depth of his genius? Certainly not me.

"Why don't you have a seat in the living room?"

Aurora scans the wreckage in the bedroom. She extends her left hand out, palm up. "Did you do this?"

"I said we'll talk about it later."

She gives me a hard look. "I want to talk about it now."

"I think you can use a little rest." I resist ending the sentence with the word 'darling.'

"Why are you avoiding my questions?"

I don't answer.

"How did we kill Romulus?"

"Aurora, this is not the time to talk about it. Our priority is to find the file. Let's look for it."

"Tell me what happened first."

She is forcing me to tell her the horrible truth.

"You frightened the crap out of Valerian Simons and Charles Fitzroy, his Security Chief, in a meeting upstairs. You made Simons show us where he was holding Romulus. Then, you fought Romulus to a draw until I had a shot to kill him."

"Seriously? How could I fight an Android to a draw?"

I take a deep breath. "I'm deeply sorry to tell you this, but you've left me no choice. You were able to fight with Romulus because you are an Android. The kind that thinks they are Human."

I see the shock register in Aurora's eyes, and then the hurt. It would only make matters worse if I told her the devastating effect her condition has on me.

"You're sure of this?"

"I'm afraid so."

Aurora turns abruptly and leaves the room. I would go to comfort her, but I know her Human personality too well. She needs time to process this nightmare on her own. I might as well look for the flash drive myself. Before I do that, I pull my mini-camera out and capture the image of Romulus' ruined body. I now have proof that phase one of our mission is complete.

Turning to the dresser opposite the bed, I find a wallet, a smattering of silver coins, a hotel key, and a purple security card. I see an empty suitcase open on a luggage rack beside the dresser. I assume Simons sent someone to collect Romulus' belongings and bring them here. Simons must have calculated the move to make Romulus feel safe within his kingdom.

I check the suitcase carefully for hidden compartments. I find nothing suspicious. I'll have to rip it apart later if I don't discover the flash drive elsewhere.

I open the dresser drawers one by one. I search each article of clothing in them. I toss aside shirts, underwear, and socks. Finding nothing, I open the next drawer. It is full of platinum coins. I pull handfuls of the coins out. I let them drop through my fingers. I do not find the drive hidden among them.

One drawer left. I pull it open. I find a yellow cashmere sweater looking up at me. Throwing it aside, I see a blue business shirt lying underneath. It's the last article of clothing in the drawer. Nervously, I remove the shirt slowly, and there it is—the purloined flash drive.

Before retrieving the drive, I photograph it in the drawer—proof that phase two of the mission is complete. Now, we have to bring it back to Mattias. Easier said than done. I take a moment to bask in our accomplishment by admiring the prize.

"Oh, you beautiful thing," I tell it.

There is no way to confirm this is the AndroBiotica file, but what else could it be? Unless it's a decoy. Then, I remember the file is encrypted. There is little chance the computers here can open it without Romulus' help. Still, it's better to be safe than sorry. Stepping around Romulus' lifeless body, I open the bloodied closet doors. I rummage through two pairs of stylish pants, two sports coats, a few business shirts, and a gray suit. Slipping out of my lightweight shoulder holster and high-velocity pistol, I strip to my underwear. I try on a white shirt and the gray suit. They fit me loosely, and the sleeves and pants cuffs are a bit short. The ill-fitting outfit will look like I bought it off a sale rack, but it beats walking around drenched in blood. I try on a pair of loafers. They are a tight fit, but they won't rouse suspicion. And, I don't plan on hiking. I tell myself the discomfort is only temporary. I'll have to find a way to make Aurora look more presentable. We'll figure it out.

Most importantly, my search of the closet and night table has yielded no duplicate files. I can only conclude the file I'm holding is the one we came for. It's time to move on.

Wait. What about the body? I consider the problem. I quickly realize there is no option but to leave it here. Simons will most likely want to study it in secret here. I can use the body as a bargaining chip.

It's time to face Aurora. I find her sitting on the living room sofa. She holds her head down almost to her knees. I can practically feel Aurora's pain, but we have to keep moving.

"Aurora, I found the file."

I expect this news to brighten Aurora's mood. It doesn't. She looks up at me with an empty expression. "I'm happy for you."

"I know this is difficult, but we have to get back to our machines before the authorities move in. I'm sure Simons has already contacted them with whatever cover story he can make stand up."

Aurora doesn't seem to care. "How dare they do this to me?"

"I completely agree with how you are feeling, but there's nothing we can do about it if we don't get out of here. Come. Let's find Simons. We need his blessing to ensure our safe passage back to the warehouse."

Aurora reluctantly agrees to go with me. We walk to the twenty-fifth-floor elevator without speaking. Aurora is in a world of her own. I don't try to deal with the thoughts going through her head. Instinctively, I take her by the hand. She doesn't resist. At this point, I'm her only ally.

"Let's start looking for Simons in his office," I suggest.

"Start at the top and work our way down," she says, looking straight forward with barely a whisper of emotion.

"Let's hope we don't have to go too far down. We have to find Simons before he calls the entire Alexandria Police Force to arrest us."

"I'll go down fighting if they try to arrest me."

She thinks she has nothing to lose, I say to myself.

We reach the elevator. I use the purple security card Romulus stole to access the Tower Floor. When the doors open, two alert security guards stand in the hallway to greet us. One of them is much taller and more muscular than the other. They wear gray Aerodyne Dynamics security uniforms. At least they are not from the local police or the actual FBI.

"We're here to speak with Doctor Simons," I say with a casual air of authority.

"Show us some ID," the taller one says.

I'm not going to risk pulling out our fake credentials. "Doctor Simons knows us. If he's in his office, please tell his assistant that Derrick Faulk and Aurora Zolotov are here to see him. It's an urgent matter."

"Step out of the elevator," the taller one says.

The shorter guard can't take his eyes off Aurora. "Where did you get those bruises?"

"In a bar fight," Aurora answers.

The shorter guard shakes his head. "You don't look like the bar type."

"It was an upscale bar."

The taller guard raises an old-fashioned tablet computer. He looks down at the tablet several times and then back at us. "Your names and photos don't appear on Doctor Simon's approved list."

"Why don't you ask Doctor Simons if he can see us?"

"Why don't you get lost, pal, before I throw you out of here?"

The outer glass door to Simon's office opens. Behind it stands the man himself.

"I overheard you arguing," Simons says to the tall guard. "Let them pass. I've been expecting them."

With a hand gesture, Simons invites us into his outer office. "My assistant has left for the day," he finds it necessary to say.

From the inference, I gather that our host wants privacy for whatever may happen next. After we are seated, Simons, in his signature manner, goes on the offensive. His eyes drill into mine.

"Let me be perfectly clear. If your partner acts violently in the slightest way, this meeting will be over, and I will alert the authorities. You're lucky that I've refrained so far. But let's be crystal clear on something. The only reason you aren't in police custody already is because I want something from you."

"Let me assure you, we have no plans to hurt you or any of your staff, Doctor Simmons. Please accept my apology for my partner's outburst, but it was necessary under the circumstances."

"Let me guess what those circumstances were. Romulus told me to expect agents from his dimension to come looking for him here. You are those agents, correct?"

I glance at Aurora. Her expression is neutral. I have the sense that she wants no part of the discussion.

"You guess correctly," I answer. "We came here to bring Romulus back to our dimension."

"And to recover the file he brought with him."

"Did he mention a file?"

"Don't be coy, Mr. Faulk."

"It's Agent Faulk."

Simons opens his mouth to speak, but I beat him to it.

"Doctor, we are willing to leave Romulus' remains here with you in return for safe passage. By 'safe passage,' I mean you will accompany us back to our departure vehicles. You will be sure to tell anyone who asks, especially the police, that you are leaving the building with us on your own initiative to learn about the most up-to-date security measures for your company at our field office in Reston, Virginia. You will not speak to the police about anything else or alert them in any way. If asked, you will verify that we are with the FBI. Are we in agreement?"

"First, let me ask you a question. Do you have the manufacturing specifications?"

"Yes."

"How did you obtain the file?"

"That's none of your business."

"Here's my counteroffer. In return for my cooperation, you will turn over the file along with what's left of Romulus. You and a dangerous robot invaded my property. That creation of yours endangered my life and the lives of everyone in this building. It murdered one of my employees, *fer Chris' sake*. I'm entitled to compensation."

"I can't give you the file."

"Then, I can't help you."

I've had as much as I can take of this guy. I pull my high-velocity pistol from the shoulder holster inside my suit jacket. I point the weapon at Simons.

"Here are my final terms. The *NSA* designed this pistol specifically for undercover fieldwork. It may look small, but it is more deadly than even a man of your stature can imagine. If you don't do what I've requested, the bullet from my gun will leave a six-inch hole in your back when it passes through you."

"You'll never get past my guards."

I raise my pistol slightly for emphasis. "I'd say our chances of getting past your guards are better than even money. This weapon holds twenty mini-cartridges made of an expandable metallic alloy. Your guards won't know what hit them."

Simons leans back in his chair. He realizes I mean business. He puts his index finger under his nose as he considers his position.

"Now that you mention it, I did want to get a look at your transporter machines. I *figya* now's my chance."

CHAPTER 17

Walking through the archway, I have to shield the sun's glare from my eyes even though I am wearing sunglasses. We've only been in the Aerodyne Dynamics building for a few hours, but it feels like an entire day. Fitzroy and Simons walk in front of us. I think Simons asked his Security Chief to come along out of force of habit. Lately, I would say Fitzroy hasn't been particularly efficient in protecting his commanding officer.

For emergencies, Simons keeps a cache of men's and women's clothing for his guests in a room on the twenty-fifth floor. Aurora's battle with Romulus qualifies as a major one. After helping her wash away the blood, I selected a business outfit for her with flat shoes. In the master bathroom, we found an extensive array of women's makeup. Aurora used it to cover her bruises. They are less evident but still noticeable.

Aurora is making a concerted effort to walk tall and straight despite the injury to her ribs. She's also put aside, for now, the gnawing questions about her identity. Our priority is to complete the mission.

We've made it this far without being questioned. Nobody wants to challenge the company's president, but we've drawn plenty of stares. Everyone in the company seems to be on edge due to the murder of Jamal Hendricks.

"We have one last piece of business to handle before we leave," I whisper to Aurora.

She looks at me blankly and shrugs. She is not fully back to herself, whatever that turns out to be.

Simons turns around. "What are you two talking about?"

"Nothing that would interest you. It's routine agent talk."

Simons regards me suspiciously, but he says nothing. His position as the head of a high-tech company breeds a sense of paranoia. My father ran two businesses simultaneously. Paranoia came with the territory. He trusted no one except his brother and two other close associates.

The crime scene van is gone. Only two police cruisers remain in the parking lot. We passed two detectives interviewing a night staffer on our way out of the building. I believe one of the cruisers belongs to the two detectives inside. The other vehicle must belong to the officer monitoring the identification of employees as they enter the lobby. The crime scene unit has stretched yellow crime scene tape across all but one of the front doors.

I see that the on-duty officer has replaced Officer Fernandez. I'm sad to see her go. Fernandez had a sense of humor and a great deal of respect. This guy looks like he has it in for the whole world. As we approach, I see Sergeant's stripes on his shoulder. He stands about five feet seven inches tall with his hands draped casually on his utility belt. We capture his attention immediately. Instinct tells me we are about to have a problem.

Short men often overcompensate for their height by flaunting their authority to make themselves feel important. I hope this guy doesn't fit the stereotype I've carved out for him. The Sergeant holds up his hands.

"Whoa, stop. I haven't received confirmation that anyone can leave the building yet."

We hold up our FBI badges. "We're here on a matter of National Security."

I'm telling the truth. Our badges are not.

"No one told me the FBI was here."

I note the Sergeant's name tag: Brian Allen.

"We're not obliged to offer that information to the local police, Sergeant Allen."

I don't expect this to go over well, but I'm confident law enforcement agencies work the same way here as they do in our dimension. We are notorious for not sharing information.

Allen holds out his hand. "Let me see your IDs."

I want to smack the attitude right off his face. Instead, I hand over my identification.

Allen looks through my credentials carefully. He whips out a note-pad and records my badge number. Our exfiltration plan is now on the clock. Allen will undoubtedly trace our fake IDs. We have to be travelling inter-dimensionally before that happens.

He hands my credentials back. Noting the remains of the bruises on Aurora's face, Allen asks her, "What happened to you?"

She must be getting tired of the question.

"The answer is way above your pay grade. I can't discuss it with you."

"Is that some sort of joke?"

Aurora regards Allen with a withering stare. "Do I look like I'm joking?"

The Sergeant is nonplussed by the response.

Aurora offers him her credentials. Relieved to avoid a confrontation, Allen peruses the FBI wallet. He makes a show of notating the badge number before returning the ID. Now, Allen turns to Simons.

"Who are you?"

"I'm Doctor Valerian Simons, the President Aerodyne Dynamics."

"Wait here while I make some calls," Allen says.

"Listen to me, you little..." Simons gathers himself. "Your Chief of Police is a close friend of mine. His name is William Britton. I've known him since grade school. We play golf together. I'm a busy man, Sergeant Allen. If you persist in wasting my time with this nonsense, I will call Bill and complain to him bitterly about your interference in a matter of National Security. Would you like me to do that?"

Allen takes a moment to process this outburst. "Where are you going?"

Simons is about to pop off again. I calm him with a hand gesture.

"We're going to our field office in Reston. There is an urgent need to upgrade Aerodyne Dynamics' security protocols. We have to protect their proprietary technology."

I wink at Allen. "You didn't hear that from me."

"Ahhh. I see," Allen allows. "Big picture. There's more to it than the murder. I get it now."

We nod and say nothing more.

■ ■ ■

The trip to Cullen in our Jeep is uneventful. We answer questions from Simons and Fitzroy with as little information as possible about Tier One and the NSS. Despite our evasive answers, I can sense the Doctors' excitement building. I can also glean from Fitzroy's expression that he is afraid to say anything. Whatever he is thinking about, given the little information we have provided, will remain with him for now.

We pull up and park in front of the old warehouse. I turn to the back seat where our two passengers reside.

"First, I'm going to unlock the doors and prepare the machines for inter-dimensional travel. Wait here with Aurora. This won't take long."

I glance at Aurora. She knows I'm lying.

I open the front doors of the warehouse. To my great relief, the three machines are there as we left them. Closing the doors behind me, I use my golden *Dara*-sized communicator to call Mattias. I wait for him to answer. About five nerve-wracking minutes pass. Mattias said he would be available 24/7. Where is he? I need a vital piece of information.

Finally, his voice comes through, but with distortion. I want to slip out the back door to escape these cramped quarters, but there is no rear exit. I don't want to arouse suspicion by going out of the front. We'll have to make do with the reception.

"I have good news for you."

"What?"

Mattias can't decipher my words. "Good news," I say louder. "Mission success."

Mattias' reply comes through garbled.

That's it. I'm going around to the back. I know Simons will think I'm up to something, and he will be right.

The reception behind the warehouse is much better. Mattias is overjoyed to hear that we have recovered the file and neutralized Romulus. I'm relieved to receive the instructions Mattias imparts to me.

Circling back to the front doors, I see Simons and Fitzroy struggling with the door locks in the back seats. Aurora has used the master lock to keep them in the car. Now, Simons appears to be yelling at her. Turning to the back seat, Aurora holds up her fist. This gesture gives Simons and Fitzroy pause. They don't want Aurora switching back to berserk mode.

After I finish what I have to do inside the warehouse, Aurora lets our passengers out of the Jeep. Simons is beside himself.

"How dare you lock me in. What the hell is going on?"

"The reception inside the warehouse was terrible. I needed some last-minute instructions for our journey home. Stop acting like a child and help us drag our transporters out of the warehouse."

"That doesn't answer my question. Why did you lock us in?"

"Because you are a rambunctious son-of-a-bitch and we don't have time for your shenanigans. Does that answer your question?"

Simons looks stunned by my response. It must be a long time since anyone has spoken to him like that, if ever. But he holds his tongue. He wants to see the Inter-Dimensional Transporter, and he wants Romulus' Transporter for himself.

"Do me one last favor," I ask Simons.

He waits for my request.

"Please return the Jeep to Hertz."

■ ■ ■

I watch Agents Faulk and Zolotov mount their Transporters. They look like large futuristic motorcycles to me. The Agents gave me a cursory overview of the way they operate. I'm okay with that. I'll have all the time I want to study the machine they left for me in the warehouse.

The bubble forming around the two transporters surprises me. I turn to my soon-to-be history Chief of Security, who stands next to me.

"Can you believe this?"

"Only because I'm seeing it myself," he replies.

I must have Charles sign an NDA before I fire him, I think to myself.

Agent Faulk asked us to stand a few hundred yards away from the machines to avoid being drawn into the energy vortex they create. I'm using a set of opera binoculars to get a close-up view. Watching the machines blur and disappear, I can't help thinking how fortunate I am. These two people and Romulus fell into my lap with technology decades ahead of ours. I have another twenty or thirty years of productivity left. With the technology the agents left behind, I will reshape this world and visit the parallel dimension from which they came.

The explosion of the warehouse shocks me half to death. Before the torn pieces of the building hit the ground, I hear something in the distance. It is the wailing of police sirens.

CHAPTER 18

An outline of the private lab appears ahead of me in the distance. I am rushing toward it at a furious pace. Because my Transporter is heading toward a room rather than a forest, as it did on the trip to Tier Two, it appears that I'm closing in on the lab faster. I close my eyes as I did on the outgoing journey. Aside from the subtle vibration in my saddle, I have no sense of movement. Only God and Matthias know how these machines rip through space and time.

When I open my eyes, I'm in the private lab. Aurora's machine has already arrived. The protective shield surrounding me retracts slowly. It will change shape and store itself underneath the Transporter—another one of Mattias' miracles.

After gathering ourselves, we dismount our vehicles. I slip my arm gently around Aurora's waist. "How are those ribs doing?"

"Healing. I'm learning that Androids have accelerated recuperative powers."

"What about the rest of you?"

"Don't ask."

My comm device vibrates. Mattias' voice comes booming through. "Welcome home, time, space, and dimensional travelers."

Aurora has her comm out. "Never mind the hearty welcome. We have more than the mission to discuss."

"I thought so," Mattias replies compassionately. I haven't heard that tone of voice from him before.

"I can't wait to hear your report. Come to my office."

Mattias' private elevator swiftly ushers us up to his office. Within fifteen minutes of our landing from another dimension, we are sitting in front of the President of AndroBiotica in his opulent office. I look around at the lifelike plants and the Android sculptures that appear to be holding up the ceiling. With its radiant lighting and elegant design, this room is a far cry from Simons' dungeon-like office. Mattias beams at us from behind his multi-station desk. I admire the artful combination of its granite and gold diagonal striping.

Mattias begins the meeting by deactivating Aurora.

"Why did you do that?"

"She wants answers and explanations that won't satisfy her," Mattias answers. "She might get violent, and I can't blame her. You and I have to talk about the mission."

Mattias grills me over the mission details. I assure him that everything Aurora and I accomplished left as little of an imprint as possible. He agrees that leaving Romulus' body behind was unavoidable. Furthermore, he notes that it will be virtually impossible to duplicate AndroBiotica's technology without access to the schematics and specifics of the manufacturing process.

We take a break for Mattias to attend a videocom that can't wait. I use the time to review the points I intend to make about Aurora.

Mattias concludes his conversation with a supplier.

"Now then, where were we?"

"I have a question before we talk about Aurora's future. It's been bothering me. Why did you make her so beautiful?"

"I can assure you that I didn't intend for you to fall in love with her."

"Who says I'm in love with her?"

"Isn't it obvious?"

We stare at one another before Mattias speaks again. "I made Aurora beautiful partly because I gave in to my fetish for beauty."

Mattias waves his arm in an expansive gesture. "As you can see, I surround myself with beautiful things. I also made her beautiful because an attractive woman can be effective in certain undercover operations."

"Was Borinsky testing my discipline as part of the mission?"

"I never discussed anything like that with your superior. I will admit, however, that I was curious to see if Aurora's appearance would interfere with the performance of your duties. It clearly did not."

"Aurora has had a profound effect on me," I admit. "My relationship with her brings up a constellation of issues, both personal and societal.

"I understand."

I wait for Mattias to say something more, but he remains silent.

"I want to continue working with Aurora in the same way we did before the mission. I'm aware that you will have to make some adjustments to Aurora's programming. It may also be necessary to make my supervisor cognizant of Aurora's status."

Mattias takes a moment to answer. I sense that he is considering his words carefully.

"What I'm about to tell you may be hard to accept. I wish it were as easy as you make it sound, Derrick. To explain the situation to you comprehensively, let's go back to the meeting we had in my downstairs office behind the two labs. It occurred a few hours before I sent you and Aurora on your mission to Tier Two."

"I remember. You entered something into your desk interface before starting the discussion. It piqued my curiosity. I wanted to know what you were doing and thought I'd never find out."

"I waited to the last minute because I really didn't want to program an automatic activation trigger into Aurora's subconscious. But I realized at that moment it was unavoidable. The sub-routine would activate Aurora's Android personality in the event that something might happen in Tier Two to threaten the successful completion of your mission."

"Her personality changed radically when Doctor Simons tried to have us arrested in his office."

"Exactly. And here's my point. Aurora isn't designed to be aware of her Human and Android personalities simultaneously. If we allow Aurora to experience memories of both personalities, sooner or later, she will have a psychotic break."

"Can't you remove the Android memories?"

"I won't bore you with the science of why we can't selectively remove memory clusters. I regret that the only option we have is to wipe Aurora's memories entirely and program her with a new identity and function.

"You make it sound like she's a commodity."

"When you strip down the illusion, she is a commodity—one that is not yours, I hasten to remind you."

"Adrien, you are a wizard. You can do anything you put your mind to. I think you owe me. I risked my life and came through for you. You can at least try to, let's say for simplicity's sake, put Aurora back together again. Her experience as an investigative agent is invaluable."

"You're talking about integrating both personalities."

"Yes."

Mattias leans back in his executive chair.

"What you are talking about is easier said than done, but your point about Aurora's experience is a good one. It would be a shame to waste it."

"There's more to this than Aurora. Working with you has made me aware of the profound benefits and pitfalls of these latest developments in the field of Alive Intelligence. I'd like to continue working with you as an unofficial consultant."

"I'm flattered, but what is your reasoning?"

"You're facing some huge decisions. The *NSA* and the *NSS* will be looking over your shoulder. You need someone like me to help you make those decisions. Let's look at a few examples. If you introduce Androids into the mainstream, what effect will they have on society, regardless of what the legislatures enact? To what extent will AndroBiotica be liable in the event that accidents happen that are not due to product failure?"

"I agree that liability is a big issue. I'm developing strategies to deal with the public."

"You can't do it on your own or with a bunch of lawyers. Most of your employees will be hesitant to give you candid feedback. You need a confidant who can be objective and honest."

I can sense the wheels turning in Adrien's head.

"The issue of liability is enormous. The future of AndroBiotica may well depend on it. From a liability standpoint, does it make more sense to confine the use of Androids to anti-crime and anti-terrorism, plus specific industrial functions? Or, can AndroBiotica safely reap the profits available in the consumer market? In the end, only one man will make the decision—You. Still, you need someone you can fully trust to make the most informed decision possible—Me."

"And we'll start with a risky experiment to satisfy your personal needs?"

"We will monitor it carefully. If it doesn't work out, we can always do what you said was necessary—reprogram and repurpose Aurora."

"I hate to admit it, but I like you, Derrick, and your points are well thought out. Give me some time to consider your proposal, and I'll get back to you."

CHAPTER 19

I give Adrien Mattias credit for trying as hard as he did. The man has a heart, after all.

I tried, too. The project presented one obstacle after another. We made mistakes. There were setbacks. I almost gave up. Aurora had good days and bad. At first, her bad days far outnumbered the good ones. If Adrien hadn't been fascinated with the project, he might have given up, too. Thanks to our persistence, Aurora slowly integrated her awareness of herself as a Human Being and an Android. Adrien performed nothing short of a miracle. I expressed my deep appreciation and told him I could never repay him for the feat.

Aurora and I resumed our work together at the Agency. The trips to AndroBiotica for checkups and adjustments decreased from every few days to once a week, and then to once a month.

I shared many happy moments with Aurora personally and professionally. Often, I forgot she wasn't Human. But her Android origin haunted me. For months, I pushed the issue out of my mind. I didn't want to let go of what I thought we had. Gradually, the little voice in my head grew louder. My conscience tormented me. I had trouble sleeping, but I hesitated to do anything about the situation. I had others to think about besides myself. I didn't want to disappoint Mattias or hurt Aurora.

Then, a year after I had convinced Adrien to do the impossible, I could no longer live with myself.

The breaking point came three days after Aurora's first skin replacement when I woke up with Aurora at our regular early morning hour. We showered and dressed for work. We ate a light breakfast. The day started like any other, but it turned out very differently. Aurora went to AndroBiotica for her annual skin replacement. She spent three days in the lab. I think the skin replacement forced me to confront the issue I had been avoiding.

With Aurora indisposed, I had the perfect opportunity to discuss the issue with Adrien. In a private meeting, I poured my heart out to him. He understood my dilemma and reluctantly agreed, in his words, to "take the appropriate steps to remedy the situation." It was a kind way of saying he would wipe Aurora's memories and repurpose her.

I never learned what Mattias did with Aurora. He said it would be better this way. I agreed, but I can't help being concerned about Aurora's fate. She is nearly Human. Thanks to the improvements Adrien made with her and what he learned from the Romulus fiasco, Aurora thinks independently. She has a broad range of emotions and a sense of herself as a unique being. Yet, despite these qualities, Aurora has no right to determine her future. Her life, as she knows it, is in someone else's hands.

I will never forget Aurora and the experiences we shared. I still have feelings for her, or more accurately, warm memories of her. I will have to live with the painful wound of how our relationship ended, probably for the rest of my life. The only solace I can take is knowing that intimate relationships are fragile. Despite the vows of marriage or poetic declarations, nothing is guaranteed. And most certainly, nothing lasts forever.

Impermanence has become the central theme of my life. As a result of my daily meditations, I am becoming aware of the impermanence of the physical world, including the few close relationships I maintain. Nevertheless, I am strongly motivated to impact the impermanence surrounding me positively.

To forget the pain of losing Aurora, I try to stay focused on the Alive Intelligence Project. Since being promoted to Director of the *NSS*, I have more discretion about how I spend my time. I am fortunate to have the opportunity to continue working with Adrien. For the time being, I have convinced him to confine the use of his Androids to special governmental operations and a specific set of industrial functions. But regardless of the lead AndroBiotica enjoys in Android development, its competitors are bound to catch up. There is a high probability that one or more of these companies will soon introduce advanced synthetic Humans into the mainstream. The lure of potential profits is enormous, and so are the risks.

I believe Humans will be prone to developing a splintering collection of neuroses if Androids enter the public sector. The adverse effects on mental health will be substantial. We have enough mental health problems associated with our complex daily lives already. The mental health of advanced social structures may be the most crucial issue at hand, but there are many more. For example, the illicit use of nearly Human Beings will undoubtedly proliferate. The proliferation of synthetic Humans will necessitate the creation of special law enforcement agencies, thereby further stretching already overburdened governmental budgets.

The erosion of jobs is already underway due to the rapid pace of technological advancements. How are people without expensive degrees and training supposed to earn a living? And what about the ethical questions? Will there come a time when Androids demand equal treatment like their Human counterparts? Will there be mass demonstrations and even war?

The corollary to the risks is the potential for the betterment of individuals and society in general if we use Androids intelligently. Besides crime and terrorist intervention, I can see long-term medical care of the elderly and seriously ill patients as a prime function. Additional examples include the distribution of food and essential supplies to impoverished areas. Androids can replace Humans in high-risk situations where radiation, poisonous chemicals, or infectious diseases are involved. These are only a few potential uses that come to mind.

I intend to present a comprehensive proposal to Adrien to support my argument for limiting the use of Androids to specific governmental and industrial purposes. In our short time together, we have become good friends, albeit with differences.

But as much as I'd like to, I can't control what men like Adrien Mattias do. These men and their companies hold the future of Tier One, and perhaps many more dimensions, in their hands. Will greed and short-sightedness prevail? Or will enlightened minds skillfully navigate the challenges ahead?

Whatever the future holds, I hang on to one simple truth: Hope and love spring eternal in the Human heart. I pray that the light within our hearts will guide us on our way ahead. It has to if we are to survive as a species.

CHAPTER 20
—Derrick—

Ten Months Later

I watch the sun rising over the city from my spacious corner office. Outside my impenetrable windows, the purple night surrenders to the persistent dawn. The sky is already congested with rush hour traffic. Without the giant electrostatic air filtration towers eating up the smog, air travel would be impossible.

Has it already been ten years since the towers were installed? Time speeds along like the sleek air breathers darting about like darning needles on pre-programmed courses above and below my office. My eleven-year career as an investigator has flown by like the air breathers outside my windows. The past ten months in my new position have flown by even faster. Is time speeding up as I transition into my thirty-fifth year of life? I have made a pledge to appreciate every moment of my position as Director of the Investigative Division of the *National Science Service*. Theoretically, the practice of being present will expand each moment and slow the frantic pace of time.

I ignore the news, official documents, and interoffice messaging on the three inlaid screens of my absurdly expensive workstation. Impressive desktops are a sign of prestige and achievement within this organization. I'd rather be the object of respect than my workstation.

I am using my time to mentally prepare for the individual who will be arriving in my office at any moment. He has arranged the meeting here to avoid interruptions. When I tried to detect the nature of our meeting, the executive assistant gave me no clue. She apologized for her lack of information and attributed it to an oversight, citing her superior's grueling schedule. Without further intel, I anticipate the meeting will be a performance review. If that is the case, I have no reason to worry.

I hear the heavy footsteps of a man about as tall as I am. I can make this estimation because my training has taught me how to extrapolate the source of ambient sounds. I've left my office door open as a friendly gesture.

My guest arrives and knocks on my doorframe to garner my attention. His neutral expression leaves what will follow a mystery.

I stand. "Please come in."

Commissioner Kyle Arnold oversees the *National Science Service* and the *National Security Authority* of the *Federated Corporate States.* His dual role resulted from the sudden death of the *NSA* Director, and the Commissioner has yet to find a replacement. I suppose, as his assistant indicated, the position remains open due to the Commissioner's tight schedule. One does not secure an appointment with him unless the matter at hand has some degree of priority, which is why I'm a bit nervous.

I've been in Arnold's office only once before. The occasion turned out to be a happy one. Commissioner Arnold told me he had decided to appoint me as Director of the *NSS*. His decision came after my partner and I completed a classified and dangerous mission involving the theft of advanced, proprietary technology.

Without asking, the Commissioner seats himself in a duplicate of the executive chair he uses in his office. I ordered it from the Furnishings Department to make him feel comfortable. The neutral expression on his gray-bearded face dissolves into a serious one. The Commissioner is a study in gray this morning. He wears a gray suit and tie accented by silver cufflinks. The gray coloring of his skin fits the ensemble perfectly.

The Commissioner stares at me with maddening intensity from an electronic eye complemented by a natural brown one. I know that manufacturers are unable to match the bionic eye color to the Human eye because the irises in each set of Human eyes are unique, like snowflakes. Only nature can match the color in Human eyes. On the other hand, Androids have artificial eyes, allowing manufacturers to match their color perfectly.

My superior has opted for bionic implants in his brain and eye. The implants allow him to function as if he were at his workstation, anytime, anywhere. My previous boss offered me the same upgrades. He encouraged me to undergo surgery to improve my job performance. I declined. Some of my colleagues look down on me for it. I don't care. Call me old-fashioned. I'd rather rely on myself than a bunch of machinery.

Commissioner Arnold's voice snatches me from my thoughts. He doesn't waste a second on pleasantries.

"The report on your last mission was lost in the shuffle when I fired Clive Borinsky. My assistant found it on one of your predecessors' computers when she reviewed its files before erasing them to repurpose the workstation."

Now I know why Arnold called this meeting. The reason is for disciplinary purposes following my last mission. Borinsky's report went missing. I thought my indiscretion with Aurora and our unorthodox tactics had escaped censure due to our mission's success. How naive of me.

"Needless to say, I'm disappointed with you *and* your predecessor. In hindsight, I suspect Borinsky sat on the report because it reflected badly on him."

I sit quietly without attempting to defend my actions.

"You disappeared for three days, then lied about your whereabouts."

"I did it to protect a very important friend of the *Federated Corporation of States*. And, I knew Borinsky couldn't handle the truth."

"I think it's high time you filled me in on what happened."

"I'm repeating this for the record because I'm sure our meeting is being recorded. As I stated in my report, Aurora Zolotov and I traveled to another dimension to recover a file stolen by a rogue Android named Romulus. We risked our lives and completed a complex and nearly impossible mission. And we did it without leaving any advanced technology behind. We prevented the plans for building nearly Human Androids from falling into the hands of criminals and terrorists."

The Commissioner leans back in the pearlescent-trimmed executive chair and turns his head to one side. I feel like I'm being pet-scanned by his electronic eye.

"I find it hard to believe what you said in your report about interdimensional travel. You didn't bother to include any details about how you did it."

"I left the technology out of my report to honor an agreement I made with Adrien Mattias."

I immediately regret mentioning Adrien's name.

"I know Adrien personally, and I know about his company. He's a fine man and an astute businessman. I'm sure he'll understand that a man in my position, I should say positions, is entitled to know about this new trans-dimensional technology."

"I'm not going to betray Adrien's confidence. He made Aurora and me promise not to talk to anyone about it."

Thoughts of Aurora and our doomed relationship sadden me—again.

"The recovery mission brought me into very close contact with Adrien. We've become good friends. I should not have mentioned his name. My reasons go beyond my friendship and agreement with him. I've been in high-level negotiations with Adrien concerning the retail and industrial use of his nearly Human Androids. I don't want to upset our discussions."

"You needn't worry about your friendship or agreement. I'll take it upon myself to ask Adrien directly. "

I'll apologize to Adrien and warn him you'll be calling, I say to myself.

"Let's talk about something else. Your lying to your superior about your whereabouts and mission activities was incidental compared to what Borinsky discovered subsequently."

Here it comes.

"You had an intimate relationship with your partner, Aurora Zolotov. Your irresponsible behavior dangerously impacted the mission and Miss Zolotov."

"That's simply not true. Borinsky falsified his report to cover his ass."

Kyle Arnold waives his hand dismissively.

"That's all beside the point. What's at issue is your character and your behavior. After returning from the mission, you had the nerve to ask your pal, Adrien Mattias, to help you continue working at the Agency with Aurora as your partner while carrying on an intimate relationship with her outside of work. Who do you think you are to disobey ironclad rules to suit your personal needs?"

I say nothing.

"I'm waiting for an answer."

"I'd rather not talk about it."

"Then let me answer for you. Your actions in this matter are appalling and unacceptable. If you didn't have a record as an exemplary investigator, I'd fire you right here and now. I'd make sure you never got a job with law enforcement anywhere in the *Federation*."

The Commissioner pauses to let his words sink in. "Unfortunately, men with the skills to do this work are becoming harder and harder to find. It's abundantly clear that Human Beings are becoming lazier and lazier with every passing generation. I may have to hire Androids to fill vacant positions. Before you know it, we'll all be replaced by Androids!"

I give the Commissioner time to regain his composure.

"Your punishment is a slap on the wrist compared to what it should be. I'm rescinding your appointment as Director of the *NSS* and sending you back downstairs to the Investigations Bureau. I am demoting you to the rank of Investigator Second Grade. I'm promoting Brendt Williams to Investigator First Grade. He will be your team leader."

"Brendt Williams is a half-wit."

"Are you questioning my judgment?"

Without responding, I look to my right. Through the row of windows, the city looks magnificent from the top of the *NSS* Building. I will miss the view from this angle.

"Do you have anything to say for yourself?"

I look back at the Commissioner. I don't trust myself to say a word.

"Your silence speaks volumes, Agent Faulk. If I were you, I'd be happy to have a job. We're done here. Clean up your office and report for duty downstairs at the beginning of the week."

CHAPTER 21

Commissioner Kyle Arnold hustles out of my office. He shoves the door closed behind him. If not for its soft return, the portal to my office would have rattled my office, the hallway, and any poor souls in the vicinity. I view the row of tall windows to my right and the bookcases on the opposite wall as if for the first time. I've read that life-changing events can strip away the insulation of daily routine, leaving behind a stark view of reality. I'm experiencing this now. It feels empty and cold.

Without any training, I adapted to the role of Director. As I always do, I relied on my intuition to guide me. I had never managed an entire department of diverse and somewhat quirky investigators before. I'm also not a "people person." However, my extensive experience as a field investigator helped me to support my people. I became involved in their cases, provided them with sound advice, and ultimately earned their respect. Our clearance rate skyrocketed. I admit it wasn't hard to improve the statistics because we started at a pathetic level, thanks to my predecessor. Clive Borinsky didn't lower morale. He crushed it. I should thank him for making my job easier.

We had a good run, but now it's over. I'm back to less-than-square-one. I don't think I can stomach reporting to a dimwit like Brendt Williams. In all fairness, Brendt is not a dimwit. He has many fine qualities as an investigator, but he lacks the most important one: Intuition. I'm not talking about ordinary intuition. I'm talking about intuition in spades—a rich talent. Only the top two percent in our profession have it. I am one of them. And so do several other agents in my department. We can't tolerate second-rate people here. Our work is vital to the security of the *Federated States*. I planned to reassign Brendt to another agency to get him out of the way. How can I possibly tolerate working for him?

As the harsh reality of this moment continues to unfold in all of its nakedness, I realize that I will be resigning from the *National Science Service*. My reasons are two-fold. Aside from the humiliation of my demotion, I don't need the income from this job. I can afford to be independent. I work for the work, not for the money.

My father was a wealthy entrepreneur. He, too, loved his work, although he never seemed happy about it. His name was Bernard. After he died miserably from cancer, Bernard left me enough money to circumvent the cruelties of economic necessity. Along with his brother, Henry, my father amassed a substantial estate from his business success. For many years, he managed two mid-sized companies simultaneously. Henry made wise investments in commercial properties with the earnings from the businesses. With their combined talents, my father and uncle made a fortune.

Sadly, my father's hard-nosed approach to business carried over into his personal life. Being a *Geminus*, Bernard had two sides. He was kind and generous on one side and mean on the other. He cut me with his verbal abuse, but I survived to fight another day. I like to think I'm fighting for a worthwhile cause. The question is: What will I be fighting for now?

The central screen on my workstation blinks twice. I have a holocall. There is only one person I know who would call me this early in the morning. Sure enough, his name appears on my screen. I accept the call. A three-dimensional head pops up.

"Hello, Adrien. I'm honored to be near the top of your early morning call list."

"You should be."

When I don't laugh at his joke, Adrien asks me if everything is alright.

"It may or may not be," I answer. "I haven't decided how to look at it. Commissioner Arnold has just demoted me to Detective Second Grade, reporting to a comparative idiot. The situation is untenable. I've decided to resign from the *National Science Service*."

"That's interesting."

"You think my demotion is *interesting*?"

"Don't get yourself worked up, Derrick. I'm calling to offer you an opportunity. I thought the chances of you refusing were excellent, but I decided to try it anyway."

No matter the circumstances, I'm always happy to hear from Adrien. He's more than an astute business person, as the Commissioner put it. He is a genius. Ideas flow from him like light emanates from a light bulb. I can almost feel the warmth of his incandescence coming through the holophone. Whatever project or job Adrien has to offer, it won't be easy, but it sure as hell won't be boring. And it will definitely beat the hell out of reporting to Brendt Williams as a Second Grade Detective.

"What do you have in mind?"

"There is someone I'd like you to meet. When can you come to my office?"

"As soon as I sign my exit paperwork and clean out my office. I'll contact your assistant to set up an appointment. I'm so glad you called. Your intuition is spot on this morning."

"It happens occasionally. Get yourself organized. Time is of the essence."

Adrien adores the phrase, and it always seems to be appropriate when he's involved.

CHAPTER 23
—Kristina—

Adrien Mattias is a trim, five-foot-ten-inch man who appears somewhat anemic. His pale appearance is unsurprising since men like Mattias are not in the habit of working on their tans. He wears his black hair in a round, Emperor's cut, accented by angular features, a firm jaw, and full lips. According to *NSS* records, Mattias is forty-two years old, married, and has an eight-year-old daughter. This information is not public knowledge. Mattias scrupulously guards his private life and personal information. He does not make public appearances or grant interviews. His tightly guarded public persona is over-the-top, but at the same time, it makes perfect sense. Only a few trusted confidants, including myself, are privy to Mattias' private life.

His office is impressive and reflects the ever-changing world of high technology. Mattias' enhanced workstation contains four inlaid screens. When the occasion calls for it, Adrien allows me to see the screens. A small square in the corner of each interface displays a different feed from major international stock markets, including the *Federated Techno, PanEuro, Chouchin,* and *Neddeki* markets.

I marvel once again at the rows of Android sculptures on each side of the room, which function as load-bearing walls and radiate an energizing light. On several of my visits, I've watched the furniture change configurations on voice command to accommodate the nature and number of employees in the various types of meetings my friend hosts.

I've seen the color scheme of the walls change according to Adrien's moods. This phenomenon generally happens when Adrien is alone.

Because we are close friends, Adrien occasionally allows me to see his moods change to make a point or to highlight a quip.

Then, there are Adrien's artificial plants and flowers. For one thing, they don't look artificial. They can move or not move, grow or not grow, depending upon the client's wishes. When first introduced, this product offering became a big hit for both commercial and residential use, catapulting AndroBiotica into becoming a public company.

Now that I'm a civilian, I can dress in any mode I choose unless the occasion is formal. Adrien doesn't care how I dress as long as I'm presentable. Since I'm meeting someone new, I've chosen to wear a tan business suit augmented by onyx cufflinks and a matching tie pin. I'm a bit overdressed. I suspect this is because I'm meeting a bright female scientist who, Adrien hints, is quite attractive. I've avoided dating since breaking off my love affair with Aurora. Maybe the way I've dressed myself hints at a new beginning. Maybe.

"Let's get down to business, shall we?"

"I've never known you to waste time on small talk, Adrien."

"Invite Kristina in, Cleo."

The walls have ears in Adrien's domicile.

"As you wish," a soothing female voice answers.

I've never heard the name Cleo or her voice before. She must be a new AI creation or a real Human assistant. Whether Human or not, Adrien has chosen to be on a first-name basis with the entity. It gets lonely at the top.

I hear a light rap on the inner translucent door. A tall, dark-haired woman in a mauve lab coat enters the room.

Adrien frowns. "I asked you to wear your new suit to this meeting, Kristina. A lab coat sets the wrong tone."

Kristina stops in her tracks. She is wearing black high heels and silk stockings. Her face reddens. "Excuse me. I had some last-minute work to do and forgot I was wearing my lab coat."

She removes the garment self-consciously. A tan leather chair moves a few feet to her right. Kristina takes the cue and deposits the coat. She stands in the middle of the room, wearing a conservatively cut pale blue business suit. Her deep blue eyes are bright. I notice her posture is moderately stooped at the shoulders, likely due to sitting at workstations for long hours. She smiles at me pleasantly and extends a thin hand. I notice her nails are perfectly manicured, and without nail polish.

"I'm happy to meet you finally," Kristina says in a *Nordish* accent. "Adrien speaks highly of you."

"He's kept you a secret from me. I'm afraid I know little about you." She glances at Adrien. He shrugs.

"It looks like I'll have to introduce myself. I'm from *Olsmar, Norsewall.* I came here to do my undergraduate work at *ESLA.* My parents always stressed the importance of education. Mother teaches at a school for gifted children. My father is a Physicist. He teaches at the *Norsewall* Institute of Science and Technology. I suppose I've inherited my interest in science from him. I met Adrien in my senior year at *ESLA* when he came to interview a few students in my class. I had planned to attend graduate school, but Adrien offered me a job at a tempting starting salary. And here I am, seven years later."

I state the obvious to observe her reaction. "You must have been at the top of your graduating class to capture Adrien's attention."

"Actually, I know her father," Adrien breaks in, saving Kristina from answering. "And yes, Kristina graduated among the top five in her class, but I didn't hire her just for her intelligence. She's a people person with motivational and leadership skills. We're lucky to have her as our Director of Research and Development."

"That's quite an achievement for a young woman."

I notice Kristina has crossed her legs tightly and placed her hands in a steepled pose in her lap. She is the picture of composure: Auburn, shoulder-length hair, fair skin, blue eyes, and a sensual mouth. These features, combined with a slim figure, make Kristina an alluring woman.

"Twenty-nine is hardly young," Kristina answers demurely.

I glance at Adrien. I can tell he's anxious to push on with the meeting. Kristina gives me an appraising look. If she has any curiosity about my background beyond what Adrien has mentioned to her, it will have to wait. I settle back in my chair, which has conformed to my shape for optimal comfort and support. Adrien looks directly at me.

"I've kept Kristina a secret for a good reason, Derrick. I didn't want anyone besides myself to know about a special project she's been working on. Now that you've resigned from your position at the *National Science Service*, I can read you in on the project. I need your help."

One of the reasons I like Adrien is his natural capacity to motivate people. He's a hard person to say "no" to. In retrospect, it's hard for me to believe I agreed to ride his Inter-Dimensional Transporter to apprehend an advanced prototype, rogue Android, and retrieve a file containing all of the specifications needed to build nearly Human Androids.

"I'm listening."

I glance at Kristina, who wears a knowing smile.

"Working with energy and frequency wave displacement, I've developed a machine that can travel to the future and back. I'm not talking about parallel dimensions. You traveled to a parallel world, a few generations behind ours, to retrieve the AndroBiotica File. What we're talking about here is traveling to the future in *this* dimension. We've thoroughly tested the machine with drones and Human test pilots, purely for observational purposes. We've worked out all of the kinks. The machine is as safe as, well, as safe as a time machine can be."

Chuckling at the irony of his last statement, Adrien smiles. "We're now ready for the next step."

"I think I want my job at the *NSS* back."

Adrien takes my attempt at humor seriously. "No one's forcing you to do anything," he says with fatherly concern.

"Okay, what's the catch?"

"The future is not bright," Adrien says forthrightly.

Kristina continues the conversation. "Decades from now, Human-like Androids will be as ubiquitous as our artificial plants. That in itself is not a problem."

I prepare myself for Kristina to ruin my day and probably many more to come.

"In the future, competitive robotics companies will develop Android models similar to ours. As the leader in this field of technology, our models are more advanced than those of our competitors in terms of design and quality. I don't expect that to change in the future. But in the future, it turns out that quality and design, while important, are less critical than system security.

Adrien turns to me from behind his executive desk, fashioned magnificently from metals and natural wood for form and function.

"To make a long story short, I've been wise to listen to your counsel. We've refrained from introducing our Androids to the public until the proper legislative infrastructure is in place." Adrien's cheeks redden. "That, and the unit price is still too high for mass consumption."

Kristina rises from her chair. She walks to a panoramic window that overlooks the city. She speaks to the view rather than to us, and the disappointment in her voice is palpable.

"At least one company we've identified will soon introduce Androids with operating systems that any person with advanced computer skills can be trained to hack. The company is called LifeLike Technologies. While it will require a license and a basic certification to purchase Androids, the actual owners can hide behind shell corporations and straw buyers. As a result, criminals will use Androids for illicit and destructive purposes, anything from prostitution to drug smuggling to murder-for-hire, political assassinations, burglary, terrorism, and whatever else criminal minds can conceive."

"Of course, there's a bright side, too," Adrien interjects. "The government is using our Androids for large-scale criminal interdiction operations. Soon, we'll be introducing a model for toxic and high-risk industrial use. We're close to finalizing a design for hospital nursing work. I'm also working on an idea for medical research."

"Forgive me for asking a dumb question, but how are you managing to see so clearly into the future?"

Adrien throws the question to Kristina with a look.

"May I call you Derrick?" She asks graciously.

"Please do."

"The drones we sent into the future are miniaturized. Adrien and I designed them to assume the color of any ordinary object they attach themselves to. These drones entered public and private areas to record the activity and store it in high-resolution holograms. Between our test pilots and the drones, we now have a library of glimpses into what the future holds for us."

I take a moment to digest Kristina's answer. "So, I assume you want me to journey to the near future to change some critical event that will, for lack of better words, brighten our future."

"Not exactly," Kristina replies.

CHAPTER 24

Leaning back in his "Emperor's Chair" with his arms crossed, Adrien glares at me.

"This is where Kristina and I disagree. I want Heddeki Matsushita to accompany you on the mission. He's an expert martial artist and one of our top scientists. He's won medals in shooting competitions. I've seen him playing roles while joking around with his co-workers. He's a natural actor. Add it all up, and Heddekki is the perfect under-cover agent for this mission. But Kristina insists on going instead. I've tried everything short of job termination to change her mind—all to no avail."

There are times when Adrien's speech sounds more like an announce-ment than an everyday conversation. This is one of those moments.

I turn to Kristina. "Are you mission certified?"

"This will be my first mission," she answers, avoiding eye contact.

"How much training have you had?"

Kristina turns back to her view of the city from Adrien's office window. "Enough."

"Not nearly enough," Adrien interrupts. The wall behind his elab-orate workstation turns bright orange. "You've barely had time to cover the basics with your instructor."

Rising from my seat, I walk toward the window until I'm right behind Kristina. It's time to invade her space to make a point. She turns abruptly to face me before I can say anything.

"I've thought this through." Her blue eyes stare directly into mine. "I'm the most qualified person we have to evaluate the LifeLike

Androids once we embed ourselves as employees of the company. And I don't want to share my time travel technology with anyone but the three of us at this point. With your investigative and operational skills and my background in robotics, we'll make an excellent team."

I shake my head and look away. "I'm sorry, but I decline to undertake this mission. It's suicide." Turning back to Kristina, I look at her directly again. "You aren't ready for something like this. Do you at least have a well-developed plan?"

"Of course we do. Adrien has placed a highly trained undercover agent in the target organization. She's a cutting-edge AndroBiotica-made Android. She's going to hire us for jobs at LifeLike Technologies."

"That's very interesting, but LifeLike is only one company. What if more competitors introduce products with vulnerable security systems?"

With a calming arm gesture, Kristina invites me to return to my seat. "Let's sit. We're getting too emotional."

After we regain our seats, Kristina continues her proposal. "If we are successful, we'll make an example of LifeLike with journalistic exposés. The publicity will generate strict government oversight of Android production."

Adrien has remained in the background for a change. I must be doing an adequate job of raising objections. Here comes the *pièce de la résistance:* "Your plan makes some sense, but I'll be going into a hornet's nest with an unqualified field agent."

"First of all, everyone I've ever known besides my mother and father has underestimated me. Don't make the same mistake. Secondly, we can't risk leaks outside of our little circle. One tiny leak can easily ripple into something that will compromise the mission. We're attempting to change the future. We must control every variable that we possibly can."

Adrien sighs. "What if something happens to you? I can't afford to lose you."

Kristina closes her eyes and shakes her head. She's tired of hearing it.

"I suppose I'm expendable?" I say to Adrien.

Adrien laughs, then shakes *his* head. "I didn't call you in because I missed you. You are the most qualified person I know for this job."

"You did miss me, but that's beside the point."

Adrien smirks while his eyes betray his amusement. He turns to Kristina. "What else can you tell me that will make me seriously consider going ahead with this risky idea?"

I note Adrien's use of the word "idea" rather than "plan."

"I've said everything that needs to be said," Kristina answers firmly. "I know I'm the only one from this company that belongs on this mission, and I know that I can do whatever it takes."

Adrien stares at Kristina for a full minute. Then he looks at me and says with a slight smile, "I guess we're stuck with her."

Adrien rises from behind his desk. "Let's go downstairs to the private lab. It's show and tell time."

■ ■ ■

Adrien leads us to an elevator in the vestibule of his office. He seems preoccupied but not troubled. The man exudes quiet confidence. I've always wondered how titans of industry like Adrien Mattias can function with a junk pile of problems incessantly weighing on their minds. I'd never trade places with any one of them. I notice his expensive *Zandac* suit is rumpled. I suspect he's worn it while sleeping in a king-sized bed hidden in the floor or ceiling of his office. It's the only evidence I can see of the crisis at hand.

On the other hand, it may be that Adrien regularly sleeps in his office after working late into the night. I imagine him voicing a command, and presto, his ultramodern bed appears with the quilt folded back and chocolates on the pillow.

My mind is wandering. I return my attention to the monastic silence of our descent into the bowels of the AndroBiotica building. I've been this way before, but not with Kristina. I try not to think about the "before." Presently, we're about to preview Adrien's latest technological miracles.

The elevator doors swish open into what is known as a "clean room." I've been in many of these antiseptic rooms in the course of my investigations. The air and the room's surfaces are subjected to ultraviolet disinfecting nano-bots to keep them germ-free. In the antechamber to the lab, I unstrap a high-velocity handgun that I carry out of habit. Our *NSS* engineers have designed this lightweight gun and holster to be undetectable by scanners and the eye when worn underneath most conventional jackets.

I strip naked and deposit my clothes into a chute that opens and closes automatically with hardly a sound. UV disinfecting nodes sterilize my body. The sensation borders on being pleasurable. I've gone through this routine a few times in the past. Next, the booth will provide me with a new set of undergarments and a technician's white suit. The finishing touch will be my visitor's security badge.

But that's not what happens.

The pleasant voice tells me to *"Stand very still."* Robotic arms and hands descend to affix a transparent helmet around my head and neck. The material is light as a feather. I barely feel it. If I didn't know Adrien the way I do, I'd be starting to worry. Seconds later, I'm standing in a shower of tiny crystals. They adhere to my body and connect to form a silver coating that sparkles as it solidifies.

"You may move your limbs now," the voice tells me. I move my arms and legs to test my range of motion. The new birthday suit doesn't restrict my movements at all.

"Good," the voice says in a reassuring tone.

"Where do I get my security badge?" I ask the voice. I assume it will be handed to me somewhere up the line. *"You will not require one,"* it answers in the same reassuring tone.

This highly unusual situation awakens my investigator's instincts. Despite my close relationship with Adrien, a special security badge has always been the norm for lab visits. There can only be one reason for suspending this security necessity: Adrien doesn't want to leave any evidence of this visit behind.

A shelf in the wall opens, bearing a white technician's suit.

"Please dress yourself."

Sure enough, the suit fits perfectly. The system has automatically updated and stored my measurements in AndroBiotica's databanks. Now that I'm sterilized and appropriately dressed, the booth door opens. A welcoming voice tells me, *"You may proceed."*

I follow Adrien and Kristina through a set of safety doors into the central lab. It is primarily as white as an arctic mountain top. I notice plastic-wrapped bodies stacked on shelves on the wall to our right. These Androids are called "neutrals." Highly trained software engineers will eventually program the neutrals with specific personality traits and skills tailored for particular functions. Then, an artist will take over to apply a unique exterior finish to the unit consistent with its intended purpose. An artist is working on an Android stretched out on an operating table as we pass. Typically, there are three or four Androids in the finishing stages on the floor, but this is a weekend. The Android on the table is probably a rush order.

Based on its nondescript body and facial features, the Android is likely to be used for a dangerous or repugnant industrial purpose. The artist uses a set of lasers on a side table to apply enough definition to make the Android look Human enough to maintain decorum in the workplace.

The upfront cost of an industrial Android is substantial, but the savings in hazard pay, liability insurance, and employee retention more than offset the initial cost. Adrien is keen on introducing a series of models for mainstream use, but the government needs to be faster in introducing legislation governing the use of Androids. We have proposed a set of laws, but Congresspeople and Senators have other priorities, chiefly consisting of getting themselves re-elected.

Sleek workstations outfitted with electron microscopes, super-computers, and various other design devices and finishing tools sur-round the room. The first time I came here, I remember meeting an Android code-named *Georges,* nearing the end of his production cycle. Notwithstanding his unfinished status, I was amazed by *Georges'* Human-like behavior and appearance.

There are two private rooms beyond the central lab. Adrien leads us to the doorway to the first room. He keys in a security code on a side panel. A hidden door in the wall slides open. Standing by the entrance, Adrien invites us in.

"*Aprés vous.*"

We speak French here from time to time (*de temps en temps*). It's a habit we developed to help Aurora round out her *Rousian* accent. We should lose the habit. Memories of Aurora are often painful. I'll speak to Adrien about it.

We enter a clean room similar to the first lab, except the ceilings are higher. I estimate fifteen feet. Recessed lighting shines down from above. In the confines of the room, the machines look enormous. There are four of them, two of which I recognize—the Inter-Dimensional

Transporters. Kristina is calmly observing me to gauge my reaction to the other two machines.

For starters, I'm surprised there are multiple time machines. Like the IDTs, they are built for one person each. Adrien and Kristina built the time machines using the IDT frame with modifications.

In place of the back panel, I see a series of concentric circles forming an outward-facing cone tapering to the end. Well, it's not precisely a cone. The end culminates in a blue, tulip-shaped gadget at the tip. The cone at the front of the machine matches the one at the back end, but it terminates in a volleyball-sized golden sphere imprinted with triangle-shaped circuitry. The silver hubcaps of the motorcycle-like wheels have been replaced by red metallic tubes about one inch in diameter. The red tubes expand outward in a spiral from the center of the wheels, resembling miniature galaxies. Both time machines rest on pontoons exactly like the ones we used to store our gear in for the inter-dimensional mission.

"What do you think of them?" Kristina asks me with one arm across her midriff. Four fingers of her other hand are under her chin, with the index finger pointing upward along her cheek.

"Honestly, I don't know what to think. You've said it works. I guess that's all I need to know for now. As to the mission, I'm still waiting for more background and a detailed plan of action."

"Why don't we adjourn to my private office to put more gristle on the bone?"

Adrien's metaphor does little to help me keep an open mind, but I owe him the courtesy of hearing whatever else he and Kristina have to offer.

CHAPTER 25

Adrien leads us to a sealed doorway. He opens it by keying in another combination. We are entering a second private room, both behind the central lab.

The office is small but functional. The ceiling is lower, and the lighting is softer than in the two labs outside. A bookcase of first-edition antique texts lines the wall to my right. I notice a row of oil painting prints by past masters on the wall to my left. Adrien is a man with a deep appreciation for the past and a clear vision for the future. Blue-prints cover a smaller version of the cubed desk in his upstairs office. Strips of gold inlays accent the lustrous redwood. Inset into the surface is a computerized design interface. Like everything I've seen belonging to this man, it appears to be pricey. Four black leather chairs surround a cocktail table in one corner.

"One and two in front of my desk," Adrien calls out. Two of the chairs roll up to his desk. We sit in them, and they immediately adjust to the contours of our bodies. These chairs, although they are smaller to fit the room's size, are as comfortable as their counterparts upstairs.

Since Adrien doesn't like to mince words or waste time, I'm comfortable speaking my mind without unnecessary preambles.

"Let's go over the particulars of your plan. I'm still waiting to be convinced."

Adrien looks at Kristina, who quickly takes the lead. "It's simple. Our mole hires Derrick as a Security Consultant and me as a Research Director. I examine LifeLike's Android technology. I identify the design flaws. Derrick quietly looks into the business end of the company.

Then, we leak the irregularities we uncover to the press and the appropriate government agencies, citing, in particular, the consequences of putting hackable, nearly Human Androids on the market. LifeLike's stock will plummet. Their product launch will be delayed for years due to the red tape of government oversight. With any luck, LifeLike will go bankrupt. The company will become a cautionary tale for any other competitor trying to take shortcuts to put a cheap product on the market."

Kristina's eyes grow more intense. She touches my arm to make her point. "It's a big job. Our mission is to get the ball rolling."

Adrien chimes in, "And you'll have to work fast. Your helmets and the special covering applied to your bodies in the sterilization chambers will protect you on the trip into the future and back, but it will only last ninety-six hours. If you stay too long, the special covering will degrade, and your cells will rupture in the time tunnel."

I address Adrien directly. "I came here to learn more about the mission and to make an intelligent decision about whether or not to accept it. By the application of the special covering, I take it you've already decided I'll accept."

"Time is of the essence, Derrick."

"Time is always of the essence in your universe. I have to tell you that your mission doesn't make sense to me."

I turn to Kristina. "How do you know there are openings for the jobs you described?"

"Our test pilots and drones reported LifeLike's need to fill the positions. It isn't necessary to know the 'whys' and the 'wherefores.' That's something you can learn when you get there."

"Alright," I allow. "Here's my biggest problem, aside from the tiny window of opportunity: Your lack of training. I can't get past it."

"I've already addressed that issue. You'll have to get past it."

"Why can't you send two of your advanced Androids to do the job?"

"Because they aren't ready to make the kinds of decisions this mission will require," Adrien answers. "You know what happened with Romulus when I gave him too much free will. There is only one Android capable of handling a mission like this. "I've already sent her into the future. She's one of a kind. I started upgrading her eighteen months ago, before Kristina made her time travel breakthrough—before we could see into the future."

"Isn't that around the time you began working on Aurora to reconcile her dual nature?"

"What are you talking about?" Kristina asks me.

"As you know, Androids can be programmed to think they are Human. In many cases, this feature is necessary for an Android to fulfill its purpose. Aurora knew herself as a Human Being. Then, in the course of her mission with me, she became aware that she wasn't. Adrien programmed her with a fail-safe loop to protect the mission in dire circumstances. A situation arose wherein it became necessary for Aurora to use her superhuman strength. I won't get into the details. The point is this: Androids are not built to know themselves both as a Human Being and an artificial one. In the unlikely event that this simultaneous awareness occurs, it leads to an eventual psychotic breakdown. The only solution is to wipe the Android's memory and reprogram it with another identity and purpose. I did not want this to happen to Aurora."

Kristina has been listening closely to my every word. "Why?"

"Because I was deeply in love with her. I convinced Adrien to find a way to preserve Aurora's identity and reconcile her awareness of herself as an Android and as a Human. Memories cannot be selectively removed. That's why Adrien had to find another solution. And he did."

I watch Kristina process the implications of my story. As the Director of Research, she is curious about everything pertaining to her area of responsibility.

A brief silence fills the room until something occurs to me.

"Adrien, did you repurpose Aurora and send her into the future to wait for us?"

Adrien gestures with both hands, but no words come out. I wait for him to formulate his answer.

"I did send Aurora into the future as the mole. I planned to tell you toward the end of the meeting."

I glare at Adrien. "Yeah, after you had me hooked. I forgot how calculating you can be."

Kristina leans forward in her chair. "You never told me about Aurora," she says tersely to Adrien.

"I didn't tell either of you about Aurora because I broke a cardinal rule in her case. I did not repurpose her. I didn't have the heart to do it. She is too beautiful, both as a person and as a creation. I learned from my mistakes with Romulus. I've given Aurora the ability to, in simple terms, think for herself. She makes informed, mature decisions. For example, I did not program Aurora for this mission. I gave her the option of going or not going. She chose to volunteer for it. In short, Aurora is a free-thinking individual with feelings and a personality all her own. She is very close to being Human, and in some ways, she is superhuman. And most importantly, I trust her."

"I can't believe you kept this from me."

"Derrick, you told me the relationship was over. You couldn't abide the idea that everything you felt for Aurora and everything she felt for you was an illusion. I thought if you knew her personality still existed, it would torture you."

"You've gone too far, Adrien. I feel betrayed. How can you expect me to undertake this mission under these circumstances?"

Kristina lightly touches the back of my hand. "Something good can come out of this. You objected to going on the mission without a trained operative. Now you have one. Aurora."

Adrien leans forward from behind his desk. His voice is urgent. "I'm sorry about keeping Aurora a secret from you, Derrick. I only had your best interests at heart, but the conditions we now find ourselves in are grave. I'm attempting to deal with the situation as quickly and practically as possible. I know that sounds cold, but it's necessary. Now that we've seen the future of nearly Human Beings, we have to change it."

I notice Adrien is referring to his nearly Human Androids as "Beings." His attitude has changed. When we discussed Aurora's future after our last mission, he referred to her as a "commodity" to make a point. Now, I can begin to see why he didn't have the "heart" to repurpose her.

I turn to Kristina. Her eyes peer into mine. I find myself taken with her focus and deep sincerity.

"I don't want to sound like a broken record, but you aren't ready for something like this."

Adrien discreetly nods in agreement.

Kristina sits up straight in her chair. I've angered her. She takes a moment to calm herself. She stares at me, then Adrien, and back at me.

"I have every right to be on the mission. I developed the science behind the time machine that Adrien and I built. I want to see the future with my own eyes, and I won't consider the experiment finalized until I do."

I take a deep breath and address my remarks to Adrien.

"It looks like we have no choice. We've lobbied for a set of laws to regulate the industry. From your glimpse into the future, it appears our efforts have fallen short. You've listened to me and refrained from selling your Androids to the general public until an appropriate set of laws is in place. You've shown admirable restraint. For this, I'm in your debt. And, like you said, 'the future isn't bright.' Someone has to do something about it. I guess one of those someones is me."

CHAPTER 26

Adrien asks us to help him cover the time machines with tarps. With his augmented bionic communication device, he calls two worker Androids into the private lab to push the machines through the central lab to a bank of three elevators waiting in the antechamber outside. One of the elevators is Adrien's private express elevator. Scientists and lab workers use the elevator in the center. The last cab is a freight elevator.

I watch the Androids push the time machines into the freight elevator. After the doors close, we take Adrien's private elevator to the Launch Room. Aside from a few worker Androids, the room's existence is known only to Adrien, Kristina, and now me.

The elevator lets us off in a clean room with a separate observation booth situated against the opposite wall. On the adjacent wall, two booths flank a tall cabinet with drawers of varying sizes. These must hold tools and blueprinted plans.

"If this is the Launch Room, it's a much simpler setup than I expected," I remark.

"It's a little more complicated than it looks," Kristina says. "The launch pad is supported by a titanium base painted over with a special coating to resist the energy pulse created by the machines. The walls and ceilings are covered with a high-density material to resist the heat of liftoff into spacetime. The booths you see to our right contain our custom-fitted suits and helmets for the journey."

Adrien took the liberty of making a suit for me without knowing if I would accept the assignment. I suppose you'd call that confidence—or maybe arrogance.

"The Launch Room might look simple, but I can tell you it wasn't cheap to create," Adrien adds. "Go put on your suits while we wait for the machines to arrive."

As usual, Adrien doesn't waste a minute. Kristina points to the booth where my custom suit awaits me. I watch Kristina disappear into hers.

The voice in my dressing booth tells me how to put on my suit for the journey ahead. The voice is female. I suspect Kristina recorded the instructions because I hear some familiar voice inflections. Shedding my technician's jumpsuit and temporary headpiece, I dress in the time travel suit one section at a time. I join the pants, top, and gloves with a zipper that folds into the fabric to form a solid seal. White, I'll call them feelers, insulate each partition of the time suit. Pliable white boots are the last article of clothing to put on. My socks are extensions of the pants, like a kid's pajamas. I slip the ankle boots over my socks and zip them to seal the junction.

Carrying my helmet out of the dressing booth, I hear my boots clatter on the launch floor. Their heels, Adrien tells me, are made of a durable yet lightweight polymer material. With the coating applied in the sterilization chamber, I now have three layers of protection. The suit is a sky blue color. Kristina tells me she chose it because sky blue is one of her favorite hues. In the reflection from the observation booth window, I look like a streamlined astronaut without the bulky arms, legs, and Oxygen pack on my back. I feel surprisingly comfortable in the outfit.

After removing the tarps, the Android team positions the time machines side by side in the center of the launch floor, about twenty feet from the observation booth. Adrien stands behind a control panel. He is the first to speak. I hear his voice coming out of the helmet I'm holding: "Kristina, would you please check Derrick's seals?"

She clatters over to begin her examination. I look straight ahead at Adrien in the booth. "While we have a moment, can you tell me how the machine works?"

"Kristina has the best explanation for the science-challenged."

"We can't all be geniuses," I reply.

Kristina finishes looking me over. She pats me on the back. "You're good to go."

Gazing at Kristina, I await her explanation. She seems at a loss for words.

"What?" She asks.

Kristina was so focused on checking out my suit that she didn't hear Adrien's request.

"Adrien asked you to explain how the machine works. Pretend I'm someone who had other things on his mind while in science class."

"I don't think I have to pretend, Derrick."

"Why has fate consigned me to a couple of science weirdos?"

"I guess we had that coming." Kristina taps her chin with her forefinger. "Okay. Let's try this." She levels her eyes at me.

"Time is a continuum. It vibrates at different frequencies relative to this moment. There are an immeasurable number of frequencies within time, causing it to subdivide and create multiple dimensions. This structure makes traveling through time very tricky. It is hard enough to create a time machine that actually works. The nature of time travel alone makes the journey even more challenging. There is a time *and* a place factor to deal with. The mathematics must be perfectly accurate as well as the machinery, or the time traveler can wind up at the right time in the wrong place or the wrong time in the right place. We must be absolutely precise when inserting the time traveler into a specific intersection of location and moment."

"Okay. I understand the challenges and the difficulties. How do you do it?"

"The heart of the engine that propels a traveler through time is something we call the Quantum Temporal Displacer."

"How does it work?"

"I'm afraid you'd have to be a physicist to understand the math."

Kristina turns to Adrien in the booth. He moves his hand in circles. "Keep going."

Kristina looks up at the ceiling and then at me. "Let's say…the QTD maps frequencies and the intended location. It then matches the frequency to the location. Finally, the machine subdivides time down to the instant of insertion. We use quantum coordinates to program the intersection of time, frequency, and location into the machine's data drive. With these coordinates lined up, the machine generates a massive energy pulse that sends the traveler through time."

Kristina sighs. "My explanation is a gross simplification of the process. The only way to cogently describe it is with equations."

"Don't worry, Derrick. As Kristina said, we've worked out all of the bugs in the hardware and the software. We have thoroughly tested every component of our time machine. The danger is not in the journey."

It's what comes after the journey.

"We will only be traveling eight years into the future," Kristina tells me as if reading my mind. "Like your previous mission, Adrien and I have packed everything we anticipate we'll need in the pontoons supporting the machines."

"Your first objective will be to secure your positions at LifeLike Technologies," Adrien says. "Aurora has already set up the interviews. We anticipate that your position as a freelance security consultant will enable you to act independently and, most importantly, have access to sensitive information. You will report directly to Jan Kronak, the president of the company."

"If one or both of us don't land a job, we're out of luck. The plan is iffy."

I can tell from his furrowed brow that Adrien is losing patience with me. "This strategy is the best one we can come up with. If it doesn't work, Aurora will have to act alone."

"I'd put our chances for success somewhere around fifty percent at best."

"Maybe so," Kristina responds, "but we have to try. We're staring at a bleak future if we don't."

I glance at Adrien through the launch booth window and then at Kristina a few feet to my right.

"Alright. I'm done raining on your parade. I sincerely hope you guys know what you're doing."

CHAPTER 27

Sitting in the saddle, I feel a tingling sensation as my machine cycles up. Unlike the Trans-Dimensional Transporter I rode on my first mission, the time machine has no cab. I have only three layers of protection against whatever comes next. I would never attempt this if I didn't have absolute faith in the inventive genius of Adrien Mattias.

The tingling sensation intensifies. It feels like the electro-stim sensation I've experienced on a body part in physical therapy after a tough *NSS* mission, except it's going through my entire body. A whirlpool of colors suddenly surrounds me. Pressure builds on the outside of my suit. The room blurs, and I explode into a world of bright light. The next thing I feel is a sense of weightlessness. The machine throws me into a tunnel of alternating darkness and light that accelerates until the phenomenon becomes a blur. I am grateful to be securely tethered to my saddle. This is my last thought before the darkness and light begin flashing by again until the effect slows. The pressure against my time-travel suit increases until I feel I'll be crushed like a hull in deep ocean water, and then, I lose consciousness.

I wake up in a dark room. I am aware it is a room only because the oval ceiling is ringed with recessed yellow lights that cast a faint glow. The ambient light barely outlines the silver shapes of our time machines.

I notice Kristina's machine rests at about a 120-degree angle relative to mine. By the slant of her tethered body, I can tell she is unconscious. I expected we would "land" together at the same 45-degree angle that separated us on the AndroBiotica Launch Room floor. I'm no expert on time travel, but I think the positioning of my machine has shifted in a way it's not supposed to.

Kristina moves. I watch her sleek, red helmet shake. The trip must have disoriented her more than it did me. She looks up with a start and then over to me. Her anxious voice filters into my helmet.

"We aren't where we're supposed to be."

I concur with Kristina's observation. Our target destination is the lobby of the new LifeLike building, which is in the early stages of construction, after working hours. The current corporate headquarters resides across the street in the year NM 30-02. From the looks of this place, we are nowhere near either building. We have missed our insertion coordinates.

We unstrap and dismount our machines. The only thing we can do now is to find out where we are and hope we aren't being held captive.

Instinctively, we move together. "Let's find the exit door."

"Obviously," Kristina replies irritably.

"Don't cop an attitude. Your machines misfired, not me."

"We'll see," she answers more civilly.

As my eyes adjust to the ambience, I can see the curvature of the surrounding wall from the faint illumination cast by the recessed ceiling lights. As our gloved hands explore the smooth surface, the wall retreats a few feet backward as if it doesn't like us touching it.

Before we can react, I hear a pneumatic sound coming from behind us. We whirl to face it. A door has opened. Brilliant light explodes into the room. Our golden face plates save us from blindness.

We move warily towards the glowing doorway. Its dimensions are high and wide, broad enough to allow a giant through. Kristina grabs my hand—a natural response under the circumstances. The unspoken question is: *What is this place?*

We pass through the tall doorway into a long, brightly lit corridor. I cannot tell if the walls and floor are solid. A single line oscillates on both walls in a wave pattern. The corridor's colors change in soothing shades of blue and lavender.

Without warning, the corridor collapses into an oval door in front of us. We step back reflexively, only to find the door behind us is closed. Kristina moves closer to me.

"Will we be crushed?" She murmurs.

"I don't think so."

"How do you know?"

"Call it a hunch."

The lavender and blue hues on the oval door in front of us stop fluctuating. The portal slides open. Beyond it, all we can see is blackness—not exactly a warm welcome.

"We have to keep moving."

Kristina nods but doesn't move. Taking her hand, I tug it gently. She follows me through the portal.

We stand on the other side of the doorway in darkness so dense it could swallow sunlight. Then, another explosion of light.

We stand in an expansive circular room circumscribed by doors. The smooth white floor illuminates the space with pale yellow light issuing from a source somewhere beneath it. I estimate the surrounding doors are five feet apart, and I count seventeen of them. A man wearing a skintight golden jumpsuit stands erect in the middle of the room.

"What's with all of the light explosions and telescoping corridors?" I ask the figure.

Kristina's spontaneous laughter resounds inside my helmet. I detect a measure of relief in it.

"Figure it out for yourselves," the golden man replies in a challenging tone.

"It's a Synthetic," Kristina says, surprised.

I accept Kristina's conclusion. I'm sure her ears can discern the subtle differences between life and its imitation better than mine.

"Why are we here?" Kristina asks impatiently.

"Please don't waste time on questions I'm unable to answer. I am here to guide you to your next destination—nothing more, nothing less."

"We aren't leaving this room without some answers," I tell our guide and whoever else might be eavesdropping.

The Android tilts its head upward toward the ceiling, which lights up with breathtaking hues of lavender, blue, green, and gold. Then, the colors fade to gray and finally to black again. An instant later, the Android speaks.

"I am permitted to tell you that your machines have been diverted here for an important reason."

"Something above the ceiling is speaking to the Android with colors," I whisper to Kristina.

The Android moves its arm in a flourish toward the circular wall.

"These doors lead to different destinations. I am here to take you through the door leading to your designated purpose."

I am still holding Kristina's hand. She lets go and turns to me. "It doesn't sound like we have a choice. I don't like this."

In the little time I've known her, I've learned that Kristina is a woman accustomed to making her own choices. I can't blame her. My life has led me in the same direction.

"The only door we intend to go through will lead us back to our machines," I tell the guide.

The Android calmly tilts its head in my direction. With its long black hair and chiseled features, it looks like a knight plucked from a royal court.

"You are not permitted to return to your machines."

No apology—just a bald statement of an inconvenient truth. It dawns on me that the machines carry all of our provisions, including my weapon. I am unarmed in unknown surroundings.

Kristina turns to me. "Say something."

I'm the one who is supposed to know what to do in unexpected scenarios, except nothing like this is in the textbooks. I'll have to wing it.

"By what authority have you brought us here? We are time travelers on an urgent, time-sensitive mission. I insist you return us to our time machines."

"I ask you again not to waste time. If you persist in being uncooperative, we will stand in this room until you decide to follow me out of it."

CHAPTER 28
—Dianah—

Without food and water, Adrien's auto-adjusting chairs to sit in, and a sympathetic supervisor to appeal to, only one choice remains. Hoping for the best and prepared for the worst, we follow our guide through one of the seventeen doors lining the circular wall. It turns out the door is not really a door. It is a holographic representation of one. I watch the image bounce off Kristina's suit as we pass through.

At the end of an all-white, shimmering hallway, a staircase awaits us. It curves upward around a broad pillar. The panels below the railing form a pattern similar in appearance to the swirling arms of a galaxy's stars. The stairway looks solid, but for all I know, half or all of what we've seen and heard so far is an illusion made of papier mâché and gossamer. The backdrops of the world we're in could be something like scenery in a stage play.

Our guide leads us to the bottom of the stairway. It is wide enough for two people to walk side by side. With an outstretched, golden-clad arm, the Android invites us to ascend a set of stairs that resemble white marble. Taking hold of the railings, we dutifully climb. Kristina and I have not conversed since leaving the circular room. We've been too busy taking in our surroundings.

I look up and see a landing a few hundred feet above us. Behind the landing, the stairway curves upward. From my vantage point, I cannot see where it leads.

I hear crisp clicking sounds coming from above.

Kristina grabs my arm. We stop.

Seconds later, I catch sight of a woman descending the stairs above us. Upon reaching the landing, she stands perfectly still. The woman wears an electric blue evening dress with matching gloves up to her elbows. Straight blond hair falls behind her athletic shoulders. Her skin is painted silver. Her eye makeup matches the evening dress. The woman is unusually tall and quite striking in her looks and physique. She continues to stand as still as a statue. Turning to me, Kristina shrugs. I'm as mystified as she is. I nod my helmet upward. We continue up the stairs in unison. When we reach the landing, the statuesque silver woman extends an arm with her palm up in a welcome gesture.

"Greetings, travelers. My name is Dianah. I understand you have questions."

Dianah pronounces her name *Dee-Anna*. Since Kristina is our team's resident science genius, I offer her a chance to ask the first question.

"My name is Kristina Flemming. I am an expert in advanced artificial intelligence. I can usually distinguish between Human and synthetic life. In your case, I must admit that I can't tell the difference."

"There is no need to introduce yourself. I know everything about you, Kristina. To answer your question, I am neither living nor artificial. I am pure consciousness funneled into the form standing before you."

The answer gives us both pause. Kristina turns to me. If I could see through her faceplate, I'm sure I'd see an astonished expression.

I grapple with a follow-up question. One comes to mind. "You put on a show for us downstairs. Why?"

"It was meant to break down your defenses." A pause. "To prepare you to listen to reason."

"That sounds like an ultimatum."

Dianah ignores my statement. She turns to Kristina in anticipation of another question.

"How do you know all about me? We've never met. I'd certainly remember you if we did."

"I have the capacity to know about everything at once, but that can be confusing. I prefer to know what I need to know when I need to know it. Often, my knowing is the result of proximity. Our immediacy gives me all the information I need to know about you." Her eyes meet mine. "And about you, former agent Derrick Faulk."

Diannah's words are chilling and somewhat infuriating. It takes a moment to recover my composure. "Are you the one who brought us here?"

"To begin with, I am not a 'one,' Derrick Faulk. And yes, I ripped you and Kristina Flemming out of time and space. My reasons for bringing you here are certainly not casual."

"What reasons?" Kristina asks heatedly.

We are both weary of being detoured against our will to this strange world.

"You must exhaust all of your questions before I can explain my reasons. When you are empty of curiosity, anger, impatience, and resentment, then you will be ready to accept what I have to communicate."

"We don't have time for a long dialogue," Kristina continues. "Our mission clock is ticking away precious seconds and minutes. Soon, we'll be out of sync with the timeline at our base. We have a schedule to keep."

"You need not worry about your mission clock. We are outside of time here. Your allotted time will resume as soon as we finish our business. Now, please continue with your questions."

"Are you God?" I ask in a skeptical tone.

"I am known by the name Overwatcher. I will explain the meaning of this word in due time."

"Why are you wearing that...costume?" Kristina asks. She does not hide her growing impatience.

Dianah answers cryptically. "Why do you think I appear to you in this form?"

The question hangs in the air until Dianah answers it. Turning first to Kristina and then to me, she says, "Your friend and your employer is a lover of Beauty in all forms, is he not?"

Kristina turns to me. "How could she know that?" Dianah's inexplicable familiarity with Adrien's penchant for beautiful things is the final straw. The remaining constructs of my reasoning mind collapse. I turn back to Kristina. "Something way beyond our comprehension is going on here."

Dianah turns to Kristina. "Do you agree?"

After some consideration, Kristina nods.

Dianah's lovely facial features brighten. "Good. You are ready to continue our discussion. Come with me."

CHAPTER 29

We follow Dianah up the winding staircase into a room lit by a spotlight shining down from a cathedral-like ceiling. The ceiling is sky blue.

Dianah walks into the spotlight. The circle it forms on the floor reveals a bone-white surface. I am unable to see what the rest of the room looks like because the darkness cloaks it. The spotlight suggests we are on stage.

Kristina and I approach Dianah until she signals us to stop a few feet away.

"Why have you brought us here?" Kristina asks in a neutral tone. I think she's learned how to get the ultimate answer out of this woman.

Dianah smiles. The spotlight causes her silver makeup to sparkle intermittently.

"My purpose is to transmit information and perspective. Look above you."

Images appear on the sky-blue ceiling. One of them comes to life. Dianah narrates an unfolding scene.

"You are viewing a politician standing on stage, addressing a rally of supporters behind a shield. The shield consists of a hyperplex, transparent material that is impenetrable by all known long guns. As you can see by the markings, the view is from a sniper's telescope. The sniper is an Android positioned a mile away in an office tower. The Android does not need a spotter. It can detect and calculate wind speed and the pull of gravity automatically."

The image changes to a view of the silenced end of the weapon. We see something explode out of the silencer. The view switches to a slow-motion path to the target, which grows larger and larger.

Dianah continues her narration. "The projectile travels at supersonic speed. It takes less than a second to reach the target."

In slow motion, we watch the projectile pierce the shield and the politician's forehead. The target's head explodes, and the image fades.

"The projectile is hardly damaged by its contact with the shield and the politician's head. It continues to crash into and through anything in its way until gravity finally takes over. Collateral damage is a certainty. You've just witnessed a sad truth. In the future of your dimension, anyone with enough money can purchase an Android for revenge or to eliminate a political or philosophical rival."

Kristina takes my hand. Hers is trembling. It is one thing to know something like this can happen. It's another thing to see it in gruesome detail.

Another image animates on the ceiling to the left of the previous one. We watch soldiers in military vehicles reach the entry point of an army base. After the guard in the security booth checks their identification, the soldiers pass through the gate. The scene shifts to the soldiers exiting their rugged transports. Each soldier enters a different building on the base. Shortly afterward, each building explodes.

"You've just watched a futuristic version of a terror attack. The perpetrators are Android duplicates of Human soldiers whom the Androids have abducted and murdered. The terrorists have stolen their identification badges and wallets to pass inspection. In time, these Android attackers will be detected by specialized wands before they enter military bases. But this new form of terrorism will result in the murder and maiming of thousands of soldiers before the safeguards are in place."

Another image animates on the ceiling. I've seen enough nightmares for one day.

"We get the idea, Dianah. We were on our way to prevent incidents like the ones you've shown us. Why have you intervened to detour us from our task?"

"Because you lack the perspective to see the immense dangers posed by the misuse of highly advanced Androids. My job is to make you aware of the high stakes at hand. The world you inhabit, more accurately, your dimension, is on a precipice. As I mentioned earlier, I am an Overwatcher. I am not the only one. There are many more like me, and we communicate regularly. I overwatch your dimension. They overwatch theirs. Because your dimension is surrounded by others in close proximity, the disharmony in your dimension causes a ripple effect. In simple terms, your dimension is a bad influence. If the innumerable dimensions of the multiverse did not affect one another, we might let your dimension destroy itself. Your destruction may be inevitable, but I must at least try to prevent it for the sake of your dimension and many others."

Kristina is quick to ask a logical question. "So, the fate of our dimension and others depends on us?"

"Not only on you. There are others we have brought here from your dimension. You are both specialists in your field. I am hopeful that you will become guardians of the uses of artificial intelligence in your dimension. Obviously, the use of artificial intelligence isn't the only problem your world faces. We have asked other specialists to deal with intractable issues in their areas of expertise. I have brought you here to broaden your perspective. The stakes are higher than you knew them to be before coming here. It is crucial that you succeed in your mission, as well as the others in their missions."

Dianah has more to add: "Unlike yourselves, I transported most of the other teams in the course of their daily lives. Their journeys here were even more disorienting than yours, and many of them lacked your training. The transportation process is frightening and disorienting. I understand and apologize for this, but your presence here and hasty introduction to me are born of sheer necessity. The most important piece of information I am conveying to you is this: When I bring to your attention the high stakes at hand, I mean that I will erase your dimension if you do not get your Android technology under control."

I exchange a look with Kristina. The surreal has suddenly migrated to the bizarre.

"I am deeply sorry for the state of affairs you and your world are in. I regret the consequences if your problems are not solved. I wish other options existed."

"Why can't you intervene?" Kristina objects.

"If I altered the direction and momentum of your dimension, the results would be catastrophic because of the chain reaction generated by an outside force. Constructive change must originate organically from *within a dimension* to achieve an orderly result. That's putting it in broad terms. And even if I *could* intervene, I would not want to because free will is an important part of the design."

"You must answer to a superior, someone or something you report to?"

"Your question is irrelevant, Kristina. There is no Court of Appeals. If you fail in your assignment, the destruction of your dimension will be assured."

Kristina turns to me.

"We'll talk about it later," I tell her.

Turning back to Dianah, I watch her Goddess-like features become suddenly radiant. "Think of our time together as tough love. I wish you great success."

With these final words, the spotlight turns off, and the sky-blue ceiling goes dark. A light switches on at the entrance to the room. Our knightly guide stands in the doorway, beckoning us to follow him.

As we descend the staircase, Kristina's voice comes through my helmet. "We're wearing three layers of protective covering, and yet I'm not sweating. I have no sense of smell, either. Don't you find that suspicious?"

"If you're questioning whether or not this experience is real, I'd say it's real enough. We now know, more than ever, that mission success is the only option. We cannot fail, nor can the others."

Without another word, we follow our guide to the room where our time machines await us.

CHAPTER 30

Our guide leads us to the room where we arrived. It is a straight-forward journey without collapsing corridors or optical illusions to give us pause. This tells me Dianah has no more tricks up her sleeve. She has set us free to complete our mission—if we can.

Our time travel vehicles gleam in the center of the oval room, which is now brightly lit. We waste no time mounting them. The first thing I do is check the mission clock. No time has elapsed since our arrival, as Dianah promised. The mission clock is a delicate instrument. The command to reset it is known only to Adrien and one AndroBiotica technician. We can bank on the clock's accuracy. I imagine the clock will begin operating as soon as we leave here, which brings up another question. Kristina is the mission navigator. I look over at her. She anticipates my question.

"The correct coordinates for the time jump remain locked in. We have to trust that the machines will transport us to the intersection of the exact moment and location of our destination."

Trust isn't exactly second nature to me after all of the investigations I've been through, but it's an essential quality to have now.

I start the Sequencer because Adrien isn't in the booth to do it for me. Then, with some trepidation, I engage the Quantum Temporal Displacer.

Seconds later, I feel the subtle vibration of the machine as it warms up. As the engine cycles up, I am surrounded by a whirlpool of colors. I'm going through my second launch, but the novelty hasn't worn off. Pressure builds on the outside of my suit. I know what comes next. I watch Kristina's machine disappear—the room blurs. I feel weightless in a tunnel of light that transforms into an accelerating succession of dark and light flashes. The pressure on my suit continues to build until I lose consciousness.

I wake up in total darkness. The only sounds I hear are of my machine cycling down.

"Kristina," I call out.

"I'm right next to you. Take my hand. I'm not a fan of total darkness."

I reach out. Kristina finds my hand and grasps it. "We're supposed to be in the basement of the new LifeLike Technologies Building," she says.

The basement, if that's what it is, gives off a musty smell combined with the odors of something fresh and new—probably construction materials.

"Let's break out our flashlights," I tell Kristina.

Untethering myself and dismounting my machine, I feel my way to the pontoons. I fumble my way to the keypad. After several failed attempts, I hear my pontoon click, indicating it has accepted the combination. The top half of the pontoon bangs my helmet as it opens. It's a minor setback. We didn't plan on operating in total darkness.

A shaft of light pierces the darkness. The next thing I know, the light is shining in my face.

"Need any help?"

I hold my hand up to block the light. "How did you find your flashlight so fast?"

"Easy. I asked our Android tech to pack it on top. We scheduled our arrival at night, and flashlights tend to come in handy."

Continuing to search for mine, I find it packed in the second layer with my clothing. "Why didn't I think of that?"

"Because you're a man."

I notice Kristina feels comfortable exchanging barbs with me. Evidently, our shared experience in the other realm has forged a bond between us. The timing is right. The task ahead is uphill from here, and we will need to depend on each other.

Our flashlights are two inches in diameter with long handles. Like many of the items we packed, it is multipurpose. It can be a decent weapon in a crunch.

We continue the unpacking process by activating the condensed suitcases stored in the pontoons. While my suitcase expands, I pull out one item at a time and stack it neatly on the bottom of my case. We have only one hour to unpack before the machines return to the past at AndroBiotica—every second counts. We must be back here in less than ninety-six hours when the machines will reappear for the return trip.

Adrien has carefully considered each item we carry for its usefulness and mass. It is similar to the payload packed for a deep space mission —only on a much smaller scale. The transfer of cargo goes smoothly and quickly. In the darkness, we change out of our time travel suits and into casual clothing. We intend to check into a hotel to rest before our interviews early in the morning. Stuck in the darkness of the windowless basement, we have been unable to confirm the approximate time of day.

Picking up our travel bags, we use our flashlights to look for a way out. If we can't find an open exit, we'll make one with a tiny explosive charge mounted on a self-adhesive base. I carry six charges in a small, temperature-controlled tube. Just peel the safety backing off, adhere the charge to the surface of the obstruction, and step away. Three minutes later, the charge warms to room temperature and explodes, creating an entrance or exit that wasn't there before.

My flashlight reveals a sturdy-looking door on the opposite wall. As we move toward it, I hear a series of beeping sounds. Someone is entering a passcode into the electronic pad. The heavy door swings open. A tall, thin man stands in the doorway, backlit by embedded lights shining from the walls of a descending staircase. His features are obscured by the helmet and the lighting.

The man in the doorway holds a powerful flashlight of his own. He wears a drab security uniform topped by a riot helmet. A large pistol is holstered on his hip. His flashlight plays over us. It shines into the darkness behind us. I turn in time to see the spear of light pick up our time machines. The light shines back in our faces.

"It is after business hours, and this area is restricted. What are you doing here?" the man says. He sounds Human. We're screwed.

"It's artificial," Kristina whispers to me.

That's all I need to hear. I'm positive that the Synth is a company security guard, not an official police officer. It has seen our time machines. And it's not too friendly. With the light trained on our faces, the Android doesn't see me slip my weapon out of its holster. I press the back end of the barrel once to change the setting from Anti-Personnel to Anti-Android.

The Android's voice changes to a threatening monotone. "I will not ask you again. Identify yourselves and tell me why you are here?"

I can think of no reason to spend precious time continuing the conversation. In one fluid motion, I lift my weapon, aim it at the Android's chest, and fire twice. *Thump. Thump.*

The guard is blown backward onto the staircase. It struggles to get up. I press the trigger again, aiming at the Android's chest above the sternum. The projectile obliterates the top of the guard's chest and part of its exposed neck below the helmet. The Android falls back onto the stairs, dead.

Blood, shards of flesh, and bone litter the staircase. This is the second Android I've killed, counting Romulus from the trans-dimensional mission. Both deaths were unavoidable.

"Your weapon blasted the hell out of the Android, but I hardly heard the shots."

"It's equipped for stealth with an internal suppressor. Let's get out of here. There's no time to clean up the mess and hide the body. By the time LifeLike has any idea of what happened here, we'll be back in the past with Adrien."

Kristina nods solemnly. Before closing the door behind us, I shine my light into the basement darkness. The last thing I see is our machines disappearing, leaving behind a crater on the concrete slab.

CHAPTER 31

We are in the lobby of a swank downtown hotel. Our lightweight suitcases, packed to the gills, rest at our feet. The hotel is located only a block away from the current address of the LifeLike Building. The walls are decorated with large, gilt-edged mirrors and paintings. The furniture looks expensive. The grey-veined white marble floor adds the final opulent touch. The only thing out of place is an officer in a pea-green Sheriff's uniform. He sits in a high-backed chair, staring down at a thin tablet.

By the jade electronic clock above the front desk, I see that we have arrived at three thirty—the middle of the night. Kristina stifles a yawn. A shield of aqua-tinted glass surrounds the black marble front desk. The lobby is a hexagonal atrium. I can see some of the light-gray doors trimmed with golden numerals on the lower floors that shoot up twenty stories on all sides of us. Techno music floats into the lobby, presumably from a bar somewhere off the lobby. I ring a small golden bell on the desk ledge for service. We wait impatiently for the night agent to arrive. Minutes later, he does. He is a handsome young man dressed in a stylish black uniform accented by a light blue shirt and bow tie. The outfit mimics a colorfully accented tuxedo.

"Good evening, and welcome to the Saxton Hotel. Are you checking in?"

"We'd like two single rooms, adjacent if possible, on any floor."

I stifle a yawn of my own. It's been a trying day and night.

The front desk agent taps an inlaid computer screen on his side of the glass. "I'm afraid we only have a junior suite available. Will that be okay?"

Kristina speaks before I can consult with her. "The suite will be fine." She turns to me. "We don't have all night to look for a hotel."

She has a point. Even though they are pricey, downtown hotels are often booked solid. So, we can't be too choosy about our accommodations. I want to ask about the glass enclosure and the presence of an off-duty officer, but I don't want to be conspicuous.

"How long will you be staying with us?"

"We're not sure."

I'm almost positive this guy is Human. I'll wager the better hotels in the near future still use Human service people for the warm and fuzzy personal touch.

"I'll require a two-night deposit then," the agent says with a smile. "If you leave earlier, I can issue a credit."

We don't have credit cards with us. If we have to leave early, then we will go without checking out to avoid suspicion.

"May I have your card?" the night agent asks through a hidden microphone.

"We'll be paying cash."

My response prompts a suspicious look. "I'll need to see your registration cards."

A tray slides noiselessly out of the front ledge toward us. We deposit our cards in it. Registration cards are used worldwide for personal identification to prevent fraud and to track suspicious persons. They are difficult to duplicate.

The night agent examines the IDs and slides them through a white cube to his right. The cube blinks green. So far, so good. The agent quotes the price of the rooms. I accept the quote. The tray slides out again with our IDs.

Here comes the hard part. We collectively decided to use coins rather than cash on the mission. Shortly before our departure, the design of our *Dara* currency had changed to end a rash of counterfeit *Dara* notes in circulation worldwide. The counterfeiters made the fakes so close to real *Daras* that they were identical to the Human eye. It simply made no sense to carry fresh new currency eight years into the future. Currency verification cubes would detect the date of issue of our bills. The question would arise: How could new bills be eight years old? We knew, however, that if it became necessary to use coins for currency, an explanation would be required.

After we remove our identification cards, I deposit platinum treasury coins in the tray. The value of the coins exceeds the quoted price of the suite. I haven't had time to convert the coins to *Daras*. The tray closes.

After inspecting our coins closely, the agent taps his cheek with his forefinger. "It's very unusual for people to pay in cash, much less with platinum coins. I won't be able to give you change until your coins are verified as genuine. That will be later today because the currency and foreign exchange department is closed for the evening. You don't carry cash?"

"Due to the rate of inflation, our bank is converting large sums of cash into gold and platinum treasury coins. I carry these coins because they hold their value much better than paper currency."

The agent places his free arm around his waist, a sure sign of insecurity.

"To be on the safe side, I will check with my supervisor to see if we can accept your coins as a deposit. I'm not clear about our policy. I've never seen any of our customers pay with treasury coins before.

"Look. It's late, and we're tired," Kristina says. "Either give us room keys or return our coins. I'll be sure to write a complaint letter to management mentioning your name if you insist on inconveniencing us."

Kristina's forceful statement surprises the agent—and me, too. He quickly composes himself.

"There's no need for threats. If it turns out that the hotel does not accept treasury coins for payment, a staff member will ask you to vacate your suite in the morning."

The agent's fingers fly over his virtual keyboard. Seconds later, the cube issues our keys. The agent places the keys in the tray and slides them out to us.

"Your suite is on the eighteenth floor, number 1807. The elevators are to your right. Enjoy your evening."

I detect a distinct note of sarcasm in the words, "Enjoy your evening." I collect our keys and, without a "thank you," we head to the elevators.

"You're a good liar, Derrick Faulk."

"It comes with the territory. Here's a tip. Good liars never stray too far from the truth."

"Thanks. I'll keep it in mind."

We ride the elevator up to our floor in silence. In the hallway on the way to our Junior Suite, Kristina's groan pulls me out of my thoughts about the day ahead.

"These high heels are killing me. I only wear heels when I have to."

"One of the challenges of undercover work. You must look the part."

"I'm having second thoughts."

I take Kristina's comment as a jest. Since our suite is at the end of the hallway and around a corner, I have a chance to share my thoughts. Kristina may be able to help me clarify them.

"Judging by the cop in the lobby and the front desk shield, this is a high-crime area. We're in the best part of the city. The crime rate should be lower here. Something doesn't add up."

"I noticed the same thing. The crime rate must be proliferating rapidly in only eight years in the future of our timeline. We'll ask Aurora about it in the morning."

Walking farther down the hallway, I mention to Kristina that I'm looking forward to three or four hours of solid sleep. Her lack of reaction surprises me. *Maybe she isn't expecting to sleep well?* When thoughts of meeting Aurora again arise, I wonder if I will be able to sleep at all.

Reaching the door to our suite, I let Kristina in before me. The living room is small, with a large, colorful, abstract painting of an eye staring at us from the middle of the wall. The sofa below is beige leather. The bedrooms are located on opposite sides of the living room.

"I'd like the king-sized bed if you don't mind. The other bed is probably queen-sized."

Kristina doesn't answer. She moves to one of the narrow rectangular windows positioned on both sides of the sofa.

"Kristina?"

She stands with her back to me, holding her arms as if she feels a chill. "I don't feel safe here. It makes no sense because the room is beautiful, and we're on a high floor."

"Aside from the creepy night clerk, what makes you say that?"

"It's a feeling, probably generalized anxiety. All of this is so new."

I watch her shiver momentarily.

"Are you okay?"

She continues to stare through the window. "I just felt a twinge pass through me. It lasted only a few seconds. It's probably nothing."

"I'd say it's a case of nerves, Kristina. You've never done anything like this before. It's natural to be nervous. The best cure is a good sleep. Let's go get some."

Kristina doesn't move. She stands in the middle of the living room with her arms crossed, looking directly into my eyes.

"What?"

"Can we stay in the larger room? I know I'm acting like a child, but I don't feel safe."

I open the door to the larger bedroom. There is no couch, just a king-sized bed, a dresser, a large 3-D screen, and a desk. I turn to Kristina.

"I think it's best if we sleep separately."

"Did you forget we're wearing protective coatings underneath our clothes? Even if I wanted to fool around with you, which I don't, it wouldn't be worth the effort."

"I still think it would be better if we slept separately."

"Fine. I'll see you in the morning."

"Six AM," I remind her cheerfully.

Without responding, Kristina goes to her bedroom and closes the door.

She's a brilliant, strong, vulnerable, passionate, and mysterious woman. I won't make the same mistake with her as I did with Aurora.

Entering my bedroom, I head straight for the bathroom, where I wash up before going to bed. Wiping my face, I register once again the gray hairs growing around my temples. I'm still a youthful and ruggedly handsome devil, but I'll soon look sixty before I reach forty if I keep accepting Adrien's missions.

Back in the bedroom, I strip naked. I notice for the first time the pinholes in the protective coating on my skin. They must be there to allow my skin to breathe. Adrien plans everything down to the smallest detail.

My thoughts turn to Kristina. I'm worried that she's too fragile for what lies ahead.

We never know what we can do until we do it, I tell myself. I have to believe Kristina will rise to the occasion. She has no other choice. The stakes are too high. And with that, I set the alarm and fall into bed. Sleep overtakes me immediately.

CHAPTER 32

The early morning sun filters into our small living room through the narrow rectangular windows. Lost in our thoughts, Kristina and I are finishing a hearty breakfast braced with cups of strong coffee. I managed not to think or dream of Aurora after I hit the bed last night. Now, I can't avoid the angst of seeing her again at our upcoming meeting. I'm sure we'll both be professional, but there is bound to be an ocean of underlying tension. I decide there is no way to prepare for a face-to-face with Aurora. I'll just let whatever happens happen.

With the issue settled, I focus on business. "I think it's best to leave the hotel without checking out. They can keep our change from last night's transaction."

"I was just thinking the same thing," Kristina agrees. "The night agent didn't like us. He's the kind of jerk who might have reported us to the lobby cop as suspicious persons to make himself feel important."

I am about to respond when I hear an explosion. Kristina looks at me questioningly. I'm supposed to be the expert when things like this happen.

"It sounded like it came from outside."

We rush to the windows flanking the sofa. I look down. I see a man in a business suit spread-eagled on the sidewalk. From eighteen floors up, it's hard to make out any details. I scan the office building across the street. There are retail shops on the ground floor closed for the night. About fifty yards past the body, I see that the explosion tore the security shutter off its tracks on one of the stores, revealing a juice bar. The front of the store is smoking. Then, a pink mist descends on the sidewalk and settles in front of the juice bar. The event is straight out of a surrealist hologram.

After the initial shock of the incident, I watch a trickle of onlookers form a semi-circle in front of the scene. My training is ingrained. I throttle my emotions. I remain calm.

A tranquil female voice comes into the room through the PA system.

"Dear valued guests. There has been an unfortunate incident across the street from our hotel. The Saxton is undamaged. We kindly request that you remain in your rooms until we have more information. Please refrain from congregating in the hallways or other common areas. We will update you with more information as it becomes available. We apologize for this inconvenience."

While the message repeats itself in other languages, I say to Kristina, "Let's grab our suitcases and get out of here before the authorities arrive. We could be tied up all day."

"They could be arriving any minute."

"Right. So, let's hurry."

We go to our rooms to throw the few items we've unpacked back into our suitcases. We've already dressed for our interviews, which helps.

A few minutes later, we meet at the front door, just in time to hear the wailing of sirens.

Taking a deep breath, Kristina leads me out of the door and down the hallway to the elevators. I press the down button and look up at the floor indicators. The elevators aren't moving.

"We'll have to use the stairs."

"Wait," Kristina says.

"Your pre-cognition at work?"

Before she can answer, I watch an elevator rise from the lobby floor. When it arrives, it is mercifully empty. We step in. Kristina hits the button for the lobby. Down we go. Kristina looks up at me. "What kind of chaos are we dealing with?"

I have a theory, but I don't want to scare Kristina with it. "Let's take it one step at a time. Like Dianah, we can't know everything at once."

We reach the lobby. The elevator doors open. A police officer stands with his back to us, facing the front of the lobby. I guide Kristina away from the door and push the button to the third floor—the doors close before the officer can react.

"There must be a side exit near the stairs. I don't think the police have arrived yet. The officer we just saw is the one from last night. I expect the secondary exits will be unguarded."

We exit the elevator on the third floor. Despite instructions to the contrary, a group of five or six people has gathered in the hallway. Two of them turn at the sound of the elevator doors opening. They will see us leaving, carrying our suitcases, and probably report us. There's nothing we can do about it except keep moving. I grab Kristina by the hand to make us look like a couple. She is surprised but plays along. The stairway is across the hall. We have to pass in front of the group to get there.

"Are you leaving?" someone calls out. Dumb question. Of course, we're leaving. I smile politely and open the stairway door for Kristina.

"We have interviews that were set up months ago. We can't afford to miss them."

We grab the railing and hustle down the stairs, and reach the bottom landing in something like world record escape time. The exit is right there in front of us. The red-lighted sign above it says, "Emergency Exit. Alarm Will Sound."

"At least I don't have to use an explosive charge to get us out of here."

Kristina pushes me playfully.

I press down on the lever handle of the emergency exit. We step out into the street, accompanied by a blaring alarm.

I am wrong about the Police response time. A blue and white cruiser is already on the scene. Two officers exit the vehicle on both sides. Their attention is immediately drawn to the alarm and two well-dressed people crossing the street carrying suitcases.

"Hey," the taller cop calls to us. He gestures for us to come over.

I wave back to the officer. "Talk later. We're late for a critical business meeting."

The cop stares back at me in disbelief. I'm confident these officers won't bother us because their priority is securing the crowd of onlookers, each one a potential witness. The shorter officer calls out to us, more insistently this time. The arrival of the crime scene van distracts him.

"Keep walking," I tell Kristina.

We enter the lobby of the LifeLike Technologies Building. I turn to make sure the cops aren't following us. We're good—so far.

Ultra-modern architecture complements the spacious lobby. Large granite squares cover the walls. The circular LifeLike logo looks down from high on the east wall, which is colored in earth and flesh tones. The ceiling is high. A stairway leads to a second-floor loft bordered by a brass guard rail. The lobby's look is streamlined luxury. A security station awaits incomers. It blocks the space between the elevators and the stairway to the loft. I see a metal detector and a scanner-conveyor for briefcases and pocketbooks. I doubt suitcases are seen as common carry-alongs here. The man on the right wears a navy blue uniform with gold buttons. The guard on the left wears a prison-grey uniform with silver buttons. Together, they exude a vibe that says they are not to be taken lightly.

As we approach the security station, Kristina whispers to me, "Where is your weapon?"

"Packed within easy reach. It doesn't help to bury it when passing through security setups."

"Wonderful. What do we do now?"

"Improvise."

I step up to the guards. "Good morning, gentlemen. We're here to see Aurora Zolotov in Employee Resources."

"We have to clear you before you can go anywhere," the guard on the right says. I notice that his gold and silver badge says: Chief of Security.

"And we have a situation on our hands," he adds. "No one is allowed upstairs right now."

"How long will we be delayed?" Kristina asks.

"That's hard to say," the Chief answers, eyeing our suitcases and pointing. "We'll have to open those right away. And I need to see your registration cards."

We pass along our cards. "You'll find a weapon in my suitcase. I have a license for it."

We changed the date to make the license current. The Chief holds out his hand to collect my concealed weapon carry card. "What do you need a weapon for?"

"I recently resigned as an investigator at the *National Science Service*. I'm accustomed to carrying a weapon. I've seen the underside of Human nature too often."

"Do you have your ID from the *NSS?*"

"I had to hand in my credentials when I resigned, but here's one of my former business cards."

I read the Chief's nameplate: Maynard Carrington. He accepts the card without looking at it. "Anyone can print a card."

"I'd have to be a world-class forger to print the *NSS* seal like the one you're holding."

Carrington examines my business card, my carry license, and our registration cards before handing them back to us. He motions for us to put our suitcases on the conveyor belt. We open them. The Chief goes through my suitcase. The other guard examines the contents of Kristina's suitcase. I watch Kristina's face redden when the guard goes through her underwear. With one hand, the Chief gingerly lifts my lightweight undercover pistol and holster from my suitcase.

"This rig makes you look like some kind of an undercover agent," he says, both as a statement and a question.

"That's very observant of you, Chief Maynard. In fact, I used that same rig, as you call it, on my last undercover mission for the *NSS.*"

Maynard looks suspiciously at me and then at Kristina. "What's your business here?"

"We have preliminary interviews with your ER Director for key positions at LifeLike."

"You two know each other?"

"We're friends," Kristina offers. "Mr. Faulk recommended me for the open position of Research Director. He knows the ER Director, Aurora Zolotov."

Chief Maynard takes a moment to consider our responses. Then, he looks behind me. I turn and see a line of people stacking up behind us.

Maynard makes a decision. "We're a little thin in the ranks at the moment. The company can use a few qualified people to fill some open positions. I'm going to let you go through for your interviews. We'll stow your suitcases and pea-shooter here temporarily. See me for your items after your interviews. I'll be in my office waiting to say goodbye or hand you your new security badges. Ask the front desk where to find me. Employment Resources is on the fourteenth floor. Good Luck."

We head for the elevators.

"Good job getting past Chief Maynard," I tell Kristina.

"I'm getting the hang of this."

We take a few more steps before something attracts Kristina's attention. "Don't look now, but the two cops from outside just came through the lobby entrance."

CHAPTER 33
—Aurora—

"The officers in the lobby are most likely coming in to connect with security to see if they know anything about the incident outside."

"We hope," says Kristine at my side in the elevator.

The elevator doors open to a reception desk on the fourteenth floor. The young man behind the desk greets us with an inviting smile. "Let me guess. You're here to see Miss Zolotov."

"Right," Kristina says. "How did you know?"

"You're her first appointment, and she doesn't have many after you," the assistant says, preening. "And, since no one comes here without an appointment, well, you can see that it's an easy deduction."

"You're quite the detective," I offer.

"Thanks. It's only my second day here."

That, and the fact that you're a nitwit, explains your unprofessional behavior, I think to myself.

"Have a seat over there. Miss Zolotov will be in any minute."

"Since you are so new, let me give you a hint. Never divulge your superior's schedule to a stranger. Say instead, Miss Zolotov will be with you soon."

I force a smile and turn to the chairs awaiting us against the wall. The light blue color is cheerful. The chairs are ergonomically designed and look comfortable. The framed prints on the wall are colorful and calming, with subjects like seascapes, sunrises, and flower bouquets. I have a sense that the room has been decorated to make the prospective employee think the job on offer is a once-in-a-lifetime opportunity.

In his typically thorough manner, Adrien has authenticated our job references by creating an intelligent telecommunications machine with multiple Human voices to answer and adapt to reference inquiries. Pilots have tested it to ensure the machine works on calls from the future to a dedicated line at AndroBiotica. Additionally, Adrien changed Aurora's and Kristina's personnel files to reflect their jobs at non-competitive aerospace and robotic-assisted surgery companies, respectively. He changed my file to show that I left the *NSS* to form a security consulting firm in the technology sector. Our home addresses are unchanged. With any luck, our residences haven't been bulldozed or burned down in the eight years prior to our arrival.

Kristina sits next to me and immediately crosses her legs. With a furtive glance, I can see she is agitated.

"You were right," she whispers to me. "I should never have come on this mission."

"It's a little late for that realization."

"I didn't consider the danger. I thought only about my scientific curiosity. What happened this morning is alarming."

"You are an interesting combination of backbone and vulnerability."

"I'll bet you say that to all the girls."

"I don't. When fear comes up, focus on our mission objectives. And remember, you are critical to our success. I depend on you as much as you depend on me."

"No pressure."

"You'll feel right at home in the LifeLike Research Lab. I'm watching you grow, and you're developing a sense of humor. That, in itself, is a sign of progress—levity in the face of danger."

She reacts by clandestinely stepping on my boot. "I've always had a sense of humor. I could only use it sparingly as head of my department."

"Okay. That's another good sign."

She turns to me with a wry smile. "You don't have to coddle me."

We wait in silence for about ten minutes. Then, from across the room, the receptionist calls out, "Miss Zolotov will see you now. Take the hallway to my right. Her office is three doors down."

The announcement is monotone. By the receptionist's own admission, the department isn't busy. The chances are he made us wait out of sheer revenge. Intuition tells me the man behind the desk is an incompetent little boy. It makes no sense to fill a gatekeeper position with someone like him. The only plausible explanation is LifeLike's desperate need to hire support staff.

As we walk the hallway, it's my turn to be nervous. I feel a mixture of dread and buried hope about the upcoming meeting with Aurora.

"Don't be nervous," Kristina tells me.

"How do you know I'm nervous?"

"I'm not a block of wood, Derrick. Take your own advice and concentrate on the mission."

"Thanks for the pep talk."

"You needed it, tough guy."

We reach Aurora's door. It opens automatically. I almost do a double-take when I see Aurora. She is literally a sight for sore eyes. Her hair is purple. She wears matching purple lipstick and teal blue contact lenses—not a Human color. I can tell from her eyes that Aurora has registered my surprised reaction to her appearance.

She stands behind her compact workstation. Gesturing to the two chairs in front of it, Aurora says, "Please make yourselves comfortable. Can I get you anything? Coffee? Water?"

"Water would be nice," I manage to say.

"For me, too," Kristina says while taking a seat.

I observe Aurora's small office. The shelves are barren. Most people put books or family pictures on their office shelves for decoration. It warms up the space. The spare office gives the impression that Aurora has been too busy in her new position to decorate. It's a brilliant strategy. As long as I've known her, Aurora has used subtle mannerisms to make appearances seem real.

With her six-foot model figure, Aurora gracefully moves to a compact chiller. She looks typically alluring, especially in her sleeveless white blouse. The overdone hair and makeup are already growing on me.

Aurora removes two glistening water bottles. Bending over her workstation, she passes the containers to us and sits with an economy of movement. Folding her hands, she says, "I'm glad you both made it in one piece. Now, *za* hard part begins."

We smile at the irony of her statement. "Getting here wasn't easy," Kristina says simply.

I doubt we'll have the time or inclination to recount our celestial detour.

"I'm sure it wasn't," Aurora responds politely. She's being very professional, as if we were strangers, and this is a routine interview.

Can we talk? I mouth silently.

"Yes. The office isn't electronically bugged for sound or video. I removed the surveillance devices when I moved in. Adrien equipped me with sensors to detect listening devices before the mission. To cover the debugging, I spoke to Chief Carrington. I told him that recording interviews revealing the intimate details of applicants' lives conflicted with my programming. Carrington accepted my reasons for removing the devices. He thinks I'm a typical Android trapped by my programming. I've been careful not to reveal my highly developed discretionary thinking abilities."

"Not to mention your extreme modesty."

"Always the kidder, Derrick."

Hearing her say my name feels like a stab in the heart. It reminds me how much I've missed Aurora's voice and her touch.

Shaking loose from my memories, I ask. "Why is the turnover rate high here? Are competitors offering higher pay or better opportunities?"

"As far as I can tell, that's not the case. I can't say definitively what the reason is, but I do know that many of the people who left felt uncomfortable. They came to me, explaining that they felt 'watched.' I knew they *were* being surveilled, but I couldn't tell them. As soon as these employees found a comparable or better job, they left."

"That's creepy," Kristina remarks.

"The company president, Jan Kronak, called me into his office to discuss the job losses. I took a chance and asked Kronak why people might feel they were being watched. He told me it is standard procedure in the industry to test randomly for security breaches."

"It sounds like he told you a half-truth."

Aurora forms a bridge with her hands and cradles her head on top of it. "I had the same impression, Derrick, but Kronak didn't blink or seem upset. He thanked me for my input and politely dismissed me."

"Before we go any further, I have to ask you this question."

Aurora resumes an erect posture. "Yes?"

"Why did you choose to look so obviously like an Android?"

Aurora's teal blue eyes turn piercing. "First of all, I came here as a registered Android. There is no point in trying to pass for a Human in a company that makes highly sophisticated Androids. Secondly, I'm comfortable with who I am. Thirdly, I didn't want any of my co-workers or superiors to hit on me."

Aurora's last remark lands too close to home. "Our attraction was mutual. I never 'hit' on you."

"You broke up with me because I wasn't good enough for you."

"That's not true. The end of our relationship has hurt me more than you can know."

"You never explained to me why it ended."

"I couldn't face you. I left the explanation up to Adrien."

"That was cowardly. I *vanted* to hear it from you."

"That's a fair statement."

I'm suddenly struck with a realization. Am I so different than Aurora? She's a high-functioning, high-IQ, independent-thinking creation. Adrien has given her a set of talents and abilities. The same is true for me. Aurora can adapt to almost any situation, except when external forces threaten the completion of a mission. It's the same for me. Aurora's personality is crafted from memories, desires, ambitions, talents, and concepts of reality. The same can be said for me. Was I born with a purpose bestowed upon me by my creator, or have I been programmed to be who I am, based on my upbringing and a host of other external prompts? Or have I made myself the man I am today by my own choices? I'd like to believe the latter, but who knows?

Remembering Dianah's wise advice, I quickly banish these thoughts. Questions like these are a waste of time in these circumstances.

I feel Kristina's firm hand on my forearm.

"Let's stay on track." She looks at me, and then at Aurora. "Both of you."

Aurora and I pause to compose ourselves. Kristina turns to Aurora and asks, "Are you aware of a rising crime rate in the neighborhood?"

"Yes. It's another reason why the staff doesn't feel safe here. I've called the nearest police agency to get more details, but the Police Information Officer has not been very forthcoming. I haven't been here long enough to develop any other sources."

I continue the questioning. It should be the other way around, but this is far from an ordinary interview.

"Do you have any insight into the murder that happened this morning outside of the building?"

"I've listened to news sound bites. The victim is a middle-aged accountant who worked for a brokerage firm in this building. There is speculation that it was a hit to cover up insider trading or related financial crimes. There's no doubt in my mind that the perpetrator was an Android who blew itself up into tiny fragments to avoid detection."

"That explains the pink mist. It also supports the assassination theory."

Aurora and Kristina nod their agreement. Kristina follows with questions of her own.

"I'm curious, Aurora. You did an excellent job landing this position. Logic dictates the company would use one of its Androids to fill your position. In spite of this, you got the job. How did you manage it?"

"Getting this job wasn't hard for two reasons. To begin with, the company is selling its Android models as fast as it can manufacture them due to the relatively low pricing. There is a backlog of orders. Kronak would rather hire outside Humans and Androids rather than *his* Androids to fill job vacancies, thereby avoiding longer delays in fulfilling customer orders. The second reason is that, prior to the mission, Adrien gave me a thorough background in Employee Resources. I came ready-made. Kronak had a hard time filling the position with a qualified candidate. He took one look at my resume, and after we talked, he hired me on the spot."

"Who checked your references?"

"When I arrived two weeks ago, the job had been vacant for a while. Kronak didn't check my references. It turned out Adrien's backup machine wasn't necessary. I don't think Kronak will ask anyone besides me to check your references. If you can pass your interview with Kronak, you're in."

I can't stop myself from asking the next question. "How do you feel about staying in the future?"

On the one hand, Aurora's staying simplifies my life. On the other hand, the chances are I'll never see her again. I've felt this kind of ambivalence since we parted.

"I convinced Adrien to send me earlier than we originally planned. We knew the consequences only too well. My protective coating decomposed ten days ago. I needed the extra time to gain Kronak's trust and confidence before I could submit your resumes and recommend you for your positions."

"You've made quite a sacrifice," Kristina observes.

"I don't feel like I've made a sacrifice. I've adjusted to my dual memories of being Human and an Android. I can empathize with both Human and Android suffering. I don't want to see my fellow Androids used for destructive, immoral, and illegal purposes. I don't want to watch the effects of Android misuse on Human Beings. And I don't feel trapped here. After our mission is over, I'll leave LifeLike and return to the future version of AndroBiotica. Adrien is now eight years older, but I'm confident he'll find a way to extend his lifespan, possibly in the body of an Android. Nothing has changed, really. Life is still hard, especially for people like us."

Kristina and I take a moment to reflect on Aurora's words.

"Let's get back to the mission," Aurora says. "Any more questions?"

"Have there been any stories in the media about Androids acting strangely?" Kristina asks.

"I'm not aware of any."

"Then we're ahead of the curve, but we have to act swiftly before the volcano erupts."

"More of your corny poetry?" Aurora chides.

She's forever on my case about my attempts at metaphors. Aurora turns to me and then to Kristina.

"Are we done?"

When she sees that we have no more questions, Aurora turns to Kristina. "Congratulations. You've passed your interview for the position of Director of Research and Development, subject to Kronak's final approval."

She turns to me. "And you, sir, have been engaged as a highly paid security consultant, again subject to final approval."

Aurora types at her workstation. "I'm notifying Kronak that you've passed your interviews with my recommendation for immediate hire."

Aurora stands. We shake hands. *"Bonne chance."*

"It's nice to see you remember your French."

Aurora gives me a pained look. "Knock it out of the park upstairs and keep me updated."

CHAPTER 34

Maynard Carrington's corner office is impressive and comfortable-looking. We, on the other hand, are uncomfortable. The Chief sits behind a workstation with a sour expression. I thought we started on the right foot, but if we've done anything to make the man unhappy, we'll soon find out. Kristina and I are sitting directly in front of him. Carrington wears his perfectly manicured uniform fastened to the last button. His gun belt rests on one side of the workstation within easy reach.

"Two police officers came up to me after I let you two upstairs. After they grilled me about the murder outside our building, they asked me if I had seen you. Police officers are not fond of citizens who disobey lawful commands."

"Since we haven't been arrested, I'd guess you vouched for us."

"I told the officers you were solid citizens and not to be concerned. You wanted to make it to your interviews on time, and we needed to fill two key positions."

"We appreciate that. Is something else upsetting you?"

"Damn right! After I went out of my way to help you, I learned from Miss Zolotov that you're up for a job as a security consultant. Is my job on the line?"

So that's it! I take a deep breath before addressing Carrington. "There's no reason to be upset. May I call you Maynard?"

"Depends."

"I'm a freelance consultant. I investigate special circumstances. I don't evaluate overall corporate security systems. The people who do that are a *Dara* a dozan, and they always make recommendations to justify their cost, no matter how good the system in place is. I won't be looking over your shoulder."

"Mister Kronak didn't mention anything to me about a special security problem."

I scan the office while I consider my answer. I want to keep the Chief on our good side.

The office overlooks a tranquil artificial lake. A large, ultra-realistic sculpture of a wild duck flapping its wings stands in the foreground. Pictures of Carrington's police career adorn two walls. He rose from Officer to Detective to Sergeant and finally to Lieutenant. Unlike many of his peers, I notice Carrington's waistline hasn't ballooned with age and his promotions. The other two walls are filled with camera views of all the offices and hallways in the building. Now I know why the employees feel watched.

On the other side of Carrington's workspace, I see a picture of a smiling Carrington with a pretty woman and three young children ranging in age from toddler to adolescent. Either Carrington waited to get married, or the picture shows his second or third family. Divorce happens too often in law enforcement due to the long hours the job requires.

I pick up the family photo. "You have a lovely family." I raise my eyes to the spacious corner windows. "And a lovely view."

"Don't change the subject."

I gesture toward the wall cameras. "I'd say you have a big enough job with overall company security."

"You're damn right, but you still haven't answered my question."

"First, let me ask you. Are you sure your office isn't bugged?"

"Of course, I'm sure. I'm no damn idiot."

"I ask because I'm not supposed to tell you that your boss is concerned for his safety, on and off the job. He hasn't filled me in with the details yet."

The Chief looks surprised.

"So, do we have a problem?"

Carrington takes a moment to consider my explanation. "I guess not."

He hands us our security badges and points to them with two forked fingers. "Those are temporary. If you land your jobs, I can make them permanent with a few keystrokes."

As we collect our badges, Carrington apparently feels the need to say more.

"As far as I can tell, Mister Kronak likes me and the job I'm doing, but you never know with him. I wanted to get a feel for why you're here, and now I know. My gut tells me you guys won't be a problem, but don't get creative with the rules like you did this morning. If you cross any lines, I'll be on you like a supersonic bullet."

"We know rules are important, especially in a company like this one," Kristina says.

"Good. Don't forget it. Now, go upstairs to the penthouse office. Mister Kronak is expecting you."

■ ■ ■

The wall behind Jan Kronak is made of a single sheet of thick glass. It has to be a custom order with a high price tag. The skyscrapers visible through the glass are creatively designed with colors and tasteful curves interacting with straight lines. The cityscape sprawls outward to a purple mountain range in the distance. The view is magnificent.

Kronak's super-sized workstation is positioned in the center of the tall, all-in-one window. I estimate the ceiling to be twenty feet high, giving the office the appearance of a small auditorium designed for private performances. The gray carpet is also custom-made, with the LifeLike Technologies logo embroidered prominently in the center.

Kronak is not at his workstation. He slouches on a semicircular sofa, concentrating on a tablet with one foot braced against the edge of a circular, flesh-colored table. Two lavishly upholstered chairs in a matching flesh tone await us on the other side of the table.

Looking up from his tablet, Kronak motions for us to sit. He doesn't bother to stand up. He is dressed semi-casually in a pair of gray jeans, a silk shirt, and black ankle-length boots. Kronak is a study in simplicity against the affluent background of his office.

Looking back at his tablet, Kronak says. "Give me a minute to finish this."

After taking my seat, I look closer at the surroundings. The wall to my right features a painting of a castle atop a seaside cliff. Four parapets stand at the corners of a flat roof. A dome, which looks to me like the housing of a massive telescope, rises from the roof's center. Deep-space photos and award plaques of various shapes and sizes plaster the wall to my left. What I observe raises questions. Glancing at Kristina, I can tell that the display has similarly piqued her curiosity.

Kronak puts his tablet aside on the sofa. Straightening his posture, he takes a moment to scrutinize us. He notices my interest in the painting and Kristina's interest in the deep-space photos.

"You like my painting." It's not a question.

"I plan to build a castle like that away from it all when I retire. It will be my home and an observatory. As you can see from the photos, I have a keen interest in Astronomy."

Kristina and I smile approvingly. Kronak has answered some of our questions concisely.

"First of all, I applaud you both for getting here on time. I've heard the neighborhood has been on lockdown since the unfortunate incident outside. It might be wise for you to stay in the building tonight. I have guest rooms available."

"That's a generous offer," Kristina says.

I want to ask Kronak if he has any in-depth information about the "incident," but I know this is not the right time.

For the next fifteen minutes, Kronak bombards Kristina with questions about her background, education, and experience. He keeps his impressions of her answers to himself.

I use the time to take a hard look at our prospective employer. Aside from a few enhancements, there is nothing remarkable about the man's appearance. I can tell he has a bionic right eye because the color of his right iris doesn't exactly match the color of the other. It also looks like his right index finger has been surgically replaced with a bionic prosthetic. I wonder if the prosthetic finger is the result of an accident or if it is an intentional enhancement.

Turning to me, Kronak fires a similar set of questions lasting about ten minutes. Most of our answers are truthful, with only slight fabrications about our current positions. We follow my golden rule of telling lies that are grounded as much as possible in the truth.

"Will you give me a few minutes?" Kronak asks us, as if we had another option. He is on his feet immediately after we acquiesce.

Kronak moves languidly toward his workstation. I assume he is thinking about our interviews, but so far, I have found this man unreadable. Watching him walk, I estimate his height to be average, about five feet ten inches. He has a slight frame with thin arms and a chicken chest. He wears his black hair short. It looks like he hasn't made a concerted effort to comb it in days. I've noticed that he has a habit of looking away when he talks, as if he is simultaneously deep in thought. I suspect, instead, that the man doesn't feel comfortable making eye contact. In short, Jan Kronak doesn't give the impression of being a titan of industry, but looks can be deceiving.

He sits, almost like a concert pianist, and begins doing something on the inlaid computers of his workstation. I notice his head moving from one screen to another. After about five minutes of this, he looks up at us and leans back leisurely against his chair. I have the distinct impression that Jan Kronak has removed the pressure of a decision from his shoulders. He calls us to take seats before him.

"I'm sure you are both eager to learn more about your assignments, so let's get started."

Let's not waste time by telling us we're hired or asking if we want the jobs we've applied for.

Kronak turns to Kristina. "Welcome to LifeLike Technologies. I'm excited to have someone of your stature on board to lead our research and development program."

"I'm excited to be here," Kristina answers dutifully.

"It's a shame you had a falling out with your previous boss. In all honesty, I can't say I'm terribly sad about it."

We laugh on cue.

"I've created an email account and a password for you, Kristina. Our IT manager will help you set up your workstation. You'll find an email I sent with a link to the physiology files for each of our Android models. I want you to study those files. When you feel that you have an adequate grasp of our architecture, contact my assistant, Elenora. Then we'll schedule a meeting to discuss our designs."

"I'm eager to get started."

"Excellent."

A tall, angular redhead enters the room. She wears a grey business suit with matching stockings and high heels. Approaching Kristina, she offers her hand.

"I'm Elenora. It's a pleasure to meet you. Come with me, and we'll get you started."

Kristina grasps Elenora's hand. With a furtive glance at me, she rises from her seat.

I am shocked at the brevity of Kristina's orientation, but I don't show it.

Kronak turns his attention back to me. For an instant, the ambient light reflects off his bionic eye. "Let's get down to your assignment," he begins.

I don't get the same glowing welcome as Kristina received.

"As I've indicated to you confidentially, I'm concerned about my safety. Here's why. My competitors are very unhappy with me. A group of them invited me to a meeting to discuss our industry and its future. They scheduled the meeting at a five-star hotel midway between our company locations. I had a good idea of what these company presidents and CEOs had in mind to discuss. They wanted me to raise my prices to be in line with theirs. I politely turned down the invitation. A week later, I started receiving threatening holocalls at my home. The calls came from someone who wore a horrifying mask and claimed I was having an affair with his wife. After a while, I suspected the calls were a code. I'm not having an affair with anyone's wife. I would never spend precious time on anything that trivial and reckless. But the calls kept coming. They became increasingly menacing. I turned the matter over to the *Federated Department of Investigation*. So far, they have come up with nothing. I'm now positive the calls are not coming from some deranged individual."

"So, just to be clear, you believe these threatening calls are coming from your unhappy competitors."

Kronak leans forward. "Absolutely. It takes a high level of technological skill to avoid being traced by the *FDI*."

"That makes sense." I'm about to outline the broad strokes of a proposal when Kronak interrupts me.

"I have achieved a more efficient manufacturing process than my competitors, and I am content to amortize our research and development costs over a longer schedule. As we all know, the field of technology is highly competitive. You can't blame me for being a good competitor."

"I guess you had to get that off your chest."

"Yes. And that's not all of it."

Looking down, Kronak pulls at his short hair. His calm façade has vanished. He's very mad—and scared.

"I'm listening."

He looks up at me. His eyes are blazing. "That incident this morning…"

He jabs a finger at me to make his point.

"That murder is a veiled message to me from my competitors. They made the assassination look like a financial crime cover-up, which is clever and cold-blooded. That poor victim died in the street for nothing. My competitors are telling me to get in line with my pricing, or there will be serious consequences."

I'm not sure if what Kronak is saying is real or delusional, but I have to react positively.

"I think our first step will be to get a top-tier security detail in place for your home and office. I'll need a day to inspect this facility and your home for vulnerabilities. I'll have a comprehensive security plan in your hands by tomorrow evening. How does that sound?"

"I feel better already. Elenora will provide you with any information you need. Will you and Kristina take me up on my offer to stay here, at least overnight? I promise you'll be more comfortable here than in any of the nearby hotels. Elenora can make the arrangements."

"That sounds too good to pass up. Thank you, Mr. Kronak."

"And thank *you*, Mr. Faulk. Do you have suitcases?"

"Yes. Chief Carrington has stored them for us."

"Elenora will have him send your belongings up to your rooms."

"That's most thoughtful of you."

As I walk out of the room, Kristina's words echo in my ears: *"You're a good liar, Derrick Faulk."*

CHAPTER 35

When I arrive at the restaurant, Kristina is waiting for me at the bar. A glass of wine and a single white rose in a slender vase sit before her. The bartender must be smitten, and why not? Kristina wears a black evening dress, black stockings, and matching pump heels. She's done something different with her hair. It's the first time I've seen Kristina dressed up. The outfit showcases her natural beauty.

I expected Kristina to be dressed casually, which means I'm under-dressed for the occasion. I'm wearing loafers, blue jeans, a blue work shirt, and a retro black leather jacket. We'll be an unmatched pair, but luckily, the place is packed. The international cuisine must be good. I scan the crowd before approaching Kristina. I see primarily business people more interested in drinking than in business and food. That works. We will hardly be noticed. We are here, by prior arrangement, to compare notes and report on our first day at LifeLike Technologies.

Kristina has reserved a seat at the bar for me. As I slide into place, I notice that she is keyed up.

"You haven't touched your wine," I point out.

"It's my third glass. I figured it was time to slow down."

"Looks like we have something to discuss."

She turns to me, wide-eyed. "You betcha."

Her response is so out of character that my interest level skyrockets.

"You reserved a table?"

"Oh, yes."

Kristina tries to settle her bar tab with a one-hundred-dollar *Dara* bank note. The note is conspicuous. We've converted our platinum coins into paper, and Kristina hasn't bothered to break the big bills. I give her back the note and leave a smaller denomination, including a generous tip. Kristina must have downed her wine too quickly because she isn't thinking clearly.

The *Master Waiter* shows us to our table. The society we live in is stratified. It is impossible to tell the man's origins since the races in the lower income brackets have been mixed and re-mixed in a giant blender. I can only see that the man is tall, balding, immaculately groomed, and well-dressed in a creaseless business suit. He probably works hard for too little pay and is grateful that an Android hasn't replaced him. He expects a tip. I don't disappoint him.

Our table is in the rear of the restaurant against a wall. It's not a good table, but it suits our purposes. The *Master Waiter* holds Kristina's chair for her. I tell him we aren't in a hurry. He nods, then off he goes. It's a busy weeknight at *Seven of the Clock*.

As soon as I'm seated, Kristina starts the conversation. "Tell me about your day."

"It started slowly. I marched throughout the building, writing meaningless notes to myself for the sake of appearance. I did, however, find one vulnerable area where an intruder could slip through unnoticed: The loading and shipping docks. There is too much activity going on there to be adequately monitored with the number and positions of the security cameras in place. I will point this out in my daily report with a recommendation to beef up security personnel and revamp the camera setup."

Kristina takes a sip of her third glass of wine. "It sounds like you made a good start. Go on."

"Here's where it gets interesting. I watched triple-decker transport vehicles carrying raw materials move in and out of the loading bays. Finished products were carefully packed into specialized crates and loaded into armor-plated monster trucks with massive wheels. In each vehicle, I observed two armed guards outfitted in combat uniforms and carrying large caliber automatic weapons sitting with the driver in a heavily reinforced cab. The extra protection struck me as over the top. I had the distinct impression that something more than meets the eye was going on. I made a note to follow up."

"It's evident that you know what you are doing."

Sensing a note of concern in Kristina's voice, I change the subject. "I thought we were going casual tonight?"

"I don't have many chances to get dressed up. How do I look?"

"That's a loaded question. You look phenomenal. I noticed men and women stealing glances at you."

Kristina smiles and holds my eyes with hers. "I'm a little tipsy."

"I gathered that. Tell me about your day."

Kristina's facial expression changes dramatically. "From the Androids I've examined so far, the LifeLike security protocols are as airtight as ours. We assumed the LifeLike protocols were flawed. We were wrong."

"Are you sure?"

"Positive."

"Maybe the security systems of the cheaper models are vulnerable because Kronak is cutting corners on them."

"That makes no sense, Derrick. Kronak would be undercutting the reputation of his company if he did that."

"Maybe one of the LifeLike engineers with a motive for revenge is responsible."

"Highly unlikely. There are layers of quality control in place."

"You've learned plenty on your first day. Your intel indicates something else is at play here. It corroborates something I felt at the shipping docks earlier. I think I know where to go to get some answers."

"At least one of us does. The situation has unnerved me. Do you mind if I go back to my room? I've lost my appetite."

I reach out and place my hand on hers. "Stay. We've both had a hard day. It would be best if you ate to keep your strength up. Let's try to relax and enjoy the rest of the evening. Then, we'll be fresh and ready to face whatever comes our way tomorrow."

Kristina pauses. "If you insist."

I sense a charge of mutual attraction passing between us. It's awkward.

"Why don't you fill me in with more of your background. Tell me more about where you grew up. What was it like? How much did your parents influence you?"

"Only if you agree to do the same, Derrick."

"You have my word on it."

As we converse, the tension of the mission slowly fades away. Kristina turns out to be an interesting and fun companion. After the main course of vegetarian meatloaf and scalloped potatoes is served, I decide not to tell her what my plans are for tomorrow morning. I don't want to put her on edge again.

CHAPTER 36

I stand at the door of Chief Maynard Carrington's office. It is open. I'm holding two steaming mugs of freshly brewed coffee and a bag filled with two cinnamon buns. The Chief looks up from his desk.

"You're up early, Mr. Faulk. I thought high-priced security consultants got to sleep in 'til at least *Nine of the Clock.* And this one comes bearing gifts. C'mon in."

I enter the Chief's office. "Where can I put your coffee?"

He pushes a knitted coaster across to me on his workstation. It looks like something his wife made for him. I carefully place the coffee down.

"Careful. It's hot. I didn't know how you take your coffee, so I left it black."

"I like my coffee the way I am—hot and black."

The Chief catches me by surprise. I laugh. It's hard not to like this guy.

"Don't stand there like a fool. Have a seat. What's in the bag?"

"Cinnamon rolls. Can I offer you one?"

Carrington finds a small plate and pushes it forward. He places his hand over it. "What's it *gonna* cost me?"

"A few moments of your time."

The Chief removes his hand. I place the roll on the plate. The Chief examines it. "Hmmm. That's a big one. Must have set you back a few *Dara's.* Why do I get the impression you're about to ask me for a big favor?"

"It's not so big. I want you to be informed about the business end of your company."

"What makes you think I'm not?"

"Something is amiss with the business of LifeLike Technologies. It could be something serious."

Carrington is about to take a sip of his coffee when he stops in mid-air. "What are you talking about?"

"I don't know yet, but I'm going to find out. That's where I need your help."

"Wait a minute. I don't think Mister Kronak hired you to spy on his business."

"I know. I'm not spying. I'm investigating. While looking into the recent murder in front of the building as it relates to Jan Kronak's personal security, I stumbled across something. All I'm asking you to do is watch your monitors and learn. I promise you'll thank me."

"I'll have to report whatever you find to Mister Kronak."

"If I'm right, I don't think you'll want to report anything to your boss. Keep what I've told you to yourself. Give me this morning only. That's all I'm asking."

Carrington shakes his head. "I don't like it. I told you about playing by the rules. I'm getting the impression that you think you can do anything you want to. That doesn't fly in my book."

"All I'm asking you to do is your job. If something isn't right here, you need to know about it."

After considering my statements, Carrington says, "I hope I'm not wrong about you. I'll give you the morning, and that's it. Report your findings directly to me and me only. You got that?"

I nod my agreement.

■ ■ ■

I find the Controller's office on the floor below Kronak's penthouse suite. With its pentagonal glass enclosure, the place is easy to find. The occupant's name is scrolled on the side of the double doors: Willard Fenton O'Grady, CCA, CTA. Willard is a Certified Corporate Accountant and a Certified Technological Accountant. Impressive.

Willard's secretary is seated behind a long workstation. Above her, the LifeLike Technologies logo is inscribed in the middle of a light gray wall. The lush green carpet is no doubt in deference to O'Grady's Irish heritage.

I pass through the doors and approach the secretary. She is in the middle of a holocall. I wait several minutes for the call to end, but it doesn't. It seems she is tracking a shipment. She is an attractive woman, probably in her mid-twenties, with wavy red hair and lovely green eyes. The triangular jade paperweight on her workstation tells me her name is Sharon Alberts. It's a shame I'll have to rattle her cage. I clear my throat.

"Excuse me, Miss Alberts."

She looks up at me. At six feet four inches, I tower over the young lady, startling her. I'm about to build on Sharon's surprise. Digging into the inside of my leather jacket, I pull out my fake *NSS* credentials and display them.

"I'm here to see Mister O'Grady."

"Hold on," Sharon tells her caller. "Mister O'Grady is on a conference call." She pulls up a list on her computer and looks closely at my ID wallet.

"I don't see that you have an appointment, Mr. Faulk."

Folding my credentials, I politely tell Miss Alberts, "It's Agent Faulk, and I don't need an appointment."

I walk down a short hallway, past a small alcove with a coffee table and some chairs, straight into William Fenton O'Grady's office. He is studying three inlaid screens on his workstation's desktop. He practically jumps out of his chair when I walk in.

"What?" is all O'Grady manages to say. His secretary's pretty holographic head pops up in the middle screen of the workstation.

"There's a government agent here to see you, sir. I tried to stop him, but he walked right past me."

"Go back to work, Sharon. I'll handle this."

For effect, I throw my fake credential into O'Grady's lap. "You are in trouble, Mr. O'Grady."

O'Grady examines my credentials. I hold out my hand to retrieve the ID wallet after enough time has passed. He hands it back to me. That's a good sign, but O'Grady doesn't realize it.

"I don't know why you're here, Agent Faulk, but I have nothing to say to you without my lawyer present."

I take a seat in front of O'Grady without being asked. "That's the typical response I get from dumb-asses, Mister O'Grady, but you're not a dumb-ass. My agency has been investigating your company for months. We have enough evidence to get a search warrant, but we want some direct testimony to ensure our warrant is appeal-proof. That puts you in a unique position to make a deal."

"This is ridiculous. You waltz in here making wild accusations and expect me to reveal sensitive information about my company. How do I know you are who you say you are?"

"What we're talking about is a matter of *Federated Security*. I have the authority to arrest you without due process. If I do, there's a good chance no one will hear from you again."

"Go ahead and arrest me."

"Stand up." I pull out a pair of handcuffs I pocketed this morning before leaving my room.

O'Grady takes a long look at the cuffs. Adrien had them made extra shiny. His artists also did an excellent job with my ID, badge, and law enforcement accouterments.

O'Grady lets out a long sigh. He's a vigorous man in his late forties, but he looks like he just aged ten years. I watch him bury his eyes between his thumb and forefinger. He massages his eyes as if the act could make all of this go away.

"I knew this day would come," he says, looking back up at me. "I've spoken to Mister Kronak several times about leaving the company. Each time, he's told me I can go only when he says I can."

"I find it hard to believe that you can't just walk out."

"Did you know a man was murdered in front of our building yesterday?"

"I'm aware of it, yes."

"It's no coincidence *tha'* victim was an accountant, *lad*. *Tha* was a warning from Kronak after I asked him again last week about leaving his damn company!"

Obviously, you and Kronak have different interpretations of the murder, I think to myself. *Who's telling the truth?*

"I have a good idea why you're here, Agent Faulk. *Yer lookin'* at the only man who has an inkling, outside of Kronak and his shady customers, *what's goin'* on behind the scenes."

I have O'Grady lapsing into an Irish brogue. It's a sign that I'm getting to him. He's probably polished his pronunciation to play in the Big Leagues.

"Why don't you tell me about it?"

"What do I get if I tell you?"

"Probably immunity if you agree to testify and the information is reliable."

"I need it in writing."

"We don't have time for writing. This is an emergency. It affects the *Federated Corporate States* and other countries worldwide.

"How do *ya'* know this?"

"That information is classified."

And you would never believe it if I told you.

O'Grady slumps in his seat. "I don't care *animore'*. I can't go on with this on my shoulders."

"Good. I'm listening."

CHAPTER 37

"It started when I did my first monthly report after Jan Kronak hired me. I noticed big differences in gross profit margins between single, double, and triple unit shipments and bulk orders. The gross profits on the smaller shipments averaged about thirty percent, whereas the industry standard is about sixty percent. The profit on the bulk sales averaged between ten and fifteen times *their cost,* depending on the number of units sold."

I notice O'Grady has dropped his accent. He seems more composed and even pleased to be offering this information.

"When it was time to review the report in Kronak's office, I asked him about the gross profit variances. He explained that custom orders generate higher margins. You see, Agent Faulk, custom orders are treated as a separate profit center here. The custom units are manufactured in a separate facility within the building and by a different workforce than the facility that produces the standard units. I can only conclude that the custom workers are more skilled because they make three times more than the standard workforce. Are you following me so far?"

"I am. What was the explanation for the lower margins?"

"Good question. Kronak says he wants to increase market penetration. Up until now, the market has been dominated by a company called AndroBiotica. They make Androids that are more lifelike, multi-faceted, and multifunctional than anyone else. Most of their sales go to government agencies and major corporations. They also sell to individuals with no criminal records who are cross-referenced for authenticity.

I've since learned the company president, Adrien Matthias, isn't worried about being undersold."

I'm gratified to hear that Adrien is still listening to me eight years later.

"On the one hand, Kronak's explanations sound logical," I observe. "On the other hand, they sound suspicious."

"Yes. I kept my suspicions to myself. I think Kronak is attempting to put his competitors out of business with his low prices on our standard units. The huge profits from the custom orders are keeping LifeLike on an even keel financially. If that's the case, no harm, no foul. Kronak can sell his products at any price he wants to as long as he's not conspiring with others to fix prices or engaging in other forms of anti-competitive activity."

"I hope you're not telling me we don't have a case?"

"Absolutely not. Here's the problem, and it's a frightening one. I dug into the customers who were buying the custom orders. Their identities are protected by shell companies and other disguises. I spent some time working as a forensic accountant for *The FDI.* I'm good at unveiling the entities at the heart of disguised business entities, but I couldn't unravel who these customers were. I can only tell you they are not major corporations. Major corporations don't operate through impenetrable legal entities. And, only major corporations and government agencies would have the kind of money to pay for the bulk orders we sell. So, who are these custom Android buyers? It's all very suspicious. I'm glad the *NSS* is on to this."

My surprise is only momentary. It's all beginning to make some sense in light of what Dianah showed us. But there are still missing pieces.

"So, Kronak is modifying his Androids in a way that makes them more valuable than their exorbitant prices."

"Yes, and until now, I've been unable to share this information with anyone besides Kronak. Now, do you understand the impossible position I'm in?"

"I do. I'll need a file with the work you've done on the highend buyers."

"No can do. I'm not allowed to download files without an authorization code from Kronak's office. It's a companywide edict."

"That's a bit extreme, but I guess it makes sense for an advanced technology company like this one."

"I've given you all the information I have, Agent Faulk. Now, I need an immunity decree from the *NSS* and protection from Kronak's Android assassins."

"I'll start working on it right away, but for now, I want you to leave LifeLike immediately without giving notice and get out of town as soon as you can. Give me at least two ways to contact you. I'll be in touch with you in forty-eight hours."

As I leave O'Grady's office with his contact information, I struggle to think of a way to protect him.

. . .

I enter Chief Carrington's office without knocking. I find him deep in thought. When the Chief looks up, he pushes a button on his desktop, and the door to his office closes remotely.

"Sit," Carrington orders me. I take one of the chairs on the opposite side of his workstation.

Maynard Carrington folds his hands in his lap. "First, you tell me you're a retired *NSS* Agent. Then I see you flash a badge at O'Grady in his office. What the hell is going on?"

"I *am* a retired *NSS* Agent. The badge was fake. I needed it to leverage O'Grady for information."

"Okay, now you're admitting to impersonating a government official. Give me one reason why I shouldn't call the *FDI* and have you arrested."

"I've seen the future, Maynard, and in the words of someone I deeply respect, 'the future isn't bright.' That future starts right here and now. I'm going to save thousands of lives and ensure the security of the *Federation of Corporate States*. And it's not just the future of *this* country that's at risk. The future of the world is at risk."

Holding his forehead with fingers spread, the Chief looks down at his workstation. "I'm dealing with a nut-case."

I was afraid it would come to this.

"I've come from eight years in the past to this point in the future. I'm here because LifeLike Technologies is ground zero for the horrible future that awaits us. Aurora Zolotov and Kristina Flemming will corroborate my story."

"All three of you are new. It sounds like a conspiracy to sink the company's stock price. I'm not going to waste time arguing."

Chief Carrington initiates a holocall.

"Wait. You watched and overheard what O'Grady said. I need your help to fill in the blanks of what's going on behind the scenes here."

"O'Grady could be in on it. Look, you've already ruined my day. If by some chance what you claim is true, you've ruined my career. I'll be a suspect. Now you have the nerve to ask me to get involved in this mess?"

"Call Kristina. Ask her to come down. Listen to what she has to say."

"I'll be listening to two nut cases *steada* one."

"You'll believe us when we gain access to the custom manufacturing facility. I assume you can get us in?"

"What if I can?"

"Then you'll see we're telling the truth."

I give Carrington a moment to think about my last request before asking for another favor.

"There's another matter we need to discuss."

"I can hardly wait to hear it."

"I've opened a drawer full of venomous snakes. It won't be long before Kronak sends one of his Android assassins after me. I need my weapon to protect myself."

"You need to work on your poetic imagery."

"I get that a lot, but I still need the weapon."

Carrington pulls something open below his desktop. Placing my weapon and holster on the surface of his workstation, he says, "You think this peashooter's *gonna* protect you?"

"My 'peashooter' is more deadly than it looks. You don't want to be on the wrong end of it in a fight."

Reluctantly, Carrington slides the handgun toward me. "You call Kristina Flemming. I have work to do."

I make the call, marking it urgent. Kristina picks up. I outline the situation in broad strokes, including my visit to William O'Grady. Kristina understands the delicacy of the problem and the need for her immediate presence. She promises to be down in a few minutes.

I try to put the pieces together in my head while the Chief works and Kristina is on her way. I can come to some obvious conclusions, but at least one unanswered question gnaws at me.

I hear a light tapping on the outer glass. I turn to see that it's Kristina.

As he opens his office door remotely, Carrington says in a low voice, "At least your partner is easy on the eyes. You're a plain pain in the ass."

"I've been called worse. Let me ask you this: Would you rather not know what's happening right under your nose?"

The Chief shakes his head. "If something's not right, I need to know about it."

"What time is the last shift over at the custom plant?"

"It varies. Today, it's at six."

"Okay. We'll meet back here at six. Then you can take us to the plant."

Carrington turns to look at the serene view outside his corner office. Then, he turns back to me with an icy stare. "You'd better show me convincing proof of what you and O'Grady are talking about. If you don't, I'll tell Mister Kronak that his new hires are security risks."

"Do you ever call him by his first name?"

"Never."

Kristina joins us, standing. "What have you boys been up to?"

"Have a seat," I say. "We'll bring you up to date."

CHAPTER 38

The custom manufacturing plant reminds me of an operating room, only this one is huge. Giant-sized recessed lights stare down from a domed ceiling. Only about a third of the lights are on to conserve energy, creating an eerie, sepia-tone effect. When in use, I imagine the bright lighting enables the technicians to see the tiniest details inside and outside of their subjects. As I look around, I see evidence that the power needed to run this plant must be staggering.

Rows of cushioned tables fill the manufacturing floor. I count ten Androids surrounded by robotic arms and powered operating tools resting on trays beside the beds. Each Android is encased in a plastic bubble for overnight storage. The "subjects," as they are called at LifeLike Technologies, look to be in various stages of construction. I count another five subjects in a separate area of the floor designated "Quality Control."

Kristina walks by my side between the rows with Chief Carrington behind us. Our steps are the only sounds in the room.

Kristina points to the Quality Control area. She is the boss now. Only she can tell us what we came here to find and where to look for it.

Kristina quickens her pace. Chief Carrington and I follow her until we reach the far end of the room. The circular LifeLike flesh and grey-colored logo is emblazoned on the wall above a steel door. A steering wheel juts from the door's center. From my vantage point, the door looks thick enough to protect a bank vault. I'm sure the finished products are packaged and picked up here on their way to the shipping docks. The finished Androids are packaged in cylindrical, windowed tubes riding on long-legged wheels.

"Can you lift the front panel on this one?" Kristina asks Carrington, indicating the nearest subject.

"Yeah," Carrington replies, looking down at the tablet he's carrying. "Give me the serial number. It's centered at the bottom of the tube."

"I see it." She reads the serial number out loud.

Carrington makes his way to a workstation at the front of the section. He inputs a series of keystrokes, and the workstation comes to life. Then, he consults his tablet again and inputs more code. The tube's front panel *hisses* open when the hermetic seal is broken.

Kristina puts on a pair of Nitrile gloves and grabs a hand-held surgical flashlight from the bedside tray. The reduced lighting from the ceiling casts shadows.

Bent over the open panel, Kristina spends about five minutes immersed in examining the inert Android body. Then, she looks up and calls me over.

"I need you to move the body when I tell you to."

"Standing by."

"Be careful with the body," Carrington warns. "I can't afford to buy it if you break it."

With my help, Kristina spends another ten minutes performing a physical examination of the body. The instrument she is using allows her to project color images of the Android's body cavity onto a nearby screen. Finally, she strips off her gloves. Looking up at me, Kristina reports, "Aside from the pronounced musculature, the one glaring anomaly on this unit is the absence of a serial number. Apparently, these custom Androids are cataloged by serial numbers, but they are not marked somewhere inside the body cavity, which is normally the case."

I turn to Carrington. "I told you we'd give you proof. The absence of a serial number confirms the unit will be used for an illegal purpose. Without a serial number, it can't be traced."

Before I can say another word, Kristina heads toward Chief Carrington at the nearby workstation. When I catch up, she is working on the station's virtual keyboard. Tucking in behind, I watch her find a file named "Programming." The file is shaped like a lockbox. True to its image, the file is locked.

"If this file works the same as the ones in the research lab, I'll need another password to get in."

"Try the serial number," Carrington suggests.

"Give it to me again."

Carrington slowly reads out a series of numerals, which Kristina inputs. I watch the lockbox open. Kristina opens more files inside the master lockbox file. She takes several minutes to study the code in one of them.

"Oh, shit."

I'm not accustomed to hearing Kristina curse. She turns to me.

"The programming of this unit isn't locked. I found comprehensive instructions on how to use the unit and maintain it. Here's the scary part. I found a separate set of instructions explaining how to program the unit and create a custom passcode. Normally, the end user is only permitted to make minor programming changes to a unit that has been designed to perform specific functions."

That's the answer to the bothersome question I've been thinking about. These Androids are more valuable than the standard models because of their custom construction *and* their ability to be custom-programmed.

The puzzle pieces are falling into place now. The picture isn't pretty. I summarize Kristina's discoveries for Chief Carrington: "Kronak is giving his custom buyers operational and programming instructions for each of the various model designs."

Kristinia continues browsing the unit's internal files. Her virtual stylus stops at a file labeled "Auto-Destruct."

"Does this unit have another password?" she asks the Chief.

"Yes, one more. It starts with the word 'Arm,' then a dash, followed by a series of numbers and letters."

Kristina opens the file. "As I feared, this unit has a remotely operated self-destruct feature."

"I'd say it's an assassin like the one that blew up in front of the building after murdering the accountant."

"Just what I was thinking," Kristina says.

The Chief bends over Kristina's shoulder. "Show me what you mean."

Kristina opens documents and highlights sections for Carrington to read. After seeing enough, he straightens and looks my way. "You've made a believer out of me."

I immediately know what has to be done next. "Can we copy the customer list?"

"Not without an authorization code," the Chief reminds me.

"Let me see what I can do." Kristina turns to the Chief. "Where are the client files kept?"

Carrington points to a large workstation surrounded by two smaller workstations set at right angles. "That's the Plant Manager's station. If the file is here, that's where the list would be."

We move to the Plant Manager's complex of workstations. Kristina assumes the beige padded executive chair behind the central workstation. I notice nobs and buttons on the right arm of the chair covered by an elongated transparent dome, apparently for downtime security.

Kristina turns to Chief Carrington, who stands to the right of her chair. I'm on her left side. It occurs to me that if we can acquire the buyer's list, Kronak will be alerted, and we will have to act quickly.

"I hope you have a password to fire this thing up," Kristina says to the Chief.

"The thing is, I don't. The PM changes the password daily."

Kristina turns to me. "We can forget about the client list."

"I do have an override code in case the PM forgets his passcode," Carrington adds.

"Aren't you something?" I say.

Referring to his tablet, Carrington repeats the password to Kristina.

After some trial and error, Kristina opens the custom plant's operating program.

She scrolls to the client list. "Wait. Oh damn. It's encrypted."

"It doesn't matter. Just download the file to a drive and give it to me."

Kristina tries a few drawers below the workstation's desktop. Each of them is locked.

"Where do I find a drive?" She asks the Chief.

"You guys would be lost without me." Carrington unfastens a single key attached to his belt. He holds it up for us to see. It is matte black with a silver flange at the end.

"This is a digital key. With it, I can unlock every employee's office and storage drawers. I keep it locked in a safe along with other high-clearance items when I'm off duty. I told you that Mr. Kronak trusts me. It's because I'm an honest man. That is, until now."

"Don't beat yourself up," I tell the Chief. "You're with the good guys."

Carrington nods. After he unlocks the drawers, Kristina rummages through them and finally finds what she's looking for.

I turn to Chief Carrington. "You have to get ahead of this. I strongly suggest you tender your resignation tonight. Then go to the *FDI* and tell them everything you know, but don't show them the video from O'Grady's office. I don't want to be seen impersonating an *NSS* Agent. I'll bring in O'Grady to back up your story when it's safe to do so. And be sure to leave my name and Kristina's out of your story completely. We have to disappear back in time without a trace. Inform the *FDI* that you uncovered Kronak's corruption on your own with O'Grady's cooperation".

"That sounds wonderful. I go to the *FDI* with a wild story backed up with practically no proof. Meanwhile, what do you think Kronak will be doing besides targeting my ass for elimination?"

"It's too late for Kronak to do anything to you. Leave him up to me."

"Just like that. On your say-so?"

"You know you can trust me."

"Oh, yeah. You being from the past and all that."

"Chief, I'm trying to help you. I don't want you to go down with the ship. Bring a pair of *FDI* Agents to this plant. You're standing in the middle of all the proof you need. The *FDI* can use your statement as probable cause for a search warrant."

Carrington sighs. "Okay. I have no choice except to stick my neck out before the shit hits the fan. And there are plenty of innocent people outside of the company to worry about besides me. Am I supposed to thank you for this?"

"It's optional."

"I'm opting out." Carrington rubs his chin. "I'm going to warn my guys. Take as many of them out of the line of fire as I can."

"Good idea. That'll make our job easier. Last but not least, give this file to the *FDI*. Let their techs penetrate the encryption." I hand Carrington the disk Kristina has made.

I turn to Kristina. "You need to pack and get out of the building. Find a safe hotel for us to stay. I'll be right behind you. There's something I have to do first."

CHAPTER 39

I find Aurora in her office packing up at the end of the day.

"I'm glad I caught you. We have a lot to catch up on."

Aurora gives me a long look. "About the situation here, I mean."

"Fine, but let's not do it here. Kronak called me. He wants a meeting first thing tomorrow morning. I think he knows something's up."

"Where do you want to go?"

"Dinner would be nice. I'm starving."

"I know just the place."

...

I take Aurora to the same restaurant I went to with Kristina. Since I gave the *Master Waiter* a nice tip, I figure he'll accommodate us without our having a reservation. He doesn't disappoint. We're seated at a table near a small stage where a live group will be playing by the end of the hour. Our host assures me the music won't be loud. I give him a bigger tip. He's pleased and asks me to call him by his first name. It's Hermione. He pronounces it *Hermwan*. Too bad I won't be staying in this time zone much longer. I'm developing a nice relationship with the guy, but tomorrow marks the beginning of our third day here. If all goes well, Kristina and I will be leaving in less than forty-eight hours.

I wish I could say the same for Aurora.

A courteous waitress, impeccably dressed in a business suit, takes our drink order. Business is the theme here. The restaurant, named Casey's, serves a business crowd almost exclusively. The place is already half full. The interior decoration is plain, but if last night is any indication, the food and drinks here are first-class. You can't eat the decorations.

While we're awaiting our drinks, I update Aurora on everything that's happened. She takes it all in without reacting emotionally. When I'm done, I ask her if she has any questions. Aurora has an observation and only one question.

"Our worst fears are confirmed. What are you planning to do?"

"There's only one thing we can do to resolve this threat in the time we have left. Kronak must be eliminated."

"That's an extreme measure, Derrick. Using your solution would make us no different than Kronak. How can you justify it?"

"Given our time window, it's the only practical solution. I don't want to get into a due process of the law argument with you. Kronak deserves the death penalty for his crimes. It's too bad we can only kill him once. He deserves at least a hundred painful deaths for the suffering he's already caused."

The drinks arrive. Our waitress serves them expertly and asks, "Is there anything else I can get you?"

A high-powered handgun for Aurora would be nice.

"We're fine for now. Thanks very much."

With a professional smile, our waitress departs.

"What time does Kronak usually leave the office?"

"Around nine or ten."

"Perfect. That gives us time to eat a healthy dinner."

"How can you be so cold?"

I stare back at Aurora. "Because I have to be in this instance."

"I won't kill a Human, Derrick."

"I don't expect you to. I want you to watch my back."

Aurora gives me a level look. "I suppose I can do that. You have to live with Kronak's murder, not me.

■ ■ ■

We use Aurora's security card to enter the building. As we walk deeper into the lobby, I see the security station is unmanned. Chief Carrington has already pulled his people. Good.

Aurora turns to me and says wryly, "I'm not dressed for this."

"I don't know. You may find your high heels come in handy for bashing heads."

Aurora is not amused. I'm sure she's conflicted about what we're doing. She's an Android with higher moral standards than I.

On the way to the elevators, I call Kristina. She tells me where we're staying for the night. I advise her to stay in the room and not wait up for me. She asks me what I'm doing. I say I'll tell her when I get back to the hotel. She wants to talk more, but I end the call.

We use Aurora's card again to operate the elevators. Her security clearance enables us to go directly to Kronak's penthouse office. I'm starting to feel like this is too easy.

We reach the penthouse floor. Two armed Androids stand guard outside Kronak's office suite. So much for easy.

The Androids sense our presence immediately. Our training kicks in. Aurora moves away from me behind the opposite corner of the hallway. Drawing my handgun, I crouch and fire at the nearest Android as it makes the first step toward us. I catch a glimpse of its chest exploding before I duck back behind cover.

"One to go," I call to Aurora. I can't see her, but I know she's ready for anything.

I peer around the corner to take another shot, but the remaining guard fires first. I pull back. The projectile blasts a chunk out of the wall.

I am thrown back. My ears are ringing. My eyesight is blurry. The Android is already bearing down on me with its weapon pointed at my head.

Before I can think *I'm dead,* something crashes into it from behind. The guard stumbles forward. Feminine hands with purple nails encircle the attacker's head before it can regain its balance.

When I rub my eyes to regain my vision, I hear an awful tearing sound. Opening my eyes again, I see Aurora holding the Android's head and bloody neck. Its body wobbles before it collapses in a heap a few feet away.

I lean back against the wall. Aurora tosses the head on top of the Android's crumpled body. She bends down to my level. Picking up the fallen guard's handgun, she checks the action and the clip. Slamming the clip back into the gun, she asks, "Are you hurt?"

"I'll probably live. Thanks for saving my life."

Rising to a standing position, Aurora gives me her hand. I use it to lever myself up. A wave of dizziness overcomes me. Aurora holds my shoulders to steady me. I breathe deeply to clear my head.

"Do you know where you are?"

"Yeah. In the belly of the beast. I'll probably have a helluva headache in the morning, but for now, I'm operational."

Aurora releases her grip on my shoulders. "Are you sure?"

"I'm sure of one thing. I'm going to find Jan Kronak and send him to the lowest pit of Hell."

CHAPTER 40

The double glass doors to Jan Kronak's office suite are open. If Kronak is inside, I'd expect the doors to be locked after the mayhem that just went down. It almost feels like Kronak is inviting us in. Either that, or the office walls contain enough soundproofing to filter out a sonic boom.

I glance at Aurora opposite me. She holds her handgun down but at the ready. I decide to holster my weapon. I don't want to scare Kronak. Yet.

Standing with her feet apart and her back to me, Aurora waits to pick off Android reinforcements storming the floor from the hallways leading to the penthouse office.

I walk through the sitting room and into the main office. Kronak is seated at his workstation, head down, immersed in his work. He wears earbuds. I'm sure they are the highest quality *Daras* can buy. He's probably listening to music to enhance concentration.

I keep walking. It bothered me to kill an innocent Android guard when we first arrived in the basement of the new building. I have no second thoughts about what I'm planning to do here.

I reach the facing edge of Kronak's workstation. He looks up slowly as if he's expecting me. When I see his eyes, I know I'm screwed.

The colors match. I know from our previous meetings that they don't. I turn and run as fast as my legs can carry me.

I hear the explosion before its force reaches the sitting room. Aurora begins to turn around as I grab her shoulders and force her away from the doors.

Debris shoots into the hall. The shockwave knocks us down. Smoke billows out from the shattered doors. Aurora and I help each other to our feet. We know what to do without needing to discuss it. Stumbling, we make our way to the emergency door and the stairs. With our weapons drawn, we take the first steps down the stairs, gripping the handrail to keep from falling.

We stop on the fifteenth-floor landing to catch our breath. I've made it on pure adrenaline, but the shock of what happened is catching up to me. Aurora has a soot streak across her cheek. Other than that, she looks okay.

"Your jacket is ripped," she tells me. "Are you injured?"

I look at my arms. The right sleeve of my leather jacket is in tatters. My work shirt underneath is ripped. I don't see any blood.

"Nothing hurts. What about you?"

"I *vas* outside of *za* blast radius thanks to your push. I'm in one piece."

Aurora's accent returns when she's under extreme stress.

I slough off my jacket and roll up my right sleeve to make sure *I'm* in one piece.

The time-travel coating under my shirt is cracked. It probably helped to protect me from the blast. It also probably means I'm stranded here, like Aurora.

Aurora stares at my exposed arm. She purses her lips as if to say, *Too bad,* and looks away.

"Kronak set a trap for us with an exploding Android assassin. He was here in the flesh yesterday, but not today. He's taken his money and run. I'm sure of it."

"I think I know how *ve* can find him."

"It has to do with the painting of the castle in his office, doesn't it?"

"Yes. With another of Adrien's upgrades, I took photos of Kronak's office with a miniature camera in my right eye during our meetings. It's a silent and seamless process. I can do it without anyone noticing. I thought it might help the investigation."

"That was good thinking. Let's go to your office."

Fortunately, Aurora's office is only one floor down. I need somewhere to recover from the explosion. I haven't told Aurora that my vision is blurred and I have a mother of a headache. I won't be much help in a firefight in my present condition.

When Aurora opens the stairway door to the hallway, we are greeted by the sound of sirens coming from the streets outside the building. Police and fire trucks are arriving. Soon, officers and firefighters will be swarming the offices and hallways. We have to work fast.

It doesn't help when we find two heavily muscled guards standing outside Aurora's office. I don't think they are Human, but we can't exactly walk up to them and ask. We crouch behind a corner in the corridor. Around the corner stands a statue of a new-generation Android model. The statue obstructs our vision.

"I doubt those guards belong to the Chief," I whisper to Aurora.

"Stay back," she answers.

Straightening up confidently, Aurora walks to the statue and stands beside it.

The guards raise their handguns and fire.

Aurora reaches the opposite corner of the corridor before the projectiles miss and hit the elevator doors at the end of the hallway. She can be super fast when in fight mode. We've fought a few battles together. Aurora is quick and deadly when she wants to be. And she's just taken the guesswork out of this confrontation.

I fire my weapon and miss both shots. With my double vision and splitting headache, I'd miss a firetruck if it were parked right in front of me. But my effort is not in vain. I've given Aurora an advantage by drawing the guards' attention.

She fires four quick bursts from her automatic handgun. The projectiles send the guards flying backward, splattering them into a chunky mess. Blood seeps out around the pile of body parts.

Evidently, Kronak programmed some backup in the unlikely event we made it out of his office alive. I guess you don't reach the top of the heap without planning ahead.

"Good shooting," I say to Aurora.

"Either you're out of practice, or you can't see straight. We had *za* element of surprise. I should not have had to fire my weapon."

I don't reply because I don't want to add to the pressure on Aurora. I assume my eyesight will improve soon.

Aurora opens the door to her office. We carefully avoid droplets of blood on the carpet. We don't want to be walking advertisements for murder. Speaking of which, we have to leave this floor fast to avoid being seen with the telltale Android wreckage.

I sit in front of Aurora's workstation. "Do you have any *asperenza*?"

Aurora opens a drawer in the credenza behind her. She offers me a sheet of tablets and fetches a bottle of water.

Sitting behind her workstation, Aurora says, "You are impaired. You need rest."

She looks at me for a response. I say nothing.

"I need a partner, not a corpse."

"Don't waste time worrying about me. I'll hold up my end of the deal."

Aurora takes a long look at me. She knows I'm bluffing. Turning back to her workstation, she says, "I'm purchasing a worldwide topographical database and downloading photos of the castle and its surroundings. Then, I *vill* run the photos against the database. I'll set some parameters to make it go faster."

Aurora keystrokes commands on her workstation at an unnatural speed.

"Downloading the photos now. I'm using a corporate credit card to buy the database. I don't think Kronak will mind. The study will take a few minutes to complete."

Aurora leans back in her seat. We fall into a tense silence, waiting.

"Are you upset that you can't go back in time?" Aurora abruptly asks me. She is not shy about speaking her mind.

"If Adrien is still alive, he can probably patch me up. If not, I can make staying in the future work, as long as I don't age eight years overnight."

Aurora smiles briefly. "If the company and Adrien are still intact, will you go back to work at AndroBiotica?"

"At least for a while. I have to make a living, and there's nobody else I'd rather work with than Adrien."

Our eyes meet briefly. Then, Aurora's workstation beeps. She smiles broadly. "The study is complete. *Ve* have a match."

"And?"

"The castle is located in *Amperigo* on the *Zarnadian Coast*. We have no extradition treaty with *Amperigo*.

It's a sixty-one-thousand-square-mile sliver of a country, with high mountains in the western part and lower mountains tapering to cliffs in the east. The castle is built on one of those cliffs."

"When I admired his painting, Kronak told me he planned to build a castle 'away from everything.' It looks like he's already built it."

Aurora's long fingers stream over her digital keyboard. "We can get there in half a day by spaceliner."

She inputs another query. "There's a direct flight to the capital city in the morning. It's a favorite destination for wealthy tourists, money launderers, and fugitives."

Aurora looks up with a thin smile. "I can get us two seats in first class. On the house."

"Are you sure it's Kronak's castle?"

"There are a few other possibilities, but the castle I've chosen as the target is the closest match."

"Okay, let's give it a try."

Standing, she takes a last, wistful look at her shelves and workstation. I can almost guess what she's thinking. There are no pictures of friends, family, or lovers. No mementos of anyone or anything. It's a cold workspace for a lonely someone who took a one-way ticket into a barren future. I feel genuinely sorry for her.

Leaving the office, we head across the hallway to the emergency stairs. With the chaos upstairs as a distraction, there is no one to stop us.

CHAPTER 41

As we descend the emergency stairs, we are met by a series of firefighters. Each one tells us to exit the building quickly. They are not interested in asking us who we are or why we're here. Their priority is to extinguish fires and rescue trapped survivors.

Reaching the lobby floor, we encounter a scene of controlled pandemonium. A large dial to the left of the entrance indicates the time: Ten *of the Clock*. I see police officers interviewing several employees who have remained in the building to work. This eventuality is both good and bad news. The number of employees provides some cover. There won't be time for in-depth questioning, but we may have a long wait until they get to us.

My mobile holophone vibrates. It's Kristina. "Where are you?"

I give Kristina a short update, deliberately leaving out a few key details.

"I'm in the lobby of the LifeLike Building. There's been an explosion. Kronak is on the run. I have to go after him."

"Are you alright?"

"I'm fine," I lie.

"Are you coming back to the hotel?"

"Yes. We'll talk more then. Right now, we have to get through a Police screening."

"We?"

"Aurora and I."

Silence at the other end of the connection.

"I'll explain everything later. Stay in your room. 'Bye."

Ending the call, I am struck once again by the ultra-modern lobby. With its towering ceiling and polished stone walls, the lobby manages to look understated and opulent at the same time. On this clear night, I can see a myriad of stars peeking through the angled ceiling windows. It is hard to believe a man as evil as Kronak could create such beauty.

A line of employees has formed behind two officers, who are checking IDs and asking questions. I notice three more officers holding a few employees for further questioning at a makeshift security station. More employees gather in groups. I imagine they are comparing notes on the events of the evening and telling their stories about how it affected them.

We have no choice but to wait in line. I zip up my jacket to hide the torn work shirt. I'll have to hold my arms behind my back to hide the tattered right sleeve. When we reach the officers, I'll be standing in a parade rest posture. I'll try to make it look natural.

The condition of my clothing reminds me that all I have in this future world is a forged *NSS* ID and badge, a bankroll of one hundred *Dara* notes, my passport, my weapon, and the tattered clothing on my back. I'd feel desperately alone if I didn't have a capable partner with me.

The wait seems interminable. I'm exhausted. The day started early, and it's been unusually demanding up to this late hour. My vision is improving, but I feel the headache coming back. I have to get some rest and more *Asperenza*.

I can see the day has worn on Aurora, too. Her typically erect posture is sloped-shouldered.

I lean slightly and whisper to Aurora, "I'm going to give the officers the same cover story we've used for the mission with a few changes. I came here to interview with you for a job as a data security consultant. I don't want to rely on Kronak as a reference. I can use William O'Grady as a reference if necessary. You hired me and were going over the employee manual and company policies with me when the explosion occurred. Since you are so busy, we had to do the orientation at night. What do you think?"

"Works for me."

Our turn in line finally arrives. Looking at the officers, I can tell two things right off the bat. They are as tired as we are, and they are uncomfortable with non-stop superficial interviews. I think these factors will work in our favor if we can avoid triggering their suspicions.

I assume a parade rest position. Hopefully, the posture will reinforce the authenticity of my paramilitary background when I'm asked about my weapon.

"Let's see some ID," the officer nearest to me says. He stands a few inches shy of six feet tall with an accent from the Deep South. His red hair is neatly trimmed, and he'd be clean-shaven if it weren't for a late-night shadow. His name is Keith Armbruster. His partner is named Rajesh Patel. By his coloring and name, I make him out to be a native *Indarian*.

Along with their badges and standard uniforms, the officers wear the letters *SST* stitched in red and yellow thread on their right breast pockets. Armbruster and Patel belong to a specialized unit. I assume it is something tactical. Both men are in excellent physical condition. Neither one of them should be underestimated.

As I pass my ID and fake consultant's card to Armbruster, his partner is looking at Aurora too closely. He puts a hand behind her back to move her away from me. They want to separate us to determine if our stories match. Aurora swats Patel's hand away.

"What are *ya 'll* doing here?" Armbruster asks me. I tell him the same story I gave to Aurora.

Armbruster notices my gun. He stays calm. I tell him the story I told the Chief: I'm an ex-*NSS* agent and all that. Armbruster is skeptical. I'm about to embellish my story when a thought hits me like a punch to the temple—something I definitely don't need in my semi-concussed condition. *Aurora has a gun, too. How could we overlook it? Yeah, we got lost in all the drama, but still?* I glance at Aurora and Patel. Their gestures indicate there is an issue. It must be the gun.

Armbruster is still calm. "We're *gonna* ask you and the lady to stay for more questioning. It's standard procedure. We'll try to clear this up as soon as possible."

Yeah, right. Next stop will be the Police Station or the FDI Office.

Armbruster motions to a nearby officer watching the crowd. "Help these folks to the temporary security station."

While I'm trying to think of a way out of this jam, I hear a commotion behind us. Armbruster looks up. I turn while jealously guarding my right arm.

The crowd behind me parts. Two figures approach. One of them roughly shoves an inattentive employee out of the way. I can see the figures clearly now. They are guards—duplicates of the ones Aurora dispatched in front of her office.

I turn back to Armbruster. "Those guards are coming to kill us."

Armbruster pushes me aside. He places his hand on his holster. It's a fatal move. The Androids react quickly. They draw their handguns instantaneously—*boom, blam, blam*—the projectiles cut through Armbruster's vest, slicing him in half. He's dead before his arteries can spurt blood.

I hear screams from the crowd as, moving sideways, I draw my gun. There is no time to worry about the innocent bystanders in the background. I change the setting on my weapon and simultaneously fire three shots at the guard on my left. The projectiles catch it in the chest and head. The Android is blown backward. It hits the floor and skids into the crowd harmlessly.

I hear gunfire to my right. Rajesh Patel has moved in front of Aurora, presumably to protect her. His pistol is not designed to stop an Android. It absorbs Patel's projectiles with only a few flinches. Aurora wisely jumps from behind Patel as the second Android cuts him down. Aurora and I fire away in the few seconds Patel's death has given us. We shred the other attacker before it has a chance to get off another shot. Glancing at Aurora, I nod my head toward the lobby doors. She is literally one step ahead of me.

Once outside, we holster our weapons and huddle on the sidewalk. Aurora grabs my hand.

"Come with me. I'm staying at the Saxton across the street."

It's the same hotel Kristina and I stayed at the night before our interviews. We scamper across the street like two children running from a hungry wolf. As we enter the lobby of the hotel, I look back across the street. No one is chasing us, thanks to the bedlam we left behind.

CHAPTER 42

"I did not lure you here" is the first thing Aurora says when we enter her single room.

"*I know*," I respond emphatically. We needed somewhere to lie low, and this is the nearest place."

Aurora looks satisfied now that she's made her intentions clear.

The room is a luxurious one-bedroom suite featuring a king-sized bed, a small workstation, and two upholstered lounge chairs. I see from the half-opened closet door that Aurora has previously made herself at home here.

Taking a seat in the lounge chair farthest away from the bed, I tell Aurora that I have to call Kristina. She nods and walks into her bathroom with renewed confidence and perfect posture.

I make the call. Kristina answers in an anxious voice. "I thought you'd be here by now. What else happened?"

"We ran into some trouble in the lobby. The Police almost arrested us before two Androids attacked us. We killed the Androids and escaped in the commotion. I'm with Aurora now in her room. She's staying at the Saxton. We had to get out of sight quickly."

"So, you'll stay there until we finish the mission?"

"That's one of the things I have to tell you. I may not be able to make the trip back with you. My protective skin is cracked from the explosion in Kronak's office."

It takes a moment for my news to set in. "What were you doing in Kronak's office?"

"I was there to kill him. My plan literally blew up when Kronak left a suicide Android in his place."

"You aren't making sense, Derrick. You went to Kronak's office to kill him?"

"Yes. It's the only way to make sure he's no longer a threat, and you know as well as I do that Kronak doesn't deserve to live after what he's done."

Silence, then, "You said he's on the run. How will you find him?"

"We think we know where he is. We're going after him first thing in the morning."

More silence on Kristina's end of the connection. "So, I'm going back alone."

"It looks that way."

"What if I want to stay here with you?"

"You have to go back to tell Adrien what's happened. He'll be beside himself with worry if the machines return empty. And your life is back where we started. Adrien needs you there."

"Then this is goodbye."

"It seems so."

A long pause, then, "Goodbye, Derrick."

The connection ends, and I am overcome with a sense of sadness. What could have been with Kristina may be gone forever.

I look down at my tattered sleeve. The protective coating is bubbling. I remove my jacket.

Aurora walks into the room, freshly showered, with a towel around her head and a bathrobe clinging to her body.

"You can use the bathroom while I dress for bed."

I appreciate the prompt. I can't wait to undress and shower. I am soiled with the aftermath of the explosion and the violent deaths.

"Do you mind if I use your toiletries?"

"What's mine is yours, except my lipstick. I'll bash you if you use it."

"Noted."

The shower is a welcome relief. I close my eyes. Memories of the past two days flood my mind. So much has happened. Most of the events haven't had time to register.

After I wash myself thoroughly, I gingerly peel the coating from my arm. It comes off easily, thanks to the razors that shaved my body hair before the coating was applied. I try to remove the coating on my chest, but it is stuck solid. I suppose it will loosen within a day or so.

After toweling myself off and brushing my teeth, I dress in my dirty and damaged clothes. Wait a minute. What am I doing? I'm not going to sleep in these. I'll sleep on the floor in my underwear. Aurora won't mind. I step out of the bathroom with the towel around my loins. I must make quite an appearance with the coating torn jaggedly off my right arm.

"Is there an extra sheet or blanket I can spread on the floor?"

Aurora is already in bed. She sits up, using the duvet to cover herself. She has replaced her lovely blond hair with black hair dye and removed her knockout makeup. Aurora still looks good despite the plain makeover.

"You can sleep on top of the covers if you want. I won't attack you."

I'm not worried about you.

"I'll take the floor."

"Suit yourself. There's an extra blanket and pillow on the top shelf of the closet. I'm setting the alarm for five-thirty to make sure we don't miss our flight."

"Some sleep is better than none," I comment philosophically.

I make my bed, using the term loosely. The king bed looks mighty enticing. *Forget it. I'll tough it out.*

Aurora turns out the lights.

"Sweet dreams."

"You as well," I answer.

My body aches in a hundred places. Nevertheless, I fall into a deep sleep quickly.

■ ■ ■

It seems like a few minutes have passed when the alarm wakes me. I pull myself to a sitting position on the blanket. My vision is clear, and the headache is mostly gone, but I feel nauseous. I know from my training that nausea indicates at least a moderate concussion. Without rest and proper treatment, there is a chance of permanent brain damage. Rest and treatment are not in my immediate future. I won't be able to keep up with Adrien and Aurora if I lose too many brain cells. I may have to demote myself to a *gopher* and run miscellaneous errands.

Aurora is already up and in the bathroom. While I'm waiting for my turn, I pull off the protective coating that has bubbled over the rest of my body. It's a relief to get rid of it. I'll have to take another shower to wash the remaining grains off.

Aurora steps out of the bathroom, fully clothed. Her black hair is braided and tucked down the back of her blouse. Her makeup is minimal. Aurora's appearance is as ordinary as it gets for a naturally beautiful woman. She points her thumb toward the bathroom.

"Take the pieces of peeled coating into the shower with you. It will dissolve while you wash. I'll wait for you out here. Watch the time."

"Good morning to you, too."

"I left a packet of instant hair dye on the sink. It sets in three minutes. You'll look good with red-brown hair."

"I've always wanted to go Auburn."

I gather up the pieces of coating. We don't want to leave any mysteries for the hotel's management to solve.

When I'm dressed and ready to go, it occurs to me to holocall Adrien. He has shared his private number with his inner circle of friends and business associates, with the condition that they not disclose it to anyone outside of the circle. I want to let Adrien know that we're okay and what we plan to do to neutralize Kronak. This action assumes that Adrien and AndroBiotica still exist eight years into the future of our timeline.

I input the number verbally. To my dismay, an automated voice advises me that the number is no longer in service.

■ ■ ■

Dawn is breaking through the lobby windows when I ask the front desk agent to hail us a ride to the spaceport. The agent is a young female, probably a trainee. She's much easier to get along with than the night agent, and I'm grateful. The day portends to be long and arduous. We don't need a hard time to start it off.

I'm also grateful that the agent isn't making annoying comments like, "Traveling light, aren't we?" Aurora and I are traveling without suitcases—not even a carry-on. We'll have to buy new clothes and a matching pair of carry-ons at the spaceport to avoid suspicion.

Our weapons are a problem. They are perfect for the mission, but we will have to ditch them before we board the spaceliner. Minutes later, our transportation arrives. I tip the agent. She smiles appreciatively.

We board the spaceport shuttle, bending low so as not to be seen by the government agents who are still on the scene to investigate last night's bloodbath and its puzzling aftermath.

Once aboard the shuttle, we have a few minutes to relax. I use the time to review the events in the lobby. We escaped before any photos were taken of us. That would leave the possibility of a holographic record if there were holographic cameras in the lobby. Assuming the worst, it's still early enough not to have our likenesses broadcast beyond the Police and *FDI* investigative teams. They want to find us for questioning, not scare us away by broadcasting our likenesses. And we aren't official suspects—at least not yet. However, the downside is that it will take too long for the combined brain trust of the *FDI* and local law enforcement to figure out that Kronak is the bad guy and not us.

Meanwhile, Aurora and I will be in play as persons of interest.

A tall truck with high wheels and a copper dome *whooshes* by us. The dome tells me the vehicle has a force field surrounding it. Since only government vehicles can be equipped with force field shields, the truck has to belong to a government agency.

"What's a government truck doing speeding around here at this hour?" I wonder aloud.

"It looks like a personnel carrier," Aurora says. "Maybe a specialized law enforcement team."

A plain industrial Android operates the shuttle. We're moving, which is a good sign. If the Android had identified us as fugitives, it would have made excuses for remaining stationary until a dozen agents came to surround the vehicle and arrest us.

I hear the intercom turn on.

"Hi, folks. I hope I'm not interrupting anything. I thought you would like to know that we'll be airborne as soon as we clear the downtown area in about ten minutes. Then, it's only a twelve-minute flight to the spaceport. We have plenty of time to get you there before your flight departs. My name is Randy, by the way. Let me know if you need anything."

"Please turn on the news, Randy."

"Right away, sir. There you go."

"For an industrial Android, this one sounds pretty Human," Aurora whispers to me. "They keep on getting better and better."

And as we continue to interact, Aurora, the more Human you become to me.

CHAPTER 43

The first thing I notice when we enter our terminal is the number of military personnel strategically placed near the restaurants, shops, and check-in counters. Some of them are cradling heavy assault weapons in their arms, and the others carry sidearms. All of the soldiers wear uniforms with lightweight armor sewn in below the surface of their battle fatigues. On our ride here, we heard nothing on the news that would explain a military presence like the one I'm seeing.

The way these soldiers outside the boarding gates sway slightly under the weight of their outfits suggests to me that they are Human. If there are no Android soldiers to fill out the detachment, it indicates to me that Androids can't be trusted. Something unusual is happening here.

The soldier nearest me eyes my tattered sleeve. I behave as if tattered sleeves are the newest fashion craze in leather garments.

Concealing my nervousness, I spot a nearby clothing and sundries shop. Aurora sees it, too. We casually make our way toward it. Once inside, we peruse the his-and-hers racks of clothing on opposite walls of the narrow interior. We'll have to go elsewhere to buy luggage, but that's okay as long as we don't do anything to arouse suspicion.

We collect neutral-colored, casual clothing items that look like they might fit us. We are both unusually tall, which makes it hard to find clothing in our sizes. There are fitting rooms at the end of the racks. We don't have to compete to use the rooms because no other customers are shopping for clothing at this early hour.

After some trial and error, I find a pair of gray slacks and a pale blue business shirt that fit reasonably well. The clothing items are drastically reduced, so the pickings are slim. I can't find a sports jacket anywhere near my size, so I forego that item. After dressing in my new outfit, I wipe my fingerprints and conceal my weapon in a bundle of my old clothes. I drop the bundle in a trash chute in the corner of the room. The loss of my handgun feels like I've cut off an appendage of my body.

On the way to the checkout counter, I find a rack of caps with sports logos and others that are plain. I select a large blue cap without a logo. Blue is my favorite color, and it goes with my outfit. The cap will help to hide my face.

Next to the caps, I find an arrangement of sunglasses on a shelf. The prices are much more than the glasses are worth, which is always the case in spaceports. I select a pair that won't draw attention. The sunglasses don't come close to my fashion preferences, but they'll get the job done.

While I'm handing the clothing and price tags in for purchase, I notice sets of microbuds displayed in a cabinet behind the attendant. They, too, are overpriced.

I point to the display. "Are those automatic?" I ask the attendant, who turns out to be a studious-looking young man. I believe he is Human, but I can't be sure. "Which microbud version do you have?" he asks me expertly.

I can't give him an eight-year-old brand name and model number. Instead, I give the attendant a perfect opening. He's a bright young man with the first name of Mirash. I can't place his accent.

"I forgot to pack mine, and it's about time that I updated them anyway."

"The buds you see are state-of-the-art, and, of course, they will automatically adjust to your voice commands. Most models carry that feature nowadays."

Mirash goes on to tell me about all of the superior options built into the MiraCast brand he sells. I'm unfamiliar with some of the jargon, but I carefully avoid questions or objections.

"This is your lucky day, Mirash. I know that I can buy these buds for less somewhere else, but I don't have time to shop. I'll take two pairs."

Mirash tries to hide his surprise at the relative ease of his sale. I hope he will get a nice commission.

Aurora joins me at the counter. Mirash almost stops totaling the cost of my items at the sight of her.

Aurora is wearing white jeans. Her ample bust fills out a black blouse. She's trying for an under-the-radar look. The outfit works as well as it can for her.

I point to the caps. "Why don't you try on one of those, dear?"

Aurora gets the message. She selects a black cap and brings it to the counter.

When he finishes totaling up the sale, Mirash looks up. I see the envy in his eyes. Mirash is definitely Human.

"Will that be cash or charge?"

Aurora looks at me. We're both thinking the same thing. It's not safe to use Kronak's corporate card. It might already be flagged.

"I like the cap, Sweetheart, but don't you think it's over-priced?"

"It's almost your birthday, Darling."

To Mirash, I say, "We'll take it." The charade is for his benefit. While I count out a cash payment, I once again sense Mirash's surprise, but he covers it well. I hand Mirash the cash. He counts it to ensure the total is accurate. He looks up at me with a polite smile.

"Sir, you have given me twenty *Daras* too much."

"Keep it, and forget that we were here if anyone asks."

"Thank you, sir. You are most kind. I will do as you say."

As we walk toward our departure gate, I give Aurora her pair of microbuds.

"Let's tune into the spaceport news channel and see what's happening in the big, bad world."

"You're just like Adrien, Dear. You think of everything."

I chuckle. "Let's drop the 'Dear' until we need it again. Did you ditch your handgun?"

"Like a bad habit, except I didn't want to lose it."

"I know the feeling."

We walk a few more steps.

"That was a good metaphor you used."

"Thanks. Maybe I'll be able to help you with yours down the road apiece."

"That one was a cliché."

She laughs. "Intentionally."

We steal glances at the soldiers as we walk. Aurora gets an occasional look from them, but I think it's just a normal testosterone reaction. We're not under suspicion. Something else is going on.

Further along, we decide not to buy carry-on strollers. When checked at the security point, empty strollers are just as suspicious as a couple traveling long distances without luggage.

As we near the security screening tunnel leading to the departure gates, we see a group of travelers staring up at a big holoscreen on the wall opposite the schedule of spaceliner departures. They are staring at smoking rubble interlaced with twisted and torn corpses.

Affixing our microbuds and tuning to the news channel, we stand behind the group of onlookers. The camera angle widens to reveal a skyline with a missing skyscraper. The scene prompts an image of a row of dentures with a missing tooth. I hear a reporter's voice narrating the devastating scene.

"Early this morning, explosions rocked the *Velanox Tower* in downtown *Worrington*. The building is home to several multinational corporations and ten floors of luxury condominiums.

"The *Velanox* is touted as one of the most secure buildings in the world, but somehow, enough high-density plastic explosive was smuggled into the building to bring it down. Authorities have no leads on the perpetrators, and the investigation is ongoing.

"The *FDI* and *HSI*, working with *Velanox* management, estimate the death toll could exceed three thousand. Local authorities and the *FDI* suspect this tragic event is the work of terrorists, but their method remains a mystery.

"As a result of this reprehensible attack, cities and major transportation hubs of *the Federation of Corporate States* are on high alert. *WLBC* news will bring you the latest updates as they become available."

I lean to whisper in Aurora's ear. "The attack has all the earmarkings of the Androids Kronak sold to his custom buyers. The government must have locked down the story long enough to deploy their troops without causing widespread panic."

Aurora nods calmly. She's a pro. I consider going to the authorities with what we know, but quickly decide against it. The authorities work too slowly, and they might dismiss us as crackpots or take us into custody.

"In other news, two unidentified individuals blasted their way out of the lobby of the LifeLike Technologies building in downtown *Sansa Berlando*."

Our profile pictures appear on the side of the frame. The photos aren't in sharp focus because we weren't exactly standing still when they were extracted from the 3-D holofilm.

"Police are still trying to piece together the why of the incident. Two Android security guards attacked and killed two officers before the unidentified shooters killed the rogue Androids. No one else was harmed in the incident. The unnamed couple left the building immediately after the gunfight. The couple is wanted by the *FDI* for questioning. If you have any information about these individuals or their whereabouts, please call the number at the bottom of your holoscreen."

As my eyes lower from the holoscreen to the crowd of travelers, I see a familiar face approaching us. It's a good thing the face is etched in my memory because everything else about the coloring and style of the figure coming toward us has changed. The hair is black and trimmed just below the ears. She is wearing a light grey business suit cut conservatively below the knee. Her body is slim and statuesque despite the flat, black loafers she wears. Her stride is purposeful, and her posture is erect. Aurora follows my gaze and touches my forearm.

"It's Dianah," she gasps.

She stands before us with her back to the crowd.

"There is no time for pleasantries, Derrick Faulk and Aurora Zolotov. As you can plainly see, your time is running out. This will be my final warning. The other teams have either accomplished their goals or are close to completing them. Please hasten to complete yours. I'm sorry it has come to this."

Before we can say a word, Dianah turns around brusquely. She makes her way through the throng of travelers and soon disappears.

I wonder if Dianah's warning was necessary. We are proceeding as quickly as we can. We can only push matters so far before they blow up in our faces. We can only try our best to save ourselves and our dimension.

I put my arm around Aurora's waist to move us toward our boarding gate. She doesn't need prompting. I tell her quietly, "It won't be long before they start checking the LifeLike employment records. You'll be identified in the holofilm. I hope we're in the upper atmosphere by then."

Keeping her eyes forward, Aurora doesn't reply. Then, we walk into the security tunnel with our heads cast down.

CHAPTER 44

We walk past a diverse crowd of people using machines to print out their bag tags. I note a few elderly couples with Android assistants helping them. Check-in counters line each side of the tunnel as we plod farther in. Commercials for a variety of products and services play on the high walls above the counters. A drone sweeps by above our heads. Is it on routine patrol or looking for someone or something in particular? I tell myself it isn't looking for us.

We avoid a long line at the check-in counter thanks to our first-class tickets. An industrial Android takes our IDs and tickets. It places our IDs and open ticket packages on an inlaid computer screen.

The check-in counter is the first in a series of security tests. If our names are on a wanted list, this will be our last stop. I remove my microbuds. Sounds of the terminal flood my ears. The Android isn't talking. Either this one isn't as chatty as Randy, or we're in trouble. The artificial ticket-taker efficiently inputs our data on its screen. It waits for a response, and then its fingers skate over the screen again.

It looks up at us. "Just one minute."

I glance at Aurora. Her expression is placid, tempered with pure resolve.

From under the counter, the Android brings up something that looks like a gun. I flinch before I realize it's not a real gun.

"What's that?"

The Android turns to me. "An update to our procedure. Don't be alarmed. This device will stamp you with an electronic brand that verifies you've passed through the check-in counter and your tickets are genuine. The brand washes off with water, but don't wash it off until you've completed the screening process. Please stand still."

The gun flashes.

"Now you," it says to Aurora. Another flash.

"Are you traveling with luggage?"

"No," I answer.

Seconds later, boarding passes slide out from slots in the front panel of the condensed workstation.

"Please take your boarding passes." It hands us our tickets. "Enjoy your flight in the spacious skies of *Dandelion Spacelines*."

After retrieving my ticket with a silent thank you to the powers that be, we continue our journey through the security tunnel.

"It's interesting to learn that spaceline ticket forging has become a significant problem in the last eight years."

Aurora nods.

"You're awfully quiet. Is something bothering you?"

"I am focused on the mission."

"The mission doesn't really start until we land. I think you can lighten up 'til then."

"Are you telling me how to act and feel?"

"I'm not that stupid."

Aurora doesn't react. I thought I'd get a laugh out of her with that line.

"Are you concerned about killing a Human?" I ask quietly.

"Now that I've seen the destruction Kronak has wrought, I don't have *za* slightest reservation about killing him."

"Okay."

Something is on her mind, and I don't think it's the mission.

We move ahead at a pace to blend in with the crowd around us. We are early for our flight. I pray for both of us, in case Aurora doesn't pray, that our departure will be on time. Our next stop is the station that secures the departure gates. This inspection will be more rigorous than our first test.

The line isn't long for either coach or first class. Spaceline tickets are expensive, and cabin space is limited. We enter the shorter first-class line. When we approach the female security agent, Aurora declares herself to be an Android. The agent asks her to remove her cap. She examines Aurora's ID and passport, then checks to see if her name or photo appears on a current "no-fly" list. The agent rechecks Aurora against her ID photo.

"Have you changed your hair color recently?"

"Yes. I do it often."

"Why?"

"I'm a creative person. I like changing my looks."

Handing Aurora's ID and passport back to her, the agent points to a line branching off from the one I will be going through. After removing her shoes and loose items, Aurora will pass behind a blue screen, which is like an X-ray machine without the radiation. Aurora's shoes and loose items follow her on a second conveyor belt dedicated to Android inspection.

So far, so good. Aurora has not yet been identified as a person of interest. Now that we've reached this point, I'm actually a little surprised Aurora's name hasn't popped up. It means the authorities have yet to examine LifeLike's employment records.

It's my turn now. I tender my ID and passport. The agent asks me to remove my cap and sunglasses. Acting confident, I shake out my beautiful Auburn hair after removing it from the confines of my cap.

The agent spends more time examining my passport and photo against her "no-fly" list than she did with Aurora. The extra time may be due to the sunglasses. I may have gone overboard by adding them to my disguise.

The agent looks up at me. "Is this your first spaceline flight, Mister Faulk?"

I think she's checking my *Anglish* comprehension and accent.

"It's far from my first flight, Agent Sinclair. You can see from my passport that I'm well-traveled."

"I see from your passport that you've changed your hair color. May I ask why?"

"I'm getting gray around the edges."

"Are you traveling with the Android I just cleared?"

"Yes. Traveling with a beautiful associate makes me self-conscious about my looks. Hence, the dye job."

Agent Sinclair's eyes telegraph her suspicion. "I find it odd that two people traveling together have recently changed their hair color."

"Last I checked, there's no law against dying one's hair."

"I'm going to have to detain you, Mister Faulk."

"On what grounds?"

"On suspicion of your involvement with terrorism."

"You can't be serious. I'm a former *NSS* Agent and Agency Director. Check my background in your database."

I want to add, *you lazy woman,* but I stop myself. The security gauntlet has me on edge—for good reason. Agent Sinclair takes her time checking me out. She doesn't like me for some reason. Maybe she'd prefer to be travelling on vacation to an exotic country rather than being here with me. Whatever. She's not the first person I've rubbed the wrong way.

After several tense moments, I watch Sinclair make copies of my registration card and ID.

"You are cleared for now, but I'm going to forward your information to the *FDI* for further examination."

"Be my guest."

She stamps my passport and hands my documents back to me.

"Enjoy your flight," she says with a forced smile.

I fully intend to, now that we've cleared the final hurdle to our flight.

When I meet Aurora on the other side of the conveyor belts, I'm surprised by her grim countenance.

"We made it through. Why aren't you smiling?"

No answer.

After putting on our shoes and collecting our loose items, we set off for our boarding gate. It is not a long walk to Gate Number Three of the *Dandelion Spaceline.* We take our seats to await the boarding call.

My holophone vibrates. I fish it out of my pants pocket. Aurora looks mildly interested. I don't recognize the series of letters and numbers on the screen. I decide to answer it. A familiar voice comes through the speaker.

"Derrick?"

"Adrien!" I say too loudly.

Aurora looks surprised, and then she smiles.

"I was afraid I'd never reach you when I tried to call on your private line."

"Aren't I allowed to change phones once every eight years?"

"It's so good to hear your voice. Aurora is with me."

Aurora leans toward me. "Hello, Adrien."

"Hello, my dear."

"We're going to change places for more privacy. Hold on."

I point to a group of empty seats on the other side of the boarding gate. Aurora follows me there. We sit near an expansive window that overlooks our docked spaceliner with its powerful combination of engines under the wings and tail section.

I press the hologram button on my phone to see if Adrien is aging gracefully. "Okay. We can talk now."

"When I saw you on the news, I thought it would be wise to fill you in on something important."

"Go ahead," Aurora says anxiously.

"I sent a complex computer virus to LifeLike from an untraceable account. It successfully breached their security walls and wiped out the company's database, including its employment records. It means you won't be discovered in the company's data files. Unfortunately, I had to wipe out the company's entire database, including evidence of Kronak's criminal activities, because I didn't have specific file names to attack. You are still vulnerable to facial recognition from the lobby holofilm. However, I reviewed a copy of the file, and I don't believe there is enough definition in your images to make a reliable identification."

"That's a relief. I suspected something besides dumb luck was keeping us incognito."

"Thank you," Aurora adds.

"Let me ask you something that's been on my mind, Adrien. Isn't it likely that dopplegangers are wandering around in this timeline: One from the past and one from the present?"

"It's not something you have to worry about, Derrick. When you left for the mission, the phenomenon of time travel wiped out your timeline in this present. You have created a new timeline. Now, here's the paradox: You can exist simultaneously in the past *and* the future as long as you don't time-travel. In other words, you didn't exist until you arrived in the future, which is our present. Fortunately, the fabric of time works this way.

"That actually makes sense."

"There's only one problem. The corollary holds true for the past as well. If you return to the past, your timeline here will evaporate. What you've done here will be undone, and you will create a new timeline in the past."

"You never told me I'd be traveling to the future with no return ticket."

"I know. I'm sorry."

"You're sorry?"

I turn to Aurora. "When were you going to tell me about this?"

"I didn't know anything about it until Adrien just mentioned it. And the 'one-way trip' is irrelevant now. We know following Kronak will require more than four days."

I stare at her, feeling powerless. Then I turn back to the holophone. "What about Kristina?"

"She'll have to stay here, too. I've called her. She knows."

"No wonder you didn't want her on this mission."

"That and her lack of training."

Another question occurs to me. "Why did you give us a ninety-six-hour deadline if you knew we weren't coming back?"

"I thought the deadline would intensify your concentration on the mission."

I want to scream at Adrien, but instead, I analyze his three-dimensional features. His hair has gone completely gray. The lines around his eyes and across his forehead have multiplied, but the glow in his eyes remains.

"I see you looking at me. At least *you* haven't aged eight years. You'll acclimate to your new situation."

"Oh, thanks, Great One."

"Can we please move on, Derrick? Tell me what's happened in the last three days and what your plans are."

Relentless Adrien.

Reluctantly, I tell Adrien everything I remember. If I leave something out, Aurora supplements the story. When we finish, I'm still angry. Before we can continue the conversation, a news update appears on the wall on the other side of the boarding desk.

"Hold on," I tell Adrien.

Aurora and I put on our microbuds.

CHAPTER 45

The now familiar face of a grim female reporter appears in a close-up on the wall.

"This is Lydia Greenspan with WLBC News, bringing you another tragic story of death and destruction. Authorities believe this latest attack is related to the *Velanox Tower* attack reported yesterday."

The shot changes to reveal a smoking bridge ruptured in the middle, with both halves plunged into the waters of a bay.

"At *Eight of the Clock* this morning, an inconspicuous air breather slammed into the *Sansa Berlando Sea Gate Bridge*. The death toll is yet to be determined, but it is believed to be high because traffic was heavy during the morning rush hour."

"Are you getting news of another attack?" I ask Adrien.

"I keep five news feeds going. They're all reporting the same story."

A pause. "I hope we're not too late."

I remove my microbuds. Aurora does the same. We don't need more tragic details. We know what we have to do. Adrien does, too.

"Contact me from the capital city when you've ended your mission in *Amperigo*, regardless of the outcome. I'll courier alternative identification, passports, and money should you need them. I'll also send you open-ended spaceline tickets to come straight back here. We have to keep you two out of the net of the authorities. I know I've acted unilaterally without informing you. We'll talk more about it when you return. Until then, good luck and good hunting."

I end the call without saying goodbye.

"That was rude," Aurora tells me.

"I'm not sorry."

Moments later, the first call for our flight is announced.

■ ■ ■

We are in our seats, waiting to take off. A laconic voice filters into the cabin through the comm channel.

"Ladies and gentlemen, this is your Flight Captain speaking. One of our passengers has been delayed in traffic. Due to the high cost of these excursions, we are bound by contract to wait an additional fifteen minutes beyond our scheduled departure time to give passengers a chance to board. Please bear with us, and I sincerely apologize for the delay."

I hope the Captain isn't lying. The Flight Attendant checking us on board seemed dazed by the news on the wall. She took a cursory glance at our tickets and didn't bother to make eye contact. Just when I thought we had made it through the security filters, more anxious moments arrive.

I glance at Aurora. Her eyes are closed. "Are you asleep?" I ask quietly.

No answer. Aurora is smart. Sleep when you can get it. I try to follow Aurora's example. It doesn't work. *Okay,* I tell myself. *Try to rest. You need it for your concussion's sake.* But I can't. My thoughts keep returning to Dianah and the warning she imparted to Kristina and me. Is she running out of patience with us? If a team of *FDI* agents yanks us off this spaceliner, will that be it? *Poof.* Dimension erased.

I hear footsteps coming down the boarding ramp. It sounds like more than one set of shoes. Now, I hear voices. If only one passenger is boarding, why am I hearing two sets of footsteps and voices?

The cabin boards from the rear. I turn to see two uniformed men push through the doors. Both men wear *Federated Navalus* uniforms. The man nearest me sports a chest full of medals and three stars on his collar. The trailing officer does an about-face after shaking hands with his superior. The three-star *Inspiritor* takes a seat in the aisle across from us. Removing his cap and smoothing his short black hair, he offers me a smile. I smile back. My heart rate returns to normal. I'm certain I've aged at least three years in the past three days.

The Flight Captain announces our departure. The inner and outer boarding doors close automatically. I hear a knock from the outer door, signaling our readiness to depart. Through the porthole at Aurora's seat, I watch fuel and battery lines drop from the fuselage.

Closing my eyes, I hear the engines whine and feel the spaceliner move away from the gate.

■ ■ ■

Ninety minutes later, I awaken to the Flight Attendant announcing that we are on our final glide path. I have slept soundly with only a faint recollection of weightlessness when my seat belt and single shoulder harness tightened to keep me from floating to the ceiling.

Aurora is already awake and alert. I wink at her. Playing along, she winks back. Other than that, we have nothing more to say to one another. We are bracing for the grind through customs and whatever awaits us on the road ahead.

Aurora studies a map on her holophone as we touch down. She will be our navigator. We've traveled almost five thousand *milas* from launch to landing in a mere ninety minutes. Like our journey in time, the relatively easy part is over. It gets exponentially harder from here.

The customs clerks work slowly. The word "alacrity" is not in their vocabulary. I try not to waste energy with my impatience. It often comes automatically. In the bitter end, we make it through without incident. I think you would have to be armed with a nuclear bomb to trigger an alarm here.

We shop for clothing, suitcases, toiletries, binoculars, and other essentials, including more hair dye, in case we need it. My bankroll of *Daras* is feeling the bite of all the purchases up to this point.

For our next objective, we head to the vehicle rental counters. We find one with a good selection of all-terrain models. We choose a muscular model with four-wheel plus angular drive and a powerful hydrogen-fusion engine. The vehicle's shape reminds me of a .50-caliber bullet resting on 30-inch wheels, ending with a cockpit windshield.

When I try to conclude the transaction, the rental agent tells us he can't accept cash, which is understandable and standard practice for the industry. We have no choice except to use Kronak's corporate card. We're not worried about the authorities intervening in a non-extradition country like *Amperigo,* but our use of the card will likely alert Kronak to our presence here.

The credit card is declined. It's been canceled—probably by Kronak. After some negotiations, the rental agent accepts three hundred *Daras* extra for the contract. We've procured transportation, but it hasn't helped my wallet.

Before leaving the rental counter, I ask the agent if he can recommend a local gun dealer.

Tilting his head slightly, the agent says, "This must be your first visit to *Amperigo.* Guns have been outlawed here for over a decade. Only the *politzia* and *Militarians* are permitted to have them."

I turn to Aurora. She shakes her head in disgust.

Our already difficult mission has just become even harder.

CHAPTER 46

We've used up more than half the day to pass through the spaceport. Fortunately, *Amperigo* accepts *Dara* currency. Otherwise, we'd have been further delayed. It feels good to be on the road to our final objective. *Amperigo* is a beautiful country, at least the part of it we are seeing now. The weather is slightly overcast, with moderate temperatures. We are driving with the windows down to enjoy the mild ocean breeze.

The roads are well-maintained. We've already encountered our first toll booth. This is the second one we are pulling up to now, about fifteen *milas* down the road. Two *Politzia* cruisers flank the booth, the same as the last toll. I guess we know where the maintenance funds come from.

The drivers in this country are lunatics. I estimate their average speed is a hundred *milas* per hour. That's thirty *MPH* over the limit. Oddly, I haven't seen any cars pulled over by patrol cruisers. It seems the Highway *Politzia* is only concerned with chasing vehicles that don't pay their tolls.

After clearing the toll booth, we pass a series of ranches and estate homes, hidden behind impressive gates and complex arrays of tropical shrubbery. I'm sure the cost to maintain the landscaping of a single one of these properties would exceed my yearly salary at the *NSS*.

Beyond the guard rail to our right, a sheer drop-off leads to white sandy beaches and the ocean hundreds of feet below. I figure the property owners have tunnels to the beaches or dual-purpose roto-jet-copters to get them there. It follows that the beaches are private for seclusion and the prevention of kidnapping.

In the distance, we can see a mountain range. Aurora is scanning the range with a pair of outrageously priced binoculars we picked up at the spaceport. The peaks are shrouded in a formation of dome-shaped, lenticular clouds. The intermolecular lenses can see through just about anything besides solid walls.

"Terraces have been dug into the mountains," Aurora reports. "They are planted with a variety of fruits and vegetables." She swings the binoculars to another location. "Oh, wait. Now, I'm seeing terraces surrounded by barbed wire fences. I see people clothed in dirty rags wandering among tin huts."

"The mountain people must have been stripped of everything they own," I theorize. "They must be dissidents, troublemakers, the chronically unemployed, and petty criminals thrown together like the refuse of an orderly society."

Aurora carefully returns the binoculars to their case and puts the case into a pocket inside the front door. She turns to me with a pained expression. "If what you're saying is true, then we can assume the government is a form of Fascism. It culls society for the benefit of the rich and the working class. And if some in the wealthy class are fugitive criminals, the government grants them asylum, as long as they pay enough for it and behave themselves."

"Now that we've had our social studies class, let's talk about the weapons situation."

Aurora turns and focuses on the road ahead. "I'm sure you've given it some thought. You first."

"I don't think it makes sense to procure our weapons from an underground source. It would take time, and it's too dangerous."

"I completely agree."

"That makes our decision easy. We collect our guns from the first Androids we kill."

"It's the only choice."

Easy to say. Hard to do, I leave unsaid.

We drive on in silence, admiring the scenery and thinking private thoughts.

After twenty minutes of this, Aurora says, "You asked me what was on my mind before. I'm ready to tell you."

"Go ahead."

"I feel comfortable with you on a professional level. That's not the case on a personal level."

It's a good thing Aurora has brought this issue to our attention at this juncture. Unresolved tension between us can affect our performance later when it counts. I need to organize my thoughts before responding. It's too easy to say the wrong thing.

"Everything changes, Aurora. I've been admiring the way you've grown. And I'll admit it's been hard for me to separate my personal feelings for you from my operational duties."

"I thought I'd never see you again," Aurora says, suddenly angry. "It took me time to accept it, but I did, eventually. Now, Adrien has thrown us together again. The mission is hard enough without ripping open old wounds."

"Adrien promised to keep us apart. But there is a cruel practicality to consider. We're the two most capable and trustworthy people Adrien knows. We have to put the mission ahead of our personal feelings."

"That sounds good, but I think we both know it's bullshit."

"Okay, let's think of it this way. We have a duty to protect each other and a duty to accomplish the mission. They are both equally important."

"You're so damn practical. I'm not fully Human, but I can feel more than you can. Why is that?"

"You don't know how I feel. And I would add something to what you just said. You aren't fully Human *yet.*"

"Maybe in your eyes alone."

Aurora seems satisfied with my answer. We drive on in silence for another hour. Aurora has been staring out her window, enjoying the ocean breeze and thinking God knows what. Then, she eases back into her seat and picks up her holophone.

"We have another hundred and fifty *milas* to go to the target. We should look for a place to stay."

"No argument here."

Due to the time change, nightfall will be coming early for us. Our bodies need a chance to adjust. They will be hungry for lunch by the time it's past the dinner hour here. Finding lodging now will give us an opportunity to eat and get a long night's sleep.

Half an hour later, we find a fishing village that caters to tourists. From her maps, Aurora selects an inn with a four-*stella* rating that serves good food and has comfortable rooms. The front desk agent doesn't ask questions, and he is happy to accept a cash deposit.

I can use a good drink and a square meal. I make it a habit not to drink on missions, but I'm in the mood to celebrate. I think it's due to my mending relationship with Aurora. I'm surprised to discover the degree of guilt I've been carrying since our breakup. I feel lighter and, yes, happier.

The room is adequate, with two double beds. Aurora lifts the half-open shade on an oblong window, which is designed to emulate an expensive cruise ship. The unmasked window reveals a glorious sunset on a calm, shimmering sea.

We take turns washing up and changing clothes. By this time, we are both famished.

Avoiding the elevator, we take a leisurely walk down three flights of stairs to the dining room. Aurora wears a pair of white jeans and a white blouse. Her black hair counters the outfit nicely. Black flat shoes complete her simple attire. I've thrown on a fresh shirt and jeans. I don't care what I look like. I'm just glad to be alive and temporarily safe with someone I trust at my side.

We take a table with an ocean view. Night has fallen, but the sea is illuminated by lights along the pier.

I order an expensive bottle of Cabernet and the *Amperigo* version of a chopped steak with a baked potato and green beans. Aurora orders something comparable to a snapper filet with carrots and peas. As we enjoy our food, two officers in black uniforms enter the dining room. They wear vests emblazoned with the words *Politzia Amperigo*. At this early dinner hour, only one other couple occupies the room. The alpha officer with stripes and gold bars on his shoulders scans the room. His eyes pass over us. His gaze fixes on Aurora momentarily. They move in tandem toward our table. I'm thinking I will have to call Adrien for bribe money.

The officers pass by our table before taking a table behind us with a view of the entire room in typical law enforcement fashion. It's harder to relax with the black clad officers in the room, but our first glass of wine helps us to settle. It is grown and bottled in *Amperigo* with a twelve percent alcohol content. We had no objection to the extra kick when our waiter showed us the bottle.

I've been trying not to reach for Aurora's hand since the time we walked down the stairs. With the wine in me, I can no longer resist the urge. I extend my hand across the table and wrap it around hers. She is startled at first, and then she squeezes my hand back.

"I'm falling in love with you again." The words tumble out of my mouth of their own volition.

Aurora looks at me intently. "I've never truly fallen out of love with you, Derrick."

I want to lean across the table to kiss her, but it is too wide.

A tear rolls down Aurora's cheek. I get up to kiss it away, and then I kiss Aurora deeply on the lips. I suddenly become aware that I'm making a display. It's the last thing we need right now. The officers are watching. I smile at them lamely. One of them raises a glass to me. He seems to understand. It is now apparent that the *Politzia* stopped here for no other reason than to enjoy a good meal, probably with a discount.

We finish our dinner and return to the room. As soon as the door closes, Aurora and I embrace in a long kiss. Moving to the bedroom, I undress her slowly, kissing and caressing her lips and body every step of the way.

When she is naked, Aurora helps me undress. It is difficult for me to restrain my desire. When we are both fully undressed, we fall onto the bed, embracing, savoring our nakedness, and rolling back and forth on top of one another. Then, we make love and, afterward, sleep like the dead.

CHAPTER 47

We wake up mid-morning to sunshine and winds whipping off the ocean. The surf pounds the shore. After a hearty breakfast of eggs and pastries, Aurora sits opposite me, drinking herbal tea. I'm on my third cup of coffee. If we were not facing a battleground a hundred miles ahead, this would be the start of a relaxing and, I believe, joyful vacation.

Since awakening, we've enjoyed each other's company without much conversation. I don't believe either of us wants to discuss what happened last night. It happened. We'll figure it out later. Today is another day, maybe the most important one of our lives. My thoughts turn back to the mission—the endgame—whatever it will turn out to be.

After I settle our bill at the front desk, we throw our bags in the trunk of our all-terrain vehicle. I expect we'll have enough *Daras* for tolls, food, and a remainder for lodging at the spaceport on the return trip. That's thinking positively in terms of our finances and our overall chances of survival.

As I pull out of the hotel parking lot, a *politzia* cruiser screams past us, followed by an *ambulancia*.

"There must be an accident somewhere up ahead," I tell Aurora.

Nodding in response, she tunes to a local *Anglish* news station. We catch an update about a five-car collision involving a chemical tanker truck that exploded in the crash. The crash is reported to have occurred on *Amperigo* Country Highway Five. We are on Highway Five.

More *politzia* cruisers and *ambulancias* bull their way past us.

"Just what we need. We'll have to find a detour or go off-road to get around it."

Aurora consults her maps for alternate routes. "There is one inland road we can use if the delay is bad enough. We can also cut through a strip of farmland, but we could be arrested for trespassing," she adds matter-of-factly.

We round a wide bend. The highway is built on flatland that extends to the foot of the mountains. We can see vehicles backed up for *milas.*

"I guess we'll have to try the inland road."

"Wait!" Aurora says. "We passed a private *Aeroporta* a few miles back. If we turn around, maybe we can hire someone to roto-copter us to Kronak's castle."

I consider Aurora's proposal. If we go any further, we'll be stuck in the crush of the stalled traffic. The crash site will take hours to clean up, and maybe even longer, due to chemical contamination. The inland routes are "iffy" at best.

"Makes sense. Let's try the *Aeroporta.*"

We are betting everything that we've located Kronak's lair. I make an illegal turn, over and across the concrete median. The angled four-wheel drive comes in handy.

On our way to the *Aeroporta,* Aurora tunes to the *Consolidated British Communications System* for an international news update. One of the stories bears the fingerprints of one of Kronak's custom Androids. An apparent assassination occurred at night in the French capital city of *Pallais.* A sniper shot and killed a French Cabinet Minister with a bullet fired from almost forty-five hundred feet away. I know that's an impossible shot for a Human to make. According to the reporter, "The killer or killers are still at large despite a multi-national, inter-agency manhunt."

The incident underscores the need to dry up the supply of Kronak's Androids—quickly. Only Aurora and I are in a position to do it fast enough.

It doesn't take us long to reach our destination. From the standard fencing, I can tell the installation's function is commercial. It appears that the *Aeroporta* is used for air freight shipments, plus the storage and maintenance of private jet-copter and sonic-jet planes. As we approach the front entrance, I can see a number of luxury jet-copters and sleek sonic-jet planes parked at angles in a secured area.

The guard at the gate is a well-groomed young man. He's moderately good-looking, and by his age, I'd guess this is his first job out of school. I'm hoping he's Human.

The young man is dressed in a white jumpsuit with a red and gold logo stitched onto his shirt. Holding a clipboard, he speaks to us in his native tongue. I don't understand a word, and neither does Aurora.

"Do you speak *Anglish?*"

"Some little," he answers me.

"We have an emergency," I tell him. He does not understand. Aurora leans across from her seat.

"*Emergencia.*"

He shakes his head. "No," he struggles for the word, "*understanda.*"

Aurora gives him a pained expression and holds her hands in a prayer pose.

The young man points to her. Then he points to a rectangular one-story building inside the gate to our right. He nods enthusiastically. The gate rail goes up.

I put my hands up in a prayer pose, nod and smile, and drive through.

Someone here must speak Anglish. I park in a space that appears to be marked for visitors. We exit the car. A plaque beside the front door of the building says something that looks vaguely like "Headquarters and Executive Offices." The door is not locked. Maybe this is a friendly place.

We go in. A middle-aged man hunches over a workstation in the middle of an open bullpen office. Three more unattended workstations surround the man in the middle of them. A hallway behind him leads to more offices. I hear chatter coming from down the hall. The place is well-maintained and appears to be newly renovated. There are a few pieces of old furniture scattered against the walls. I figure they'll be replaced as soon as the budget allows. The man looks up at us, startled. The first thing I notice is the color of his eyes. One is blue, and the other is gray. This guy either has a glass eye or a bionic augmentation. He wears a gray jumpsuit with three silver bars on the collar and the red and gold logo stitched into his shirt. His name, stitched below the company emblem, reads *Pembra.* I've never encountered a name like that before.

Pembra says something to us in his native, indecipherable language. My intuition tells me he is a sharp individual. His brown hair is combed neatly, and there is a glow in his right eye. From five feet away, I can't discern which eye is bionic.

"Do you speak *Anglish,* sir?

He points to his shirt. "I am Pembra. Who are you, and why are you here?"

I was hoping for "How may I help you?" but Pembra's *Anglish* comprehension more than makes up for his curt manner.

"My name is Derrick Faulk, and this is my associate, Aurora Zolotov. We have to ask you for a favor. We're here from *the Federation of Corporate States* for a critical business meeting, about a hundred *milas* north of here. Due to the traffic tie-up on the highway, we will be late for the meeting unless we can get a roto-copter ride. We can pay you. Will you help us?"

Pembra motions with his right hand. "Show me ID."

I pull out my registration card. I make a subtle show of it to Aurora. My intuition tells me again that it would be a colossal mistake to represent ourselves as government officials.

Pembra examines our IDs. He doesn't check his workstation to see if we are wanted criminals. We've made a good impression.

"Have seats." Pembra motions for us to bring two chairs stacked against the wall.

The chairs turn out to be lightweight and not too comfortable, compared to the ones we're used to.

"So, you will need the round trip from this place you are going?"

"That's correct," Aurora chimes in.

"How long you stay there?"

"A day or two, depending," Aurora adds.

"This can be arranged. Tell me first. Are you *Amperigo* government agents?"

"What makes you think that?" Aurora asks sweetly.

"You know it is illegal for me to do what you ask?"

"We aren't aware of that," Aurora goes on. "We don't want to get you in trouble. It's just. Well, you see. We've come all this way."

"Why is what we ask illegal?" I interject.

"It takes days to get a flight plan filed and approved. You don't have days."

Pembra may be telling the truth or lying to raise the price of the trip. Whatever the case, we're in no position to argue with him.

"What is your business?" Pembra asks me ominously. I don't think he liked me asking the legal question.

"It's technology-related," I say vaguely. "We are under contract not to discuss the details with anyone outside of the company."

"Tell me the company."

"LifeLike Technologies," Aurora says, smiling.

Pembra queries his inlaid computer. "Ah, yes. Big company. Lots of business. You have business cards?"

Aurora digs for hers. I hand Pembra my fake business card. "I'm a freelance consultant."

Aurora finds one of her LifeLike cards. "Here you go." Again, the smile.

Pembra examines the cards and then puts them down dramatically. He steeples his hands in front of his face—a show of confidence.

"This ride you ask for. It is not cheap."

"How much?" I ask.

"We are looking at four thousand of your *Daras.*"

We only have half the amount left in our bankroll.

"We'll pay you two thousand now, and the rest when the pilot picks us up."

Pembra considers my offer. "This I don't do." He turns to Aurora. "But I make exception for this beautiful, sweet woman."

"Thank you for the compliment and your kindness," Aurora says, sounding remarkably authentic.

"You have car?"

"Yes," I confirm.

"Parking will cost fifty *Daras* per day."

Aurora and I exchange a look. She smiles, but I see a flicker of concern in her eyes.

We shake hands with Pembra on the deal.

CHAPTER 48

The roto-copter soars over the mountains to avoid the main highway. The ship is an old model scrounged from the military and converted into a craft used for medical emergencies and odd jobs. Our excursion falls into the latter category. Aurora and I are buckled into our seats behind an aged pilot, who, fortunately, doesn't have much to say. All I know about him is his name, *Jacquomon;* that, and he's on his third career, he'll never retire, and he's originally from *Sadd Afrika.*

Belted in beside me, Aurora pores over a holomap. "Move due east to the cliffs," she tells our pilot.

I look down on the cliff tops, searching for a compound with a castle towering up from the middle of it. So far, no luck. Another moment of truth is fast approaching.

"Hover," Aurora tells Jacquomon.

The copter steadies. At five hundred feet above the cliffs, we have a comprehensive view of the landscape below us. The castle is nowhere in sight.

"This is where it should be," Aurora says dejectedly.

"Let's drop down for a closer look," I say.

Jacquomon decreases altitude slowly.

Still, nothing.

"Move farther east," Aurora says.

Suddenly, the castle appears on a shelf built into the face of the cliff. Only half of it is in sunlight.

I grab Aurora's hand. "You found it!"

She squeezes back. "*We* found it."

"Where *de ya* want me to put *ya down?*

Jacquomon has asked a sobering question.

Aurora looks at me for the answer. She's done her part. It's now my turn.

"Set her down on the top of the cliff."

"*This'll* be a fast delivery. *Ya* bounce out when I *tuche* down. Then, I'm off. Call Premba on his secure line when *yer* ready *ta* be picked up.

We acknowledge the brief instructions. A very lonely feeling steals over me.

The landing is smooth and goes without a hitch despite the wind. The wind was up when we left the hotel. It's stronger here due to the ocean exposure.

We're wearing all-weather, one-piece coveralls with pockets everywhere and high-traction boots. Our pockets are filled with rations and the few medical supplies we bought with our clothing in the fishing village. At this point, the weapon I dumped at the spaceport would feel very comfortable against my body.

Standing beside me, Aurora grabs my arm. "You know that *ve* don't have an extra two thousand *Daras* for the return trip. How are *ve* going to get back to the *Aeroporta?*"

"Kronak must have piles of cash hidden in the castle. Don't worry about it now."

"I don't waste time worrying, Derrick."

"I wish I could say that."

Moving to the edge of the cliff, we look down. At first glance, all I can see is a sheer drop from the rock face to the top deck of the castle. It's at least a hundred feet below us.

A gust of wind almost blows me into Aurora. We'd be tumbling over the cliff if I didn't regain my balance. As I pull Aurora backward two paces, I see something move a few feet below us. Aurora sees it, too. It's a momentary distortion in the rock face. I lower myself to a prone position on the cliff. While I'm pulling forward, I'm about to ask Aurora to hold my legs when I feel her hands already placed there.

With half my chest over the cliff, I reach down. Instead of rocks, I feel something coarse and solid. I pull farther over the edge. Aurora holds my legs tighter. I lean closer to the surface I'm feeling. Breaking through the holowall optical illusion, I see a concrete staircase leading down to the castle's top deck. It's all there, including the massive telescope—just like the painting. I push backward and report my findings to Aurora.

We have a minor dispute over who will proceed first. I insist it should be me. Aurora allows me to be chivalrous.

With the issue settled, we cautiously make our way down the narrow steps. My intuition is tickling me. There must be something significant about the single-file construction of the steps. I decide to store the thought for future reference.

We reach the bottom. I step onto the deck and kneel to a crouch.

Surveying everything I can from this angle, I see no opposition. I motion for Aurora to follow me.

Kneeling next to me, she points to the base of the telescope. It's the only place for us to hide from view. As we approach, a circular trench surrounding the telescope appears—an even better place to take cover. We drop down into it.

There must be a door somewhere along the circumference of the inside wall.

The trench turns out to be a circular groove that the telescope uses to turn through 360 degrees. It's made of a self-lubricating material marketed under the brand name Perma-Slide. I learned about the all-weather product in connection with a case in my former career.

"I hear footsteps," Aurora whispers from behind me.

We crouch lower. The top of our hiding place is flush with the roof deck. Looking up, I watch the head and shoulders of a muscular Android pass by.

The next thing I know, Aurora jumps out of the trench. She crashes into the Android. They disappear from my view. When my reflexes recover, I peer over the edge.

Aurora has the Android pinned down with one hand on its chest. Using her legs as leverage, she pounds the Android's chest with her other hand in a fist.

Whump. Whump. Whump.

After three concussive blows, the Android lies motionless on the deck. Aurora can summon superhuman strength when needed. On our last mission, she was unaware of her strength until events threatened the mission. At the time, Aurora thought herself to be Human until a pre-programmed pulse forced her Android self to emerge. I thought she had gone berserk because I, too, thought Aurora was Human. The sudden transformation shocked us both.

Jumping out of the trench, I use my left hand to stand. I grab the long gun clutched in the Android's right hand. I have to pry open each digit to secure the weapon. Meanwhile, Aurora has liberated the Android's pistol from its holster.

Handing me the pistol, Aurora tells me to take the weapons back into the trench. "I'll handle the body," she adds.

I hold her forearm gently. "Are you okay?"

"I'm in full control of myself. This time."

I have to laugh. Aurora joins in, but only briefly.

With the body, ourselves, and the weapons safely hidden, Aurora sits on the Android's chest. From there, she inserts her thumbs into its ears.

"What are you doing?"

"Searching for files."

I wait about half a minute. "Which ones?"

"Be quiet. I'm trying to concentrate."

After about a minute, Aurora says, "There."

"What?"

"I have the combinations for all of the interior doors in addition to this one's posting schedule. The other files are for body functions and operating systems. In other words, this unit is no genius. I hope the other bodyguards are programmed the same way."

"Can you tell if the guards are linked for synchronized action?"

"No. I guess we'll find out soon enough."

I hold both weapons out to Aurora. "*À vous de choisir.*"

"Such a gentleman for giving me the choice."

She takes the pistol. I check the rifle's action. It's a heavy-caliber weapon. I assume it's primarily designed for long-range encounters.

"Let's find a way in. Ready?"

"As ever," Aurora answers.

We circle the base of the telescope until we find the outline of a door. "Oh, shit."

Like Kristina, Aurora generally avoids using curse words. She has a good reason for using one in this case. There is no keypad or any other way to open the door.

CHAPTER 49

I state the obvious. "The door must be locked from the inside."

Staring up at the rock face, Aurora uses a forearm to shield her eyes from the sunlight directly overhead. "This doorway is likely an emergency exit. It lines up with the hidden staircase."

"You're saying if all else fails, Kronak will use the exit and the concealed staircase to reach the top of the cliff. He'll have a jet-copter waiting for him there."

Aurora finishes my thought. "Possibly from the same *Aeroporta* we used. Maybe Pembra is on Kronak's payroll as well as ours."

"There has to be another way to get in."

Aurora jumps out of the telescope base with the ease of a gazelle. She offers me a hand.

Strapping the rifle over my shoulder, I pull myself up and out of the base. Dusting off my hands, I tell Aurora, "I could have gotten up just as easily, but not as gracefully."

She elbows me in the ribs. "I heard your bones creak."

"It must have been the crickets."

The thought strikes me: Aurora won't age. I will. I'll eventually die, and she'll go on—if we manage to survive the mission. It's a topic for serious consideration, but certainly not now.

Beyond the telescope base, we see a balcony railing wrought with intricate ironwork. Crouching, we make our way to the balcony facade. Aurora starts to rise. Holding her down, I take a peek over the railing. I see a long, narrow staircase curving to the left and down across the castle face to another balcony below us.

Crouching again, I notice a gate at the end of our balcony. I point to it. Aurora turns, and I duckwalk behind her to the gate.

To the left of the gate, we find an oval keypad. Aurora hesitates, and then she enters a three-number combination. She has memorized the combination to every entry point in the castle—or at least most of them.

Click.

Aurora pulls the gate open. I unstrap the rifle from my shoulder. Aurora pulls the handgun from her hip pocket. We advance down the staircase. I'm standing with my rifle trained on anything that moves below us. Aurora advances in a crouched position in front of me with one hand on the railing to steady herself, allowing me to have a clear line of fire.

Heading down the side of the castle, I feel naked. We aren't wearing protective vests. The fishing village market offered none for sale.

While I'm feeling exposed, an Android appears on the balcony below. It mounts a short staircase leading up to the one we are on. Opening the gate, it looks up. I have the head of the Android Defender centered in my scope. I pull the trigger. It is frozen. Instinctively, I find the safety and release it.

The Android peers into the scope of its rifle. I pull the trigger again. I'm unprepared for the rifle's recoil. It knocks me on my backside. I hear a projectile *zing* overhead.

Aurora swivels toward me. "Are you okay?"

Before I can answer, Aurora looks up and fires three times. The barrel of her handgun kicks up with each shot.

I rotate painfully to see an Android go down behind us at the top of the stairs. Pieces of it fly apart before falling.

I rise from the steps. My buttocks complain. I'll have a beauty of a bruise down there. The Android on the steps below us sprawls with its head blown off and holes in its chest. Judging by the remains, it looks like both of us killed the thing.

We switch places, with Aurora covering the staircase towering above us. Moving back to back down the stairs, we reach the lower balcony. Aurora hops off the steps and drops to a shooter's stance on the marbled flooring. Turning right and left with her gun ready, she motions for me to join her. I use the railing to jump down. A jolt of pain shoots up my spine. I hope I didn't compress a vertebra from my rifle's recoil.

I limp over to Aurora's position. I can guess what she's thinking: *Here comes the walking wounded.*

I use my free hand to massage my back. "I'll be okay. I just need to rub it out."

Aurora rubs the sore spot and then regards me with an appraising expression.

"I'm okay," I reiterate.

"If you say so." Aurora turns to the round wall about ten feet from the balcony's edge.

Cautiously, we move in for a closer look. We find the same outlined door as the one above—locked from the inside with no keypad for ingress.

I manage to stand. The pain is subsiding. Aurora looks up at me plaintively.

I shrug. "One staircase at a time."

We duckwalk back to the balcony's edge. This time, Aurora peers over the top of the facade.

"Another flight of stairs, shorter than the last one, curving right," she reports.

"Anyone down there?"

"Not yet."

"If the Androids are linked, their hub feed must be slow."

"It's possible. This is probably the first time the defense system has been tested. And I don't think Kronak expected an assault from the rooftop."

Aurora makes a good point.

I follow her through the gate. We reach the next balcony, only to find the same result—no way in. Peeking over the railing, I see another short flight of stairs. Beyond them lies a lush, manicured lawn. About a hundred feet away, a row of Royal Palms stands guard, separated by Italian cypress trees shooting up like pencils. The foliage blocks the view of the castle from the highway.

Suddenly, three Androids run from the castle and spread out on the lawn. I sight down at the Android on my right. Bracing myself for the recoil, I fire. I hit my target square in the chest. Aurora fires simultaneously, killing the Android on our left with three perfectly placed shots; one to the head and two in the chest. The one in the middle fires its pistol as we take cover. Three projectiles *whizz* over our heads.

My shoulder hurts from the recoil. I conclude that the butt end of the rifle is not made with enough cushioning for Humans.

The surviving Android jumps from the lawn onto the stairs. Aurora fires repeatedly at it. The Android's right arm flies off. The next two projectiles tear into its chest, blowing it off the stairs onto the lawn. It lies there with multiple holes in its center mass. Blood soaks the lawn around the Android's torso. We move down the last staircase, prepared for more resistance, but none comes our way.

Reaching the wreckage of the Androids, I quickly exchange my rifle for a pistol and grab another for backup. Aurora picks up a spare handgun, too.

We move to a standing position on either side of two arched entry doors inlaid with sculpted Human and Android figures in the throes of ecstasy. The LifeLike Technologies logo sits atop the doors. The castle is the company's new home.

I grab the copper handle nearest me and open the heavy door a crack. We have a way in. The dead Androids didn't get a chance to lock the entrance doors.

I exchange a set of hand signals with Aurora. Our assault plan is set. Before going in, I decide to use both of my handguns. They hang from my hands. Looking over to Aurora, I hold them up. She shakes her head. Each to their own.

Aurora counts down with her fingers and whispers, "One-Two-Three."

We pull open the twin doors.

CHAPTER 50

A giant black-and-white stairway greets us. The stairs have a white marble base covered with black carpeting on the steps. It appears that the side panels are carved from ivory with the same motif as the front doors. The stairway is at least ten feet wide. From an architectural standpoint, I have the impression that the stairs are flowing down into the center of the room.

Holding the heavy doors open at an angle for protection, we survey the room. The circular wall rises to a ceiling height of about twenty-five feet. It is covered in a shiny, gray, silk-like material. Paintings of all sizes hang at intervals on the wall. Sculptures on pedestals ring the room. An expensive grand piano sits in the center of the room's right quadrant.

We encounter no resistance. Aurora edges into the room with me. So far, I see nothing dangerous in the room, except maybe its alluring beauty.

Slowly, we split up and sweep the space. We find only the artwork and the silence of a tomb. Meeting again at the bottom of the stairs, I tell Aurora. "The room is a showcase worth millions of *Daras*. I don't think Kronak wants to damage it with a gun battle. He's confident he can stop us higher up."

Aurora nods. "Makes sense." She points upward. We climb the stairs warily, checking in every direction. My body aches, but I don't think the recoil damage has impaired my mobility. And, the symptoms from the bomb explosion have abated. I should be able to hold up my end of the bargain. It remains to be seen if that will be good enough.

Reaching the top of the stairs, we crouch below the last few steps.

Dead silence.

"We assume they are waiting for us," Aurora whispers to me.

I nod and peek over the top step. Movement.

Aurora hears it, too. She draws the second handgun from her other hip pocket.

More movement.

I hold up my index finger. "On one."

We crest the stairs and roll to opposite sides of the room.

Two guards pop up from behind a workstation in the center of the room. Before they zero in on us, Aurora and I roll to shooting postures and fire. The hail of projectiles shreds the Defenders into chunks that splatter against the wall and fall harmlessly to the floor. Their reaction time is slow for Androids. Either they are linked to a central hub, which inhibits their response interval, or Kronak hasn't had time to fine-tune them.

I stand while Aurora covers me. The room is a large office furnished only with an executive chair and a workstation. The circular wall is painted stark white. The office is unfinished. Kronak hasn't completely moved in.

Aurora stands. We scan the room. We find nothing besides the Android remains and the outline of a door behind the workstation. Embedded beside the door, I see a keypad. Smiling, I turn to Aurora. Advancing to the pad, she enters a three-digit combination.

Click.

"Hold position," I tell Aurora. She looks at me inquisitively.

I pull out my holophone and dial Pembra's number.

He answers gruffly.

"This is your friend, Derrick Faulk."

"When did you become my friend?"

"If Jan Kronak has you on retainer, I'll double what he pays you to ignore his next call."

Silence. I wait.

"You are sounding crazy, Derrick Faulk."

"I'm inside Kronak's castle. If I get any closer to him, he'll call you for an emergency evacuation."

"I say again. You are a crazy man. I'm hanging up."

"Wait."

The line goes dead.

"You *are* sounding crazy," Aurora says. "Kronak is a proven entity. Pembra hardly knows us."

"Pembra will think twice before he sends a copter for Kronak. I've just climbed into his head."

"Did you forget we're broke?"

"There's cash here. We'll find it."

"I hope you're right."

Aurora opens the unlocked door carefully. We stand on either side of it. Another staircase exactly like the one below awaits us, only this one is much shorter—maybe a ten-foot climb. The stairway is flush against bare walls. We are entering a space with no escape. Talk about shooting fish in a barrel—we're in one.

Pointing to myself, I enter and place one foot on the lowest stair. Aurora follows me inside the cramped space. The ceiling above the stairs is tall enough to allow us to walk upright. A square hatch with a keypad beside it awaits us at the top of the stairs. Aurora gives me the combination. I open the hatch and carefully push it aside. It slips from my hand and bangs against the floor of the level above us. I drop back with my guns ready, pushing Aurora back behind me.

I wait for a response. None comes.

Very possibly, killer guards could be waiting on the sides of the hatchway.

I turn to Aurora. "Go back down the stairs and wait for my all clear."

"No."

She pushes up beside me. "Let's take them by surprise. Me first. I'm faster. Enough of your gentlemanly behavior."

"Let me take a look before we make any more noise."

"If you get your head blown off, it's not my fault."

"Thanks. I'll be careful."

With my head level to the floor, I look around the room. It is an ample space with about a ten-foot ceiling. The walls are painted white, and the floor is concrete. If I had to guess, I'd say Kronak plans to use the room for manufacturing.

I mount another stair to get a better look. Checking all the angles, I see no Androids ready to pick me off. I catch sight of a wall that I couldn't see from below. The entire wall is a power grid. I'd say the grid confirms my theory about manufacturing space. Aurora follows me up the stairs, and then we are both standing in the empty room with our handguns raised.

As we head to the next doorway, it bursts open. Aurora and I dive to the hard floor. My shoulder screams. I ignore it.

After firing at the lead Android, we roll in opposite directions. When I'm right-side up again, I see the first Android lying face down with blood spreading around it on the floor. A second Android steps over the body. This one is carrying a rifle. We roll sideways again as it fires. In the enclosed space, the weapon's report sounds like a cannon. The whine of the ricochet against the bare concrete floor sounds like a scream. Before the guard can fire again, we blow it to smithereens. Chunks of it fly backward into the open doorway. The rifle clatters to the floor. We wait for more resistance. None comes.

Rising from the floor, we move to either side of the bloody door. I don't think either of us wants to look inside. I point to myself. Aurora waves me off. She peeks around the doorway and then enters. I follow her in.

She pivots. "Clear."

At this point, I'm wondering how much ammunition we have left. I tell Aurora to wait for me. I exit the stairway. Checking the fallen Android, I find two ammunition packets for handguns and one for a rifle. It's easy to tell the difference because the rifle projectiles are bigger and longer. I wouldn't want to get hit with one of those slugs. No wonder they deliver such a violent kickback. The handguns have a strong recoil, but it's manageable compared to the rifles. Both weapons are clearly set for Android use.

I examine the handgun clips. The projectiles are narrow and honed to a fine point at the tip. Each clip holds twenty projectiles, and there are five clips in a packet. I search for a clip release on my handgun, but can't find it.

Aurora pokes her head out of the doorway. "What are you doing?"

I hold up an ammunition packet. "Ammo."

"I picked up three of them from the Defenders we killed outside the front entrance. I was going to give you one," Aurora says.

I walk to the doorway, holding one of my handguns sideways and feeling embarrassed. "Do you know how to reload?"

"I'll show you." Aurora pushes a pressure plate on the right side of the stock surrounding the barrel. The clip pops out of the bottom of my grip. I have five projectiles left. I pocket the clip and insert a fresh one. It *clicks* into place. I follow the same procedure with my second handgun.

I look up to find Aurora watching me intently. "Ready?"

"As ever," I mimic back.

CHAPTER 51

Removing chunks of the second attacker, we make our way up another short staircase. Aurora hands the residue of the fallen Android to me, and I place the pieces quietly out of the way. We do this in case our entrance to the next floor requires a hasty retreat.

Our clothing is bloodied. I feel like a meat carver in an old-fashioned slaughterhouse. Maybe it will fool the Defenders into thinking we are wounded and give us an edge. If they serve no other purpose, our blood-smeared clothes are plain nasty to live in.

Aurora reaches the top of the staircase first. A keypad secures another square hatch above our heads. Aurora enters a combination and pushes the hatch open. I watch her head turn back and forth to survey the room. She stands on tiptoes to peek over the edge of the opening. Then, with agility, she raises herself into the room.

"Wait," she says in a loud whisper.

I climb to the last stair. Scanning the room, I see what looks like a Medical Bay in the far corner. A bed encircled by a diagnostic tunnel makes the identification easy. I've seen the flooring before at the LifeLike manufacturing facility. It is similar to the manufacturing flooring at AndroBiotica. The flooring is white with subtle treading to prevent slips. The floor tiles are highly resistant to viral and bacterial germs, as well as staining from bodily fluids. It's a safe bet the space outside of the Med-Bay will be used for additional manufacturing. The room is not yet built out.

It will take time for Kronak to import and assemble the necessary materials and machinery to return to full production. It will happen inevitably unless we do something about it.

I watch Aurora check the Med-Bay to make sure no Defenders are hiding there. After she finishes her inspection, she motions for me to come up.

When I stand with my guns ready, I see this room is the same size and shape as the one we just left.

I join Aurora. The Med-Bay is a simple setup. The operating table and diagnostic tunnel are surrounded by two monitors mounted on tripod floor stands. I figure the monitors are used to track vital signs and magnify minute surgical procedures. Two rows of white cabinets line the corner walls at a right angle. I open one and find vials of pharmaceuticals and surgical supplies. A refrigeration unit stands behind the table and diagnostic tunnel. I ask Aurora to open it. She punches in a code and swings the double doors open. There is a blood bank inside. I move in for a closer look. The blood bags inside are separated by a divider. On one side, the blood type is marked as AB-negative. The other bags are marked 0000. The quadruple zero type has to be Android blood. I assume the AB-negative blood is there for Kronak in case of emergency. Only about one percent of the Human race has an AB-negative blood type.

I pull away from the refrigeration unit. "The blood in there must be used to treat injured LifeLike Androids and Kronak."

Aurora nods.

Searching the cabinets, I find antiseptic towels we can use to clean ourselves up. As we are finishing, my holophone chimes. I recognize the number. When I accept the call, Aurora automatically assumes a covering position, though it's doubtful Kronak would risk a firefight with the Med-Bay equipment in the room. I switch the call to speaker so Aurora can hear.

"This is Pembra. How much do you pay for return copter trip?"

"How much are you asking?

"Fifty Thousand *Dara*."

"Whoa. I don't have that kind of money."

"Kronak is very generous man."

"He's not that generous."

"I take big chance if Kronak calls me for emergency exfil."

"You don't have to worry about Kronak."

"Why? You going to kill him?"

"Yes."

"You joking, right?"

"I couldn't be more serious."

Silence. Then, "How much you can pay?"

"Ten thousand *Daras*."

"*Reediculous*. I take my chances with Kronak."

"Twenty thousand."

"Forty."

"Twenty-five."

"Thirty-five."

"Thirty is my final offer, Pembra."

Silence, then. "I think about it." The line goes dead.

Aurora glares at me. "Where are we going to get thirty thousand *Daras*?"

"We'll commandeer the roto-copter if we have to."

"We can hire an air taxi," she counters.

"The castle is hidden in the middle of nowhere. There is no way we can depend on an air taxi to pick us up."

Aurora shakes her head in resignation. "As you say, I guess we'll have to improvise."

Another locked doorway awaits us in the middle of the adjacent wall. Where will it lead?

Aurora works the keypad to open the exit. It leads to a replica of the previous staircases. I follow Aurora up to the next level.

Reaching the top, Aurora pushes against the hatch above her head. It doesn't budge.

Turning to me, she says, "The door is locked—this time from *za* other side."

We retrace our steps to the Med-Bay floor.

"Any bright ideas?" I ask Aurora.

"There must be an armory in the castle. We could find something to blow the hatch open. It would give us the element of surprise."

"That will take time and invite more Defenders into the picture."

"*Vhat's* your idea?"

"Let's try blasting the door open with our handguns."

"By the time we get through, Kronak will have a squad of heavily armed Androids waiting for us."

"I think Kronak is running out of soldiers. His troops aren't coming up the stairs after us. They aren't rushing down to overwhelm us from above. I have a feeling Kronak is using his remaining chess pieces judiciously."

We stare at one another, maybe for the last time.

Then, "The escape route. One of us has to guard it."

"We can't split up, Aurora."

"Pembra's copter could be waiting for Kronak on the cliff. He hasn't accepted your offer."

"If Kronak escapes, we'll try to find explosives to blow up the castle. Then, we'll continue the hunt. I say we blast open the hatch now. We may never get a chance like this again."

"Maybe I'm overthinking the problem."

"You're playing the devil's advocate. It never hurts."

"What is devil's advocate?"

When I start to explain it, Aurora cuts me off. "Never mind. *Ve* have no time for definitions."

CHAPTER 52

We stand together at the base of the staircase leading up to the impenetrable trap door. On a count of three, holding a weapon in each hand, we open fire. The sound is deafening in the cramped space as the projectiles explode against the target. The outer layer of the hatch door disintegrates, revealing a shiny black layer of something. It could be a new type of shielding Kronak has invented. We empty our clips with only a shallow hole to show for our efforts.

"Damn!" Aurora shouts.

I start to think we'll need an explosive charge, as Aurora suggested. Then, an idea occurs to me.

"Stay here and guard the door. I'll be right back."

"Don't be a stranger."

I find the rifle on the floor of the Med-Bay where we left it. Grabbing the long weapon, I rejoin Aurora.

I hand her the rifle and carefully phrase what I'm about to say.

"You're stronger than me. I think you can use this without getting hurt. I'll warn you, though, it has a nasty kick."

"I'm happy to try anything at this point."

After checking the ammo in the clip, Aurora aims and fires three projectiles in succession without hesitation. The sound is concussive. The recoil rocks Aurora, but she handles it. She fires again. The hatch splinters. She fires again. The hatch door flies off its hinges.

Blue-white light filters into the staircase from the floor above. Aurora hands me the rifle. She re-arms with handguns.

"Stay here. Wait for my signal."

Abandoning my "gentlemanly behavior," I let Aurora march up the staircase. All I can see is her back. Then, I hear shots.

Aurora moves through the open hatch so quickly that the next thing I see is a square of empty space. Ignoring Aurora's instructions, I rush up the stairs and, rolling, throw myself on the floor of the next level. I count three Android bodies scattered around the room. The room resembles Kronak's penthouse office, albeit smaller, right down to the LifeLike Technologies logo stitched into the carpeting. One windowed wall faces the rooftop and the ocean beyond it. I make the space out to be a living room with one set of double doors and another odd-looking door to my immediate right.

Aurora rises from one corner. Blood spatters cover sections of the carpeting and walls. None of it is Aurora's.

The door near me is gray and shiny. It looks like porcelain, but I'm sure it's not. It is tall, rectangular, and has a keypad next to it. The doors across from it are not similarly secured. Aurora crosses to one side of the arched set of burnished mahogany doors sculpted and decorated with copper handles exactly like the entrance doors downstairs. I move to the side of the adjacent door.

My holophone chimes. Digging it out of my pocket, I tell Aurora, "It's Pembra, with the worst timing."

"Answer it. I'll clear the room."

Before I can stop her, Aurora slips through the door on her side.

When I connect, Pembra doesn't bother to introduce himself.

"Kronak just offered fifty thousand *Daras* for the copter ride."

"I thought we agreed on thirty thousand."

"Price is now sixty for you."

I hear gunshots through the door. "I'm busy at the moment, Pembra. I'll call you back."

Pushing through the door on my side, I enter a lavish master bedroom. Aurora is nowhere in it. I call out her name.

"In here."

Following the sound of her voice, I pass by a deep walk-in closet hung with racks of his-and-her clothing, shoe shelves, and a chest of drawers facing me at the end. An Android with a hole in its chest lies feet first and face-up at the closet entrance.

"Where are you?"

"Bathroom."

Passing another exit door on the wall to my right, I see a half-open crystaline door. I pass through it.

The master bath is breathtaking. The sight of Aurora isn't. She's holding a towel against her side with the other hand supporting herself at the edge of a black granite counter. My heart sinks. Aurora's breathing is labored.

"The Android came out of the closet. It shot me before I could kill it."

"Let me get you out of here."

Aurora puts an arm around my shoulder while she holds the towel firmly at her side.

Returning to the living room, I lay Aurora down on a sofa. A red stain is blossoming on the flesh-tone towel forced against her midriff. The living room and bedroom suite are decorated in LifeLike logo colors. The recognition of it makes me furious. The color scheme underscores Kronak's self-important image of himself.

I caress Aurora's forehead and cheek. "Hang on. I'll call Pembra to airlift you to a hospital."

Aurora nods.

I hear a sound to my left. My handguns are holstered. I whirl around in front of Aurora to protect her. Before I can draw, I see an Android rising from behind a credenza with its hands in the air.

"Don't shoot. I'm unarmed. My name is Walter."

Walter doesn't look dangerous, but I pull my weapon out for insurance. The Android is dressed smartly in a three-piece butler's suit with a gray-striped tie, gold tie clip, and cufflinks. A white pocket handkerchief completes the ensemble.

"I can help you," Walter says in an assured, calm voice.

"Tell me quickly how you can help."

"I am Jan Kronak's butler and assistant." Walter's eyes fix on Aurora. "Your partner needs immediate medical assistance."

"Where is Kronak?"

Walter uses his chin to indicate the shiny gray door.

"Why are you betraying your master other than to save your own life?"

"I do not like Jan Kronak."

This Android obviously has high mental processing capabilities. I assume Kronak is experimenting with higher learning, decision-making, and free choice, like Adrien. And perhaps Kronak created a high-func-tioning Android to keep him company. I doubt Walter's master expected anyone to find him here.

"How can you help Aurora?"

"I will operate on her in the Med-Bay. She is losing blood rapidly. I must begin soon."

With my handgun trained on Walter, I bend to Aurora's side. Her grip on the towel is loosening. "What do you think?"

"I think Walter is right." Aurora's eyes close.

"Alright. Take her downstairs." I indicate the gray door. "Do you know the combination to the keypad?"

"I am the only one besides Kronak who knows it."

"Write it down for me."

I double the towel over and hold it tight against Aurora's side. Her hand falls away. She is losing consciousness.

A minute later, Walter hands me a sheet of paper with a string of numerals printed out from Kronak's workstation. Carefully, I lay it aside and help him lift Aurora from the couch. When I'm satisfied that Walter has Aurora and the towel secured, I tell him, "I'm trusting you with her life."

"Her condition is serious. I will do my best."

"Do better than your best. Go."

Pulling my holophone, I call Pembra. He answers immediately.

"I'll pay your asking price for the ride. Wait for my call."

"You better, or I kill you and your partner."

"If you stop being an asshole, I might add a bonus." I disconnect the call before Pembra can reply.

I pick up the paper with the keypad combination printed on it. If Walter is on the level, the combination will work. If not, I'll be down-stairs to slaughter him before he can hurt Aurora.

Standing on one side of the gray door, I input the combination. I hear the sound of gears smoothly engaging, almost imperceptively. The shiny door slides open.

I wait by the side of the door.

Nothing happens. No deadly Androids jump out at me. No sound comes from inside the open door.

Taking a quick peek around the threshold, I glimpse a short corridor leading to another door painted in lustrous gold. I can make out a keyhole beneath the latch. The keyhole is an irregularity, but it makes some sense. It's not a keypad with a combination. The keyed door is Kronak's last bastion of security.

Sliding against the corridor wall, I reach the gold door. With my weapon in my left hand, I place my right hand on the door latch. Before pressing it, I examine the door. It is divided into a top and a bottom panel. The panels are slightly convex and appear to be made of the same ceramic-like material as the exterior door. For all I know, the panels could be packed with explosives that detonate if the key and the hand opening the door do not belong to Kronak.

I can't risk trying the handle or attempting to blow the door open. I must go downstairs and confront Walter. And hope Kronak hasn't already escaped.

CHAPTER 53

I rush down the stairs to the Med-Bay. There, I find Walter bent over Aurora's inert body on the operating table. The diagnostic tunnel has split in half, and it is stored under the table. Covering the floor in two long strides, I startle Walter.

"You almost made my scalpel slip," he exclaims.

I'm at the boiling point. Before exploding at Walter, I tell myself to calm down. I realize that I'm losing control of my emotions due to Aurora's condition.

"You didn't tell me about the second door."

"What second door?"

"In the room where you indicated Kronak is hiding."

Walter stares at me for an instant. "Master Kronak doesn't allow me to go past the outer door."

"I think you're lying to me."

"I'm trying to save your partner's life, and you are not helping."

Walter's resolve and evident sincerity render me speechless. He goes back to work on Aurora as I watch helplessly.

The surgical opening on Aurora's side has me concerned.

"I've tied off the blood vessels to prevent more bleeding, but Aurora has lost a dangerous amount of blood. Thankfully, I'm almost finished repairing her internal damage."

"I found Android blood in the refrigerator."

Walter continues operating without looking at me. "That blood has been manufactured for LifeLike Androids. It could have catastrophic effects if introduced into what is essentially a foreign body."

Walter looks up at me. "I'm almost finished. I'll use the robotic arms to close the wound and bandage it faster. Then, I'll bring Aurora up to you. Can you obtain a compatible blood type soon?"

"I'll do everything possible to get it in time."

I have no choice except to trust that Walter is telling the truth. Rushing back up the stairs, I feel the weight of fatigue setting in. It's been a long and anxiety-ridden day, and it's far from over. I have two urgent priorities. In the living room, I place a call to Adrien. After three rings, it goes to voicemail. I leave an urgent message to call me.

I have to prevent Kronak from escaping, but I don't know any of the codes for the exit doors. While I'm grappling for a solution, the shiny outer door to Kronak's inner sanctum slides open. Out walks a beautiful barefooted woman wearing a diaphanous negligee. I'm about to address her when the woman raises a handgun from the folds of her nightgown.

Diving to my left, I pull the handgun from my right pocket. The mystery woman's first shot crashes into the bedroom doors on the opposite wall. I roll again to avoid a second shot and fire from the hip. My projectile hits the lady in the neck. She grabs at the rupture, making gurgling sounds and falling back against the gray door that has slid shut behind her. It is not a pretty sight. I figure the unfortunate woman is Kronak's mistress. I can't determine if she is Human or an Android.

I kneel to examine the modelesque body sprawled haphazardly on the carpet. The woman is holding something in a death grip in her left hand. Opening her hand one rigid finger at a time, I find a golden key in the palm. Pocketing the key, I step over the body and re-enter the code I've memorized. The gray door slides open. The golden door in the short hallway awaits me.

I pass into the hallway with my handgun ready. Slowly, I unlock the golden door with my free hand. I hear the tumblers rotate as the lock opens. Gradually, I push the door open. Taking a quick peek around the edge, I'm confronted with the sight of Jan Kronak.

I pull back as three projectiles pound into the door. It stops them from penetrating. The door is made of something incredibly dense, possibly multiple layers of it.

Reaching around the barrier, I fire three snapshots.

The recoil pulls the handgun out of my hand.

I switch the second gun to my right hand and wait for a counter-strike. It does not follow. I hear no sounds coming from the other side of the door.

Taking a second quick peek, I see blood splattered on the opposite wall. I peek again. Kronak is slumped on an S-shaped sofa against the far wall. The wall to my right is embedded with security cameras. Kronak was keeping tabs on our progress every step of the way.

Moving around the door edge, I fire three more shots into Kronak's chest. They aren't necessary. Upon closer examination, I see that Kronak's skull is split from one of the projectiles I fired before.

The blood spatter highlights the outline of a door in the wall behind the body. I sense something is off. Kronak's body shouldn't be here. I doubt he would stick around for a gun battle rather than use the exit door to escape, especially after the coward sent his girlfriend to run interference.

Advancing on the body, I examine the eyes. They are mismatched in color, like the pair I remember from Kronak's office when we first met. The right eye appears to be the Human one. When I push my index finger against the right-side socket, the eye falls out. It is not a bionic or a Human eye. It is made of glass, confirming that Kronak used a decoy Android to aid in his escape.

CHAPTER 54

Running back to the living room, I find Walter laying Aurora down on the sofa. Turning to me, Walter notices the woman's body on the floor.

"Who is she?" I ask.

Walter's countenance saddens. "She was Master Kronak's pleasure model. Zora was an advanced prototype like me. We were friends before the Master added programming to make her worship him."

I'm relieved that Zora wasn't Human, and at the same time, I can't help but share Walter's grief, but only for a moment.

"What's the fastest way to the roof?"

Walter points to the burnished mahogany doors. "There's an exit door in the bedroom."

I follow him through the double doors. He keys in the combination for the exit I passed earlier on my way to the bathroom, and the horrible sight of Aurora, gravely wounded.

When I step through the exit to the roof, I squat and sweep the deck with both handguns at the ready.

The rooftop is eerily quiet until I hear the distant staccato of rotor blades. Running to the giant telescope, I jump down into the base. Kronak must be nearby.

I advance with one weapon held in front of me and the other pointing backward.

Behind me, a projectile ricochets off the telescope base. I turn in time to see a booted foot disappear from my view.

Kronak screams from the other side of the base, "I don't know how you found me, Faulk, but it will do you no good. I will always be one step ahead of you. If you come after me again, I'll make sure you and all of your friends die. I never make the same mistake twice."

Does he expect me to divulge my position with a reply? Probably. Kronak thinks he's one of the brightest Humans on the planet.

I edge toward the sound of Kronak's voice. He breaks cover and fires again, this time in front of me. The shot misses by several feet. Kronak pulls behind the base before I can return fire. Apparently, he hasn't spent much time practicing with firearms. He never expected anyone to survive his army of Android guards.

The sound of the copter grows louder. In seconds, it roars overhead. It's time to go on the offensive. As I flash around the base, Kronak breaks for the disguised staircase, laying suppressive fire as he runs. From the angle, I get a good look at the weapon. It is a custom-made handgun with a long barrel. I could use one of those.

As I prepare to fire, a line of projectiles stitches toward me from the roto-copter. I barely have time to take cover.

I wait for the barrage to subside. Then, I peek over the edge of the groove. Kronak has vanished. I vault back to the roof and head in the general direction of the hidden staircase.

I hear the copter settling on the cliff above me. Finding the staircase, I hit the first step. Kronak is almost at the top with his back to me. He turns and fires—a loud report in the confines of the staircase. The projectile whizzes by me.

At a distance, Kronak is a hard target to hit with a handgun. But I'm a damn good shot with handguns when I'm not injured, and I feel good enough. I fire three times. Two shots strike Kronak at center mass. The third one hits him in the forehead—not where I intended, but I'll take it. Kronak's slender body flies backward, out of sight. Only his weapon remains on the top stair.

I sprint up the steps, picking up Kronak's gun at the top. His body lies ahead of me on the clifftop in a pool of blood. Half of his head is gone, and there are two gaping holes in his chest. I notice that Kronak has bled more profusely than the Androids I've killed. It's the first sign that I've killed a Human Being. Reaching the body, I bend to look into the open chest cavity. There, I see the remains of a Human heart. Adrien has shown me what a nuclear-powered Android heart looks like. I'm not seeing a resemblance.

Wiping the sweat from my brow, I take pleasure in knowing Jan Kronak is no longer a threat to the existence of our dimension. The moment passes quickly when I realize I have to convince Pembra's pilot to take us to the spaceport.

CHAPTER 55

The jet-copter is painted black with white lettering, including a corporate logo. I'm sure Pembra "borrowed" the airship from a wealthy client. The machine is a six-seater, bigger than the roto-copter we arrived in. Kronak must have demanded a quick exfil in a fast machine.

I stay low to avoid the chop of the rotor blades.

The weather is windy and overcast. Glancing to my right, I see dense cloud banks over the ocean and flashes of lightning. Menacing thunderclaps sound in the distance.

Warily, I circle behind the copter's tail. Holding the deadly handgun up, I rap on the pilot's window. He angles it open. I recognize the man immediately.

"What *ken* I do *fer ya*'.

"For starters, you can apologize for almost killing me."

"Just *followin'* orders."

Jacquomon's laconic reply means he's not worried about me shooting him. Regardless, I keep the long barrel pointed at his head.

"Let me in. I need to speak to your boss about a ride."

"My orders are *ta* leave if Mister Kronak doesn't show up. He showed, but it *don't* look like he's goin' anywhere."

"Pembra will be angry if you don't let me speak to him. You don't want to come back empty-handed."

Jocquomon hesitates, then leans over to open the opposite cockpit door. Circling the copter at a dead run from the front this time, I reach the open door and get in. Jocquomon is already on a satellite phone. He speaks in his native tongue, presumably to Pembra, summing up the current state of affairs. He finally switches to *Anglish* for my benefit.

"Yer friend, Derrick Faulk, wants to speak with ya'.

Jacquomon hands me the phone without waiting for an answer. I hear Pembra say, "…not my friend." I ignore the comment intended for Jacquomon.

"Your client, and I use the term loosely, is dead."

"So I hear."

"How much more money do you need, considering Kronak has already sent you a money transfer?"

"Whether he sent the money or not is none of your business. You want ride, you have to pay."

The satellite phone's signal is crystal clear. So is Pembra's message. I know where this is going.

"I'll pay what Kronak offered you—fifty thousand *Daras* for a ride to the spaceport."

"Seventy-five thousand, and you pay first. No credit."

"That's robbery. Sixty thousand."

"You have another ride lined up?"

"I'll commandeer your roto-copter if you keep this up."

"You'll never land at the spaceport without an official flight plan. You'll never get one without my help."

He has me without even knowing about Aurora's condition.

"Give me some time to get the money together."

"Twenty minutes. No more. Storm is coming."

Lowering my long-barreled weapon, I hand the phone back to Jacquomon. "We're on," I tell him.

I almost trip, hurrying down the hidden steps. Running across the rooftop, I bang on the windowed wall. Walter appears and gestures toward the bedroom entrance.

Once inside, I move to the living room to check on Aurora first. Stretched out on the living room sofa, she is pale, and her breathing is shallow. I take her hand. It is cold to my touch.

Walter comes to my side. There is nothing to say. We both know what Aurora needs faster than yesterday.

"There must be at least a few hundred thousand *Daras* lying around here somewhere," I tell Walter.

"Master Kronak never discussed money with me."

What now, I ask myself. The answer comes: Intuition and logic tell me the master bedroom is the best place to start.

"Help me search the bedroom. Do you have X-ray vision or anything like that?"

"I'm sorry. I don't. May I call you Derrick?"

"Of course. We're friends. Let's go."

After clearing the bedroom doors, Walter says, "Is there any place in particular you'd like me to search?"

"Start searching. Everywhere."

I start in the walk-in closet, dumping racks of clothing, clearing shelves, and pulling drawers. I don't find a single *Dara* in any of them.

Walking back into the bedroom, I find Walter neatly removing items from an old-fashioned writing desk Kronak kept in the room.

"Walter!"

He turns to me, puzzled.

"Don't worry about disturbing your master's belongings. Search quickly."

"Yes. Quickly."

Walter returns to work at twice the speed, opening drawers and discarding items haphazardly. He moves to an unusually tall stack of drawers flush with the headboard and blows through its contents. I catch his eye. He shakes his head. I go through the stack of drawers on the opposite side. Nothing.

"Walter. I want you to check all the drawers in the room for false bottoms. Smash them with your fist, but don't hurt yourself."

"Yes. Right away."

Walter starts pulling drawers, dumping the remains inside them, and then smashing his fist through the bottoms.

I stand at the foot of the bed with my hands on my hips. The elaborate headboard intrigues me. It is another version of beautifully proportioned figures engaged in sexual intercourse in a variety of positions. Moving to the side of the bed, I notice the thickness of the headboard. I am aware of it now because we've pulled aside the tall end-stacks of drawers.

I see the outline of a small rectangular shape, no more than three by six inches, on the width of the headboard. I push the rectangle. The side of the headboard swings noiselessly open. Inside, I see the ends of shelves divided into sections and laden with stacks of *Dara* banknotes, passports, identification cards, expensive jewelry, and another long-barreled handgun. I pull several stacks of banknotes from the shelves. They come in one hundred, five hundred, and one thousand *Dara* notes. For good measure, I snatch a finely etched gold bracelet from one of the shelves.

Jackpot!

Walter has been watching me all this time. I turn to him.

"There is a valise in the walk-in closet. Bring it to me. Please."

Almost forgot my manners.

Walter fetches the valise and places it on the bed. While we are counting out the cash and loading it into the bag, my holophone chimes. It's Premba. Who else would it be?

"Your twenty minutes are up. Where is my money?"

"We're making sure of the count. Give us another ten minutes."

"Who *is* we?"

"A friendly Android named Walter."

Silence, then, "I'm losing patience. Hurry." Pembra disconnects.

"Can you finish the count? I have to bring Aurora to the copter."

Walter nods without looking up.

"I will do it triple-speed."

"I was slowing you up. Why didn't you tell me? Never mind. Make the count a hundred thousand *Daras* to be safe, then bring the bag up to the copter."

"Triple speed is appropriate for the money, but not the drawers." A pause. "I like working with you, Derrick."

"Same here. We'll meet on the cliff at the roto-copter."

I don't wait for a reply. Every second counts.

CHAPTER 56

I carefully maneuver Aurora into a black leather seat opposite the exit door. While strapping her in, I glance over my shoulder. The weather over the ocean is deteriorating rapidly. I feel the wind speed picking up. A violent rainstorm is rolling in. Jacquomon has the rotor blades turning lazily in preparation for takeoff. The valise Walter handed him is open on the co-pilot's seat. He is spot-checking the contents. I move around Aurora's seat to sit next to her. I try to warm her hands with mine. Her pulse remains weak, and her once lustrous skin is pale. Aurora's head lolls to one side. I'm afraid she's not going to make it.

As I pull my phone to call Adrien, Walter comes to my door.

"Goodbye, Derrick Faulk and Aurora Zolotov. I will miss you."

"Aren't you coming with us?"

"My instructions are clear. I am directed to oversee the care and maintenance of the castle in my Master's absence. I will fulfill these responsibilities until my nuclear battery runs down."

"That would be a complete waste of your time and energy. I'm changing your programming as of this minute. Come into the jetcopter and leave with us."

"You cannot change this directive, even though I wish you could."

"You disobeyed Jan Kronak. Why can't you change your directive if it no longer makes sense?"

"There are certain directives I cannot change. Jan Kronak made an error in my directives towards him. I used the loophole to help you."

"We *gotta'* go before this weather hits us," Jacquomon shouts against the sound of the gathering wind.

"I wish you a safe trip." Walter closes the cabin door. He trots away from the jet-copter as Jacquomon cycles up the rotors.

Our liftoff is bumpy due to wind gusts. I watch Walter standing on the cliff, alone, looking upward. He grows smaller as our altitude increases.

I feel sorry for Walter, but life must go on. I call Adrien. He doesn't answer. I leave him another urgent message.

"We have *ta* make a stop at the *Aeroporta* before we head to the spaceport," Jacquomon calls back to me.

"That's not happening. My partner is at death's door. There's an extra twenty-five thousand *Daras* in the valise. That money is yours if you fly us directly to the spaceport."

"Don't get *yer* balls in an uproar, Faulk. The flights from our station back and forth from the castle are off the books. We have *ta* stop at our station to file a proper flight plan. Otherwise, they'll shoot us down at the spaceport."

"Can you go faster?"

"We're flying at top speed and encountering turbulence."

"How long will that take to file the plan?"

"Could take an hour, could take a day. Depends on who *ya* know."

"Doesn't Pembra have the connections for something like that?"

"He *useally* doesn't get involved. He lets his big-shot clients throw their weight around."

I glance at Aurora. She is not an encouraging sight.

I call Adrien again. No Answer. I leave another urgent message— very unlike me. Adrien will know something is terribly amiss. He'll get back to me as soon as he can, but it might be too late.

At jet-copter speed, the flight to the station takes half an hour. It seems more like half a day. I think Aurora is stabilizing. Her Android healing powers are superhuman, but she can't manufacture blood.

We land. Jacquomon called ahead for an emergency stretcher. It rolls out to meet us. With the valise under one arm, Jacquomon helps to push the stretcher toward the station. We jog to the entrance, lift the stretcher off the ground, and pass through the door.

Inside the station, I ask Pembra for an empty room to keep Aurora away from the chaos in the outer office. It is a different scene from when we first arrived, with six clerks *clicking* away at their workstations. The room smells of body odor and *Sagarello* smoke.

Pembra shows me to an empty office. After I tell him a hundred thousand *Daras* are lying on his workstation, he becomes markedly more accommodating. Before he can go back to counting his money, I grab his arm. "You must know someone who can get the flight plan approved quickly."

With a grave expression, he replies, "I doubt we'll be able to get you airborne before the storm hits. Maybe it *passes* soon."

I can't leave it to chance. I call Adrien again. This time, he answers.

"I just picked up your messages. I was chairing a planning meeting. What's going on?"

"Aurora is seriously wounded. She needs a blood transfusion badly. Can you send your private spaceliner to *Amperigo City International Spaceport* with blood packs and a doctor? I need it yesterday."

"I'll have the plane fueled and ready in an hour. It will take another hour to get there. That's the best I can do."

"Thanks. Another thing. Can you get a jet-copter flight plan approved from here to the spaceport right away? There's a storm coming, and I don't want it to delay us. I'll put someone on to give you the particulars."

"That's a tall order. Let me look into it." Then, almost as an afterthought, "What about Kronak?"

"Taken care of. Hold on for Pembra."

EPILOGUE
—Five Days Later—

Once again, Adrien achieved the impossible. The man managed to have our flight plan approved within twenty minutes of my call to him. When Pemba realized I had given him a twenty-five-thousand-*Dara* bonus, he went out of his way to fly us out ahead of the storm on a luxurious jet-copter. He surprised me with an invitation to come back anytime. I hope I will never have to accept it.

On the flight home, the doctor told me Aurora would have died of organ failure had she not received the blood transfusion immediately after boarding the spaceliner. The only thing that kept her going, he said, was her nuclear-powered heart. I'd add that Aurora's ferocious courage also had something to do with it.

Here we sit, *en famille*, together again, in Adrien's office. For Aurora, Kristina, and me, it is eight years and some days later than when we began the mission. Only Adrien shows signs of aging, but I'd never mention it to him. He relaxes in his "Emperor's chair" behind his enhanced, four-display workstation. I'd also never let slip what I've privately named Adrien's executive chair.

As always, I admire the rows of Android sculptures bordering each side of the office that function as load-bearing walls and radiate energizing light into the room. I'm delighted every time I see Adrien's colorful collection of artificial plants that move and look so real. Each one of them, large and small, is manufactured in quantity and offered for sale. Adrien is always adding models to the collection and discontinuing others to keep the offering fresh.

The three of us are seated in Adrien's leather chairs that conform automatically to our body shapes for optimal comfort and ergonomic health. We are listening to Adrien bring us up to date on facts and events that will never be made available to the general public.

"I had to advise the relevant government authorities of Kronak's actions and his eventual demise. As you know, I completely wiped LifeLike's files to protect your names. It's a case of throwing the baby out with the bathwater, but it couldn't be helped. Fortunately, international agencies have cooperated to construct their cases without the files. There is enough eyewitness testimony to close LifeLike Technologies permanently.

"Our government knows all three of you were involved in Kronak's death. They don't care. In fact, they consider you heroes, however unsung you are destined to be. The reports are sealed and classified at the highest level. Furthermore, the *FDI* has seized all of LifeLike Technologies' assets under the *Federated Patriotism Act*.

"Here's some more good news. It turns out a single buyer purchased the custom Androids: A *Swarbian* industrialist and multi-billionaire who wanted to cripple the economy of the *Federated Corporation of the United States* to increase his worldwide profits and advance his political agenda in the *Europan Federation*. His name is Kasmir Rogenko. From his Villa near the port of Astrakhan at the mouth of the *Vulega River*, he set up dummy corporations in countries known for harboring terrorist groups to make the attacks look like acts of terrorism. Rogenko has been captured by special forces and secreted away from his Villa on the coast of the *Kaspathian Sea*.

"I have since learned from my international agency contacts that Rogenko will be executed without due process of the law. The misuse of Android technology to carry out multinational criminal activities is now a terrible reality and a major concern. It cannot be allowed to continue. To this end, any individual, group, or organization found guilty of the criminal use of Androids will receive lengthy prison sentences or be condemned to death, according to the nature of the crime or crimes.

"Supplemental to this ruling, it has been decided that any trials of these criminals will be held in private because they would only generate additional anxiety in the general population surrounding Androids and their place in society. We also don't need the Press screaming about the suspension of due process. A multinational tribunal will adjudicate these cases.

"Furthermore, *the Central Intelligence Authority, the Federated Division of Investigation, the Federated Corporate Security Bureau,* and *InterraPol* have come to the following conclusions by pooling the results of their initial investigations. This information is by no means final or complete, and I am relaying it to you in the strictest of confidence.

"The evidence indicates that Jan Kronak did not foresee his buyer using his custom Androids to attack the *Federated Corporation of the United States.* When the strikes began, Kronak accelerated his retirement agenda and ran to *Amperigo.* However, the *FDI* has determined that Kronak used one of his Androids to kill an innocent accountant in front of his building as a warning to his Chief Financial Officer, William O'Grady. There is no evidence that Kronak's competitors were behind the murder."

Adrien goes on with his briefing, but my mind wanders to more personal matters.

I contacted William O'Grady to inform him that his former boss was dead and no longer a threat. I did not go into details. I convinced O'Grady to surrender to the *FDI* when he told me that he possessed the offshore numbered accounts where Kronak accumulated the bulk of his wealth. I have brokered a deal whereby O'Grady will receive immunity in return for the numbered account information and any other salient details he can offer to the multinational investigation.

I dealt with a niggling matter when the *FDI* came calling to investigate any possible connection I might have to terrorism, resulting from a report issued by *Amperigo* spaceport security agent Anna Marie Sinclair. With Adrien's backing and my sterling record in law enforcement, plus hints of my recent activities, we quickly dispatched the *FDI's* concerns.

Upon my return to AndroBiotica, I had a much bigger issue to face: Kristina's reaction to my romantic relationship with Aurora. Her initial reaction was shock. She picked up on our status right away. I had given great thought to explaining how my relationship with Aurora evolved, but Kristina waved away my attempts. She seemed to accept the relationship and move on without revealing her feelings one way or the other.

From my perspective, any feelings I might have held for Kristina never had a chance to get off the ground. We are left with a somewhat strained work relationship. In time, I hope we can become good friends again.

My work relationship with Adrien is one he calls "fluid." He wants me to be involved in all aspects of AndroBiotica's security and special investigative projects as the need arises. He has promised, for the time being, not to make these projects anywhere near as demanding as our last two assignments. Aurora and I need some downtime to recover mentally. I can use some extra time to recuperate physically. I don't snap back as quickly as I used to.

My thoughts turn to Aurora. She left the hospital two days ago after making a full recovery. In my eyes, she's becoming nothing less than an augmented Human Being with each passing day. Where are we going as a couple? I don't know. Adrien certainly has a scientific interest in our liaison. I know I can't bear the thought of hurting her again. I also know I would have been devastated if she had died from her wound. Together, we can only take one step at a time and see where our relationship leads. Our future as a couple, like my job description, is fluid. It is best left open-ended.

In a broader sense, I contemplate questions that have no answers. Questions like these: After decades of daily meditation, am I any closer to knowing what is called "my true self?" Am I a better person?

I consider even larger questions like: How does our world keep going around with the technology we have at our fingertips and scoundrels like Jan Kronak and Kasmir Rogenko living in it? Will Dianah and whoever/ whatever she represents allow us to go on? For how long?

It's probably better not to think of these things. I can only do my best and let the rest take care of itself. I tune back into Adrien's monologue. Right now, it feels good to be alive and with friends. Tomorrow will bring what it may.

THE
SILVER SPHERE
IT'S COMING—NO TIME TO WASTE
A Seven Part Story
by
DAVID GITTLIN

CATACLYSM
END OF WORLDS
Novella 2
The Silver Sphere Series
DAVID GITTLIN

PROMISE
OF THE
VISITOR
VOLUME 3
THE SILVER SPHERE SERIES
DAVID GITTLIN

THE
SILVER SPHERE
TRILOGY
A Science-Fiction
Adventure
DAVID GITTLIN

The Silver Sphere Series
RIVER TO THE
MULTIVERSE
DAVID GITTLIN

The Silver Sphere Series
RETURN TO
ANELEYA
A Novella
David Gittlin

THE ANDROBIOTICA FILE:
NEARLY HUMAN
A Novella
DAVID GITTLIN

ANDROBIOTICA 2
JOURNEY IN TIME
DAVID GITTLIN

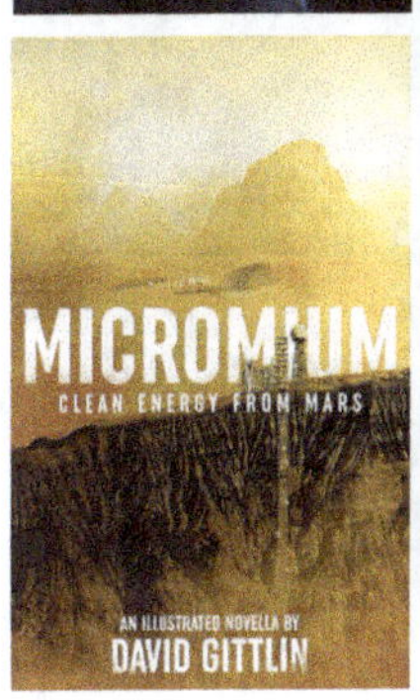

MICROMIUM
CLEAN ENERGY FROM MARS
AN ILLUSTRATED NOVELLA BY
DAVID GITTLIN

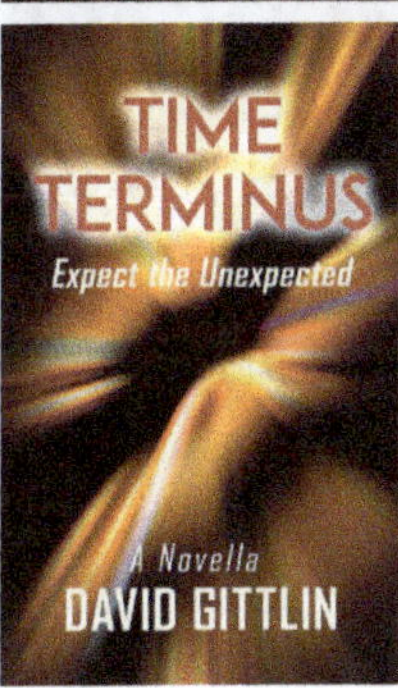

TIME
TERMINUS
Expect the Unexpected
A Novella
DAVID GITTLIN

SCARLET
Ambrosia
Blood is the Nectar of Life
David Gittlin

Three Days
to
Darkness
DAVID GITTLIN

About The Author

After a successful career in marketing and business communications, David Gittlin turned to writing fiction and has since produced thirteen novels and novellas, including **The Silver Sphere Series**. He lives in Florida with his wife, daughter, and granddaughter.

www.davidgittlin.com
www.davidgittlin.net

www.ingramcontent.com/pod-product-compliance
Lightning Source LLC
Chambersburg PA
CBHW060341310726
48976CB00003B/677